Praise for
EDGE CASE

"*Edge Case* delves deeper than your typical missing-person's mystery. It's also a book about a woman trying to understand who she is on her own and where she belongs in the world. . . . Chin is interested in the idea of home as both a cherished place and a complicated destination. *Edge Case* doesn't lack for interesting characters and complications, which Chin spreads generously throughout the novel. . . . The result is a touching, introspective story about identity, belonging, and the effects of long-term transience on both the heart and soul."   —*Washington Post*

"What interests Ms. Chin—and what she so skillfully dramatizes—is rather the eternal conundrum of being a human among other humans . . . and, more specifically, of being an immigrant at the mercy of a volatile host. . . . Chin expertly directs the shifting currents of emotion and of memory that sweep us along in this affecting novel."

—*Wall Street Journal*

"One of the first great novels to examine the grinding effect of US anti-immigration policies during the Trump administration. . . . Chin is superb at describing the tumult of a woman being psychologically knocked about like a pachinko ball. Every chapter bears witness to Edwina's pain, befuddlement, and sheer exhaustion, while also revealing her snarky sense of humor, resourcefulness, tenaciousness, and capacity for love. *Edge Case* shows what can happen to ordinary people when they're caught up in systems beyond their control."   —*BookPage*

"A quirky exploration of marriage, immigration, identity. . . . Her voice from the edge—perceptive, funny, introspective, smart, wry, calling to us from the margins—is one worth listening to."

—Washington Independent Review of Books

"Chin makes an impressive debut with this sharp take on faltering romance, the American dream, and self-realization. . . . Edwina's wry outlook and wrestling with thoughts about what it means to make it in America will resonate with readers. Those who enjoy the work of Charles Yu should take a look."
—*Publishers Weekly*

"Chin's novel is littered with genuinely funny moments; Edwina's voice is a chatty, engaging one that belies her depth. . . . The novel also presents a layered view of racism. . . . An endearingly offbeat story with particularly timely themes."
—*Kirkus Reviews*

"*Edge Case* is a beautifully subtle novel about precarity and dislocation. YZ Chin writes with wisdom, precision, and humor, tracing the routes by which we become strangers to one another and to ourselves."
—Katie Kitamura, author of *A Separation*

"YZ Chin's eerie and brilliant novel looks closely and tenderly at the margins of life for answers to pressing questions of love and self. *Where do I belong? Who am I in the face of loss? What am I willing to do for my precarious place in this world?* The result is a totally engaging and emotionally resonant story of one woman's alienation, ambivalence, defiance, and humor in the face of turmoil—I won't soon forget it and can't wait to read what Chin writes next."
—Alexandra Chang, author of *Days of Distraction*

"A quirky story of loss and limbo, *Edge Case* immerses us in the worries, hopes, and absurdities of life on a work visa in America. As a woman's marriage disintegrates, YZ Chin examines her complicated, ambivalent quest for American citizenship and lays bare her indelible feelings of foreignness and unbelonging. This is a timely, intimate novel unlike any I've read."   —Chia-Chia Lin, author of *The Unpassing*

"The great tension of YZ Chin's *Edge Case* is that it's always pushing in two directions at once. It's a domestic mystery wrapped in the international pressures of immigration. It features a narrator whose interior informs her surroundings (or she worries that it's happening the other way around). Chin has written a wonderful debut that excavates how the US oppresses its white-collar migrants, offering them stability that is dependent on marriage and the workplace, but has rendered it in an intimate, human story that I flew through in two days."

—Kevin Nguyen, author of *New Waves*

"On the surface, YZ Chin's debut novel is about a woman's search for her missing husband, but her quest also speaks to so much more: what it means to belong to a new country and to disentangle yourself from another, how relationships and memory change with time, what it means to be alone. Funny, smart, and questioning, *Edge Case* is a glorious read."

—Tash Aw, author of *We, the Survivors*

EDGE CASE

ALSO BY YZ CHIN

Though I Get Home

EDGE CASE

A Novel

YZ CHIN

An Imprint of HarperCollins Publishers

HarperCollins books may be purchased for educational, business, or sales promotional use. For information, please email the Special Markets Department at SPsales@harpercollins.com.

Ecco® and HarperCollins® are trademarks of HarperCollins Publishers.

A hardcover edition of this book was published in 2021 by Ecco, an imprint of HarperCollins Publishers.

FIRST ECCO PAPERBACK EDITION PUBLISHED 2022

Designed by Angela Boutin

Library of Congress Cataloging-in-Publication Data has been applied for.

ISBN 978-0-06-303069-5 (pbk.)

22 23 24 25 26 LSC 10 9 8 7 6 5 4 3 2 1

For David

Her memory, like her guilt and early love, is involuntary, but her choice of the United States is willful.

—Shirley Geok-lin Lim, *Among the White Moon Faces*

EDGE CASE

Day One (Wednesday)

I know I can *really* talk to you because you're a therapist. You'll keep everything I tell you confidential, I'm sure.

Yes, I know, you've said. You're not a therapist yet. But as far as I'm concerned, it's close enough. My friend Katie SooHoo said bouncers started letting her into clubs with her real ID two or three months before her twenty-first birthday. Your situation is isometric. You're basically a therapist at this point. All you lack is paperwork. You did say my story sounds fascinating, so here it is, everything leading up to the disaster.

By the way, I realize I sometimes have the foreigner's way of speaking too formally—believe me, I'm self-conscious about that. But I grew up reprimanded by elders for mixing up my T-V distinction (as in *tu* and *vos* honorifics, which exist in both Chinese and Malay), and that has caused me to default to formality in America. When you are a foreigner, everyone else can take on the intimidating aura of an elder, especially if they are in uniform. Being very polite to train conductors and building security guards for the past decade has made my deferential way of speaking second nature. Though what an odd saying. What is my first nature?

But back to the story. It all fell apart the day of the steam pipe explosion. I was at work. The air-conditioning was cranked up too high, even for July. Someone came by our coworking pod to announce that we should go home early. This was unusual: the launch date for AInstein was in September, less than two months away, and we were behind schedule.

"Check the news."

I pulled up a *New York Daily News* article and read that a steam pipe had exploded near our office.

"Did you hear it happen?" Josh asked, pushing a button to lower his standing desk so that his face was slowly revealed, hairline first, then blinking eyes, all the way down to his jaw. Our desks faced each other, but his question wasn't directed at me.

"I thought that was just one of your famous earthshaking farts," Darren cracked from behind me. I did not bother pretending to smile at the joke. Being the only woman in the entire startup, I'd long given up trying to participate in the men's banter.

They surrounded me, the software engineers, engaged in a lengthy and loud debate about whether it was better to go home early as suggested or to stay in the office. They kept saying "smarter," never "safer."

"Think about it. If an explosion just happened, and we can't rule out terrorism, then it's a much smarter move to lie low instead of running around out there. The Twin Towers were hit by more than one plane, remember?"

"Okay, but acting on the information available, we know that the city evacuated people from a small radius around the explosion. Why would they do that? Hmm, let's see, maybe a small thing called asbestos, which was used to line these old steam pipes? So the smart move would be to quit the area while we're still not completely saturated by poison."

"Really? 'Poison'? Such a lazy and inflammatory word choice."

"Fine, smart-ass. Hazardous airborne material, whatever."

The debate had the tone of people placing bets on Fantasy Survivor brackets. The way they squabbled, it was like the incident had no possible chance of affecting their lives, or anybody else's lives for that matter. I left them to it and made for the exit. I would not be missed. The only reason they even created a quality assurance analyst position in the first place was to appease VC investors after a code release gone wrong, one that had angered the company's first customers and cost the investors a nice chunk of change in make-good credit. My job was to write tests that would catch the engineers' bugs before they could make their way out to customers. The men regularly referred to me in the office as "the tester." It always made me think of the sad labeled tubes of lipstick at Sephora, mauve heads battered and ready to transmit oral herpes.

It wasn't that every single man on my team was virulently sexist. In fact, more than a couple of them seemed quite decent on their own. Whenever something cringeworthy happened, the better ones hunched over their keyboards more, and their typing grew a little louder. I am sure that if I ran into them outside of work— grocery shopping at Eataly, let's say—we would have perfectly civil exchanges.

The problem was that as a group, the tone was set by the two or three guys who seemed to think women were ill-equipped by nature to do certain things, like coding. The others did nothing to rein in the "jokes" or the snide condescension dressed up as "constructive feedback," the holiest of communion in tech startups. The men congealed bloblike around me every weekday, viscous and suffocating. It made no difference that some ingredients of the blob were less harmful than others—when they were all mixed together, a uniform consistency took place. The texture ran throughout.

Outside on the streets of the Flatiron District, ash was falling from the sky like celestial dandruff. The breaking news report had mentioned an enormous plume of smoke that developed in the explosion's aftermath. My instincts told me to steer clear, but I still felt a strange desire to see the plume with my own eyes, mainly so I could tell my husband, Marlin, about my brush with death. Things hadn't been great between us. I was hoping the threat of physical danger could get him talking to me again.

"America is getting more and more unsafe," we might say to each other, shaking our heads, his palm sketching calming circles on my back. We'd take turns bringing up other recent incidents in Flatiron, like the suspicious package outside a hardware store that turned out to be a decade-old hulk of a printer, abandoned on the sidewalk. Or the real, actual bomb found in a dumpster outside a facility that serves the blind. We sighed over the calculating cruelty of banking on blind people being less likely to discover the bomb. It chilled our hearts. "America," we would say, looking at each other, our mouths downturned.

This kind of talk soothed us, made us feel slightly superior to our fates. We were both on H-1B work visas, and we were running out of time. Unless our employers could be persuaded to sponsor green cards, we would soon have to leave the country for Malaysia or become undocumented when our paperwork expired. But if America was so rife with danger, then leaving was no hardship, right? Exiting would be the safe thing, the *smart* thing, wouldn't it?

I decided not to go toward the flashing lights and police tape. Instead, I walked into a Duane Reade far from its namesake streets, wondering if it too felt helpless, so removed from home and yet bearing such obvious marks of it. I paid for a box of surgical masks advertised as "99% effective."

On my walk home from the subway station I sweated and practiced my "America," intoned with fear, disappointment, and flippancy. I huffed the word into the moist cave created by the mask. Overtaking a couple of slow tourists, I texted Marlin: "You won't believe what happened. What do you want for dinner?"

No answer. When I left our apartment that morning, he'd told me he was working from home, which wasn't unusual for a software engineer like him. In this tech hub sometimes referred to as Silicon Alley, engineers were treated like kings (from my perspective as a nonengineer, anyway), and flexible work arrangements were part of the bare minimum requirements for attracting coding talent, especially for the kinds of companies that could not afford Google or Facebook compensation packages.

So I didn't worry right away. I thought about getting something a little extravagant for dinner, like sushi. I'd walk in with this luxury incommensurate with hump day, and he'd ask what for, and I'd go through a dramatic telling of my narrow encounter with mortality. Maybe, in deference to a force such as loosed asbestos, he would act like his normal self tonight. We could have a nice tension-free evening like we used to, united against our host country.

But he wasn't there when I got home, paper bag dangling heavy from one hand. I sensed his absence as soon as I unlocked the front door. A weak glow suffused the otherwise dark entryway. It took me a second to realize that Marlin had left the light on in the hallway closet.

"Hello?" I put the sushi down by our shoe rack so I could knock on the closet door. Marlin might be holed up in there. Nothing would surprise me anymore. Over the past six months, his behavior had grown so erratic, I wouldn't put it past him to be sitting on the closet floor in a trance.

I opened the door. My head brushed the light's pull chain, setting it going in a pendulum rhythm. It swung meaningfully overhead, indicating a bare patch of floor marked off by a border of dust. No Marlin. My heart responded first. By the time I remembered that a suitcase used to stand where the clean square was, my chest was growing hot from racing, tripping beats.

A book lay just outside the blank space, forlorn and dusty. The title made me flinch. It was K. S. Maniam's *The Return*, a novel we had both been assigned to read at seventeen by the Malaysian government. Was the book his copy, or mine? I saw that it had fallen off a tottering tower of books we couldn't fit on our shared bookshelf. When we moved in, we'd jammed them into a corner of the closet, optimistically telling ourselves it was only a temporary arrangement.

So it had come to this. He'd left me. I sat heavily down on the shoe rack, the toe boxes of Marlin's winter boots digging into my butt. What should I do? Should I give him some time apart? To cool off, as people say, as if my husband were a piece of bread fresh from a toaster. "Absence makes the heart grow fonder," I mumbled. The aphorism seemed to echo back at me, a phrase as empty as the apartment.

I lifted a plastic tray of cucumber and avocado maki from the bag by my feet. I ate a piece reflexively, hoping that food would make me feel better. As I swallowed, I eyed the tray of sushi. The negative space where the piece had been looked like a suitcase disappeared.

Maybe that was what Marlin needed at this time—space. Manhattan real estate being what it was, we'd been penned together for two years in our six-hundred-square-feet apartment. He would come back to me once he'd gotten a chance to stretch his limbs and take some big breaths. I wouldn't launch myself after him. He would get a taste of life without me, and maybe that would be enough to bring about his return.

The incomplete tray of sushi presented an intolerable visual. I ate the rest of the pieces quickly, hastily chewed blobs forming knots in my throat on their way down. On my last piece I choked, spraying rice as I coughed.

I made for the bathroom, one fist pounding my chest. In the mirror, the folds of skin on my neck made shadows so deep I almost questioned my breathing. They looked like rings choking my throat, suffocating me. I hacked into the porcelain sink, waiting for the pain to come.

I used to fret, when I looked at myself in our bathroom mirror, that I was aging rapidly, but Marlin insisted that the lights were unflattering. He said it wasn't just me; they brought out the worst features in him too. We both crowded into the bathroom at once, looking back and forth at our mirror images and at each other in the flesh. The lighting made us sallow, almost actually yellow, which was quite a feat considering Marlin is half Indian and half Chinese, his skin a dark brown. In the mirror, my uglier husband grinned at me: *See?* When he raised his eyebrows, the lines on his forehead looked like the ruled exercise books we'd grown up using.

We conjectured: Perhaps the lights were designed with milder skin tones in mind. Perhaps, just as TV had its color girls, bathroom illumination technology had its mirror models who set the tone for all of America.

Later, when he first started acting strangely, Marlin told me that if a person had a wrinkly neck, it meant they had been suicides in their previous lives. The more rings, the more times they had taken their own lives, the opposite of how rings on trees worked. That was one of the first signs I was about to lose my husband. The Marlin I knew would never have said something like that.

I turned off the bathroom light. In the darkness, I thought about wandering the streets shouting Marlin's name, like someone looking for their lost pet. But the odds of success were so low. Maybe we could both use a break. I was exhausted by the daily adjustment of reality Marlin had been imposing on me during the past months. Day after day I came home wondering who my husband would be at that moment, bracing myself to find out how much further he'd drifted away from the person I love. Just the previous week he'd told me I was harboring a lot of unresolved negativity within my heart.

"That's why you're so anxious and angry all the time," he had said. "It's a vicious cycle."

"What are you talking about?"

"I consulted the charts on your behalf. It's not too late. I can help you."

Six floors down a fire truck wailed, and I became aware of how hot it was. I groped my way to the AC unit next to our bed and found it nearly warm to the touch. When the AC came on I listened to its cranking, sweat running down my temples.

I pulled my shirt over my head, wiped my armpits, and tossed the shirt on the floor. Then I saw it, our Difficult Fruit and Vegetable Knife lying on the bed. A duplicitous jolt of hope sparked through me as I imagined that Marlin had simply stepped out for groceries, that he would return soon with a bag jostling with firm vegetables, ready to make me dinner.

"What's a huge butcher knife doing in the home of two vegetarians?" dinner guests would ask, when we used to have them over. "Actually, it's one vegan and one vegetarian," my husband would say. "For now," I'd pipe up tartly, tilting my chin. They lapped it up, our guests, especially the ones who found the idea of not eating meat absurd. A vegetarian trying to corrupt a vegan into loosening his dietary restrictions! It was funny to them.

Marlin and I would explain. The Difficult Fruit and Vegetable Knife came into our lives after a frustrating day trying to cook dinner together on our first wedding anniversary. It was fall and gourds were in, according to food bloggers. We'd planned on butternut squash soup and "pasta" in the form of spaghetti squash. Per Instagram, it seemed like the appropriate middle-class American thing to do. We were just two immigrants trying to fit in.

Except we never got past the first step of the recipe, which was to peel and cut the vegetables. The butternut squash bent our only knife crooked. The spaghetti squash body-slammed the coffee maker before escaping onto the floor.

"Gourd damn it!" I exclaimed dramatically, while Marlin rolled his eyes. We took off our gingham aprons and went out, resigned, for our usual pan-Asian fare. On our walk home, sated by "Singapore" noodles and Tiger beer, we passed a gentleman hawking wares on a street corner. He was wearing a bow tie, and we were just tipsy enough to stop and listen.

"Cuts anything," he promised.

"Even butternut squash?"

"Anything!" He held up a block of wood, threatening to demonstrate. Already there were wood chips and splinters all over his lap, spilling onto the tarp he'd spread out under him. "Or, sir, if you still don't believe me, hand over your shoe and I'll prove it to you! Cuts anything!"

We bought the knife. It looked like a horror-movie weapon and worked like a charm. We obtained all sorts of difficult fruits and vegetables just for the sake of testing the knife. We had the pleasure of eventually conquering not only all manner of squashes but also fruits from home we'd missed, like jackfruit and durian, though not without some bloodshed for the last of these. Marlin and I turned to each other and joked: Is it still vegetarian if it's spiked with blood? Well, surely our own blood doesn't count?

But I hadn't seen the DFaVK for a while. We hadn't cooked together in months. Really, we hadn't done much of anything together for a while.

On our bed, the DFaVK seemed almost to shine. An A4-size index card lay pinned under it. I slid the card out, and it spawned a copy of itself. No, it split off in the middle, one half in my hand, the other still trapped under the knife. The card's mutilation was executed cleanly, the border of severance straight and neat. Dread settled low in my stomach as recognition struck. Over two years ago, Marlin had proposed to me using the card. Now he'd sliced it in two.

It had been a Saturday, the day he proposed. I can't recall anything of the day outside. We had sex first thing in the morning, and then we let the shades stay drawn into evening, both of us half undressed and optimistically yelling, "Sex all day!" with bravado from time to time. It was a long, lazy afternoon of streaming videos while absentmindedly petting each other until arousal turned into rhythmic comfort. I was contented, sprawled out on the couch with my head nestled on his shoulder.

When Marlin shifted his weight under me, I thought he needed to go use the bathroom. Instead he maneuvered himself onto his knees and pushed a card into my hands. I fingered its crisp edges and read:

MARLIN % EDWINA == 0

"What is this?" I asked, completely bewildered.

"That percent sign means you're looking at a modulo operation," he said.

I no longer recall his exact explanation, but my understanding is that the modulo is used to find the value left over after division. For example, 5 % 2 == 1, because five divided by two yields two, given two times two equals four, and five minus said four equals one. That one was therefore the remainder, the output of the modulo operation left untouched after division. A kind of surviving figure.

"So you see," he said, "I'm trying to tell you that if you and I were to be divided, there would be absolutely nothing left. Zero. You are everything to me."

My laughter came out as a shout, followed right away by tears.

"That's . . . so corny," I gasped.

He grinned and admitted that he'd planned it this way so he could see the exact moment I realized I was being proposed to, the turn of my face from confusion to joy. He wanted to see my happiness in its entirety, right from its very first arrival.

Now our memento of that singular day had been chopped up. I turned over the piece I was holding.

MARLIN %

Had he replaced me in the equation? Fingers trembling, I flipped over the other half from under the knife.

EDWINA == 0

I got up and paced. If this was a riddle, then it was one with a blatant answer. He was clearly communicating I was nothing to him. A big, fat zero.

I walked in circles, too agitated to stop. I strode from one corner of the apartment to another, listening to the AC's hiss and hum, wishing it would grow louder and louder until my ears rang with its static. Then I was back at the hallway closet, squeezing the door handle so I could feel my hand hurt. The suitcase that was no longer here—it was lime green, a color we'd strategically chosen so it would stand out on luggage conveyor belts. That had been Marlin's idea, a "hack" as he called it, to make our travels to and from America more efficient. Over the years the suitcase had acquired a smattering of barcode stickers, many of them printed with "PEN," for Penang International Airport.

I let go of the handle and looked to our microwave for the time. It was after eleven at night, which meant it was almost noon in Malaysia. My mother-in-law would have just started preparing lunch, dicing onions, laying out little bowls and pewter trays for her mise en place. It was her unfailing routine, or at least it had been until Marlin's father passed away.

The phone rang on the other end. After four rings someone picked up, but said nothing. "Mummy?" I whispered. The syllables were strange and lumpy in my mouth. I called my own mother something else. Marlin's mother had cornered me before our wedding ceremony, holding both my hands in a tight grip, and insisted I start calling her Mummy. While she spoke, I kept peering over her shoulder. Whenever a man rounded a corner into view, my heart lurched. I was expecting my father to somehow appear to surprise me, announcing that he hadn't been dead for eighteen years after all. Only much later would I realize how oxymoronic it was, to expect a surprise.

"Mummy?" I tried again.

"Edwina, is that you?" On the phone, Mummy finally spoke. "Can't hear you well. The line must be bad."

It sounded like an indictment. I swallowed saliva and tried to follow through on my hastily thought-up script. I was just calling to check on her, to see how she was doing in the wake of her husband's passing. Six months was not at all long ago. There was nothing suspicious about a concerned daughter-in-law calling.

"How are you doing, Mummy? Making lunch?"

I sensed a hesitation before her "Yes."

"What are you making?" Memories of her hands, busy, proudly showing off herbs fresh-plucked from her garden. Her shooing me out of the kitchen, from which she produced elaborate dishes of kangkung with belacan and sizzling Japanese tofu.

"Actually I'm just microwaving some noodles that I tapau."

"Oh? How come you're not cooking?"

"There's not much point, isn't it, now that I'm all alone."

The resigned sadness in her voice made me ball up my body, dizzy with relief. My head was almost in my lap, phone wedged between ear and thigh. She was speaking to me normally, as far as I could tell, even revealing some vulnerability. No anger or iciness. It meant Marlin hadn't said anything about the end of us. And if he hadn't, there was a possibility our marriage wasn't over. This break, this breach in normality, it could be temporary. All I had to do was find him and convince him—of what? I wasn't sure yet, but right then it felt like I had the beginnings of a plan.

February 2014

Start from the beginning? Impossible to know when that was, but I'll begin somewhere, if you think it'll help.

It had seemed, at first, like just another lunar New Year spent away from home. I showed up for a party in a fellow Chinese Malaysian's one-bedroom apartment. A dog brushed against my jeans on its way after a ball. I simultaneously wished to be *home* home and happy that I wasn't. At *home* home, the TV would be blaring all day with variety shows from mainland China and Hong Kong, so that we in the diaspora could, for one week, feel as brassily Chinese as possible. The women would be in the kitchen cooking a double-digit number of dishes, and I would again refuse to join them because I didn't want to be part of a stereotype. Then everyone would get annoyed at me but would have to hold it in because it was new year, a time when we were all supposed to be one happy family, back together for 团圆, pronounced "tuan yuan," a phrase that, appropriately, manifested tight, fencelike boundaries.

That particular year of the horse in Tom's Upper East Side apartment, there was a similar plenitude of food, minus the guilt. This gathering, too, was a keening for authenticity, but softer, gentler on the ears. The attendees were all from some country that was neither the United States nor China, and we all identified (or were identified via peer pressure) only with the aesthetics of being Chinese. We wanted the five-thousand-plus years of culture, the history of world-changing inventions, and the somber respect due a sophisticated ancient civilization, but we disavowed the clichés of squatting on toilet seats or spitting on sidewalks, not to mention the Communist Party. Certainly we wanted nothing to do with the Falun Gong people at Union Square whose expressions signaled life or death as they performed their deliberate exercise moves.

My contribution to Tom's potluck was kailan (hideously termed "Chinese broccoli" by Americans) and mushrooms in oyster sauce. This was a self-preservation tactic, knowing Tom's network of meat-eating friends as I did. If I didn't make and bring my own vegetarian dish, I'd go hungry until I couldn't stand it anymore, and then I'd run downstairs for a "quick cigarette" in the form of a dollar pizza slice.

I noticed Marlin right away, of course. He stood out, his skin a shade that I had seen compared to food items like chocolate or coffee in American books. Looking at him, I thought not of food, but of a neutral coolness that disguised something else, like an envelope that contained either really good tidings or earth-shattering bad news. Marlin sat next to a man with the crispest collar I had ever seen, and I thought at first they must be partners. Marlin was perched uncomfortably on the arm of a sofa, his right leg bouncing up and down with the impatience of someone corralled into attending a social function.

The room was loud. Faces shone bright with Asian alcohol intolerance, but no one was really drunk. No one ever got that drunk at these things. I took a picture of the crowded space so I could later show my mother just how unmiserable my new year was, how I had an entire community while being so far away from *home* home. I was applying a horse filter and a red festive border to the photo when Marlin snuck up on me.

"Spying on someone?" he asked, his voice soft, his emphasis on "ying" letting me know that he was from back *home* home after all.

"Just capturing the moment," I said, a pleasant kind of shock tingling in, of all places, my left elbow.

"You know that is not possible, right?"

"Oh?"

"At least Husserl thought so. You see a moment you want to capture, but by the time you act on your intention, that original moment has already passed, so all you are really capturing is the next moment, or the moment after that, depending on how quick you are with your hands."

He looked down at my hands. I had never known my fingers to blush.

Tom swept in, playing the host, clapping Marlin on the back. "Marlin, my favorite Chindian! Talking cock again?"

Turning to me, he rattled on, one pointer finger aimed at my plate of kailan. "Edwina! Surely you're not dieting on Chinese New Year?"

"I'm vegetarian, remember? Why do you always forget? Am I your only vegetarian friend?"

Both Tom and Marlin's eyes lit up. They talked over each other excitedly, a jumble of "Him, him—" and "I thought—." Tom's finger now jabbed aggressively at Marlin, joined by Marlin's thumbs poking himself in the chest.

"Okay, I'll leave you two birds of the same flock," Tom said, eyeing a newcomer through the door. "Or"—he delivered his parting shot—"whatever the veggie equivalent of that saying is."

"Kailan?" I said to Marlin, lifting my plate with a flourish.

"Sure." He beamed. "Is it vegan?"

"Yes," I said automatically, the word a response to his smile, his big black eyes, rather than to his question. Then I caught myself. "Wait, actually there's oyster sauce."

"Oh." He deflated. "So you're not a real vegetarian."

"Oysters are like one step up from single-cell organisms."

"Yes, and that's a huge step, probably millions of years of evolution."

I didn't want to debate him. What I wanted was to see him smile again. So I said: "I can't wait for the movie called *Assault on the Planet of the Bivalves*."

"If I were you, I would *clam* up on that idea. Someone might hear you and steal it."

Laughing, I pretended my lips were hinged mollusk shells. I clasped and unclasped them all night, until, eventually, he kissed me outside a dollar pizza joint.

Day One (Wednesday)

You'd assume otherwise, but I did sleep, a little, the night Marlin disappeared. After I got off the phone with Mummy, I resumed pacing the apartment. The relief I'd experienced while speaking to her quickly wore off. While it still felt like the door to repairing my marriage had been left slightly ajar, I had to wonder why Marlin hadn't announced our separation to his mother. He was close to her—had been close to both his parents, in fact. He'd taken his father's death very hard.

Unsurprisingly, Marlin did not pick up when I called.

"Marlin, please pick up. We have to talk about . . . whatever this is."

When I called a second time an hour later, a chirpy voice announced to me that the person I was calling had not set up their voice mailbox. He'd turned it off. I looked around our bedroom, unsure what to do. Then I noted, numbly, that I hadn't seen our cat.

Marlin must have taken him too. It was probably better that way. Marlin was always good at taking care of Buster.

Sometime after midnight I sat down in front of Marlin's desktop computer. Should I? He had built it with his own hands, curating and assembling various parts into the quiet machine in front of me. One panel of the computer chassis was see-through. I peered into the machine's innards. A fan was spinning so fast it looked like a solid, static circle.

No, I decided. I wouldn't do it. It would be an invasion of privacy to snoop around his digital life. I ran a thumb across the chassis as I stood up. Dust smeared across my fingerprints. Something was wrong. Something missing besides Marlin and the suitcase. I looked at the microwave again. Too late to call Katie. She was the one person I'd semi-confided in about Marlin, but she had a toddler and a demanding job. She'd have been asleep since ten.

My mother? The thought of baring it all to her made me crumple onto the bed, narrowly avoiding the DFaVK. My mother, who had never remarried since my father passed away in her late thirties. Who remarked, when I'd casually brought up the demise of Brangelina as small talk to fill the silence during one of our Skype calls: "It's his second marriage, isn't it? It's like this: people in the West don't know how to love. They're always divorcing!"

Impossible to admit the huge question mark hanging over my own marriage now. Especially since she'd taken to Marlin immediately, from the moment he'd waved to her through a computer screen. "You're very lucky," she kept reminding me on my wedding day.

I WOKE TO A LOUD, ECHOING CLANG. RUBBING SLEEP FROM MY EYES, I realized I'd kicked the DFaVK off the bed. The knife glinted, menacing in the faintest of dawn's light. When I moved to pick it up, I saw a nick on my left foot, a streak of blood underscoring my ankle.

The microwave had the time as 5:56. Seeing the rich red against my skin, I felt suddenly afraid. Even though the missing suitcase indicated that Marlin had left of his own volition, flashes of violent scenarios lit up my mind. Marlin backing away at knifepoint, his hands raised. Worse: bright steel held stark against his own wrist.

I scrambled back to his desktop. There might be a note if he were thinking of hurting himself. Half of me vehemently denied the possibility; not a chance, Marlin would never take such a step. The other half provided reminder after reminder that my husband had changed so much, I no longer knew what he was capable of.

The monitor screen's harsh glare made me squint. Marlin was not an idiot, so I could dismiss things like "12345" or "qwerty" as possible passwords. Same for birthdays. He was too sophisticated for that.

"Husserl," I typed. Incorrect. "NicolDavid." Malaysia's most famous squash superstar, whose career Marlin had closely followed. No good. I tried "DatukNicolDavid" for good measure, tacking on her honorific title. Still wrong. I pounded the keys. "YangBerbahagiaDatukNicolAnnDavid." Asterisk stars rushed in a row, taunting me.

It was foolish to think I could ever guess a software engineer's password. I picked up a loose stack of papers by his keyboard and rifled through them, searching for a clue. Even though he was too savvy for it, I hoped against hope that he might have written his password down.

Receipts. A flyer for a Women in Tech meetup at his office. A menu from our favorite restaurant, Keep Calm and Curry On.

I glanced at the hours. Maybe I could stop by tonight, on the off chance Marlin would be there. But no, he had taken a suitcase with him. Didn't that indicate he was somewhere far away by now?

Not really. He could be anywhere. The Holiday Inn five minutes from our apartment. An Airbnb in New Jersey. Under a bridge. No, no use being morbid. He simply needed some time off from us. Maybe he was just taking a long-needed vacation. Right at this moment he could be touching down in Hawaii, ready for his lei and the first of many tiki drinks. No, wrong again. Hawaii was my dream vacation, not his.

Think logically. Think like an engineer, like Marlin before his personality change. I turned over a Best Buy receipt and starting making a list of places where I might find my husband.

- Hotel (impossible, too many of them to search)
- Vacation (also impossible, unless I can find a booking confirmation or a brochure?)
- Home with Mummy (unlikely, based on phone call yesterday)
- His office (possible, though need an in to get past building security)
- Crashing with someone?
    - Best friend Eamon (possible, all the way out in College Point)
    - Friends from work (possible, could verify by visiting office—see above)
    - Climbing gym partners? (can't remember names other than Eamon)
- Climbing gym (possible, given three-times-a-week routine)

- Favorite restaurant (too close to apartment? worth a try anyway)

The list somewhat quelled my paranoid fears. Some of these were concrete locations that I could physically visit, one after another. There were numerous possibilities to check off before I had to consider the void of death or other unknowns. But first—I glanced at the microwave—I still had to report to work. Now, of all times, I could not afford to be fired, voiding my work visa. I had to be at my desk.

AFTER

Day Two (Thursday)

I squeezed onto the subway, sucking in so I would fit. The Cortlandt station was right by a Hilton, and I'd had to tamp down a wild desire to rush in and demand the concierge give up Marlin's hiding place. The World Trade Center memorial across the street did not help either, conjuring up images of dust and ash.

I texted Katie on the train, one elbow hooked around a subway pole. "Can we meet up soon?"

In an instant: "Sure! Brunch this weekend?"

The lightness of her reply distressed me. I had assumed my five-word text message would convey the magnitude of my emotional turmoil. It must be lack of sleep. I wasn't thinking clearly. I tightened my grip on my satchel, trying to gird up for the workday ahead.

It hadn't always been like this. When I got the job last year, I'd been beside myself with excitement. I would be working not just in tech, but at a company focusing on artificial intelligence. AI was hot, a sexy buzzword on par with *blockchain* or *big data* a few years ago. The cherry on top: my new workplace had a mission to bring laughter into people's lives via the power of AI. I would be part of a team of young, smart people developing a robot that told jokes to those who needed some joy in their lives—the bedbound, the lonely, those who woke up each day wondering how to spend their hours. Thanks to our innovation, the halls of nursing homes and hospital wards would ring with cheer.

I was particularly sold on this idea because of my early months in America. I'd arrived in the fall of 2008 with what Americans called "an accent," which apparently rendered me unintelligible to many of them. That first despairing year, I repeated myself often and dejectedly. I was here for college, to learn, but I found this difficult to do when professors and TAs couldn't understand my questions. The less they could comprehend me, the more polite with mortification I became, which meant my sentences became longer and even harder to parse, embellished as they were with pleases and thank-yous.

"Watch more TV!" my mother advised from half the world away. "It's like this: you have to learn to speak like them."

I started tiptoeing into my dorm's common room at the end of my long days. Often the TV would already be on, half watched by shadowy figures slumped sideways, homework piled up on their laps. So began my acquaintance with late-night talk shows. It started off bewildering. Men wearing suits and ties, telling jokes that were often childish or uncouth? That was not what I'd previously associated with formal attire. But something happened as I watched. I began to understand that, for Americans, making others laugh was itself a kind of elegance. What do you think? Is that an accurate read? The men wore suits because they wielded power and demanded respect, stemming from their ability to elicit an involuntary physical reaction from their audiences.

It solidified in me an ambition I have carried since: if I could make Americans laugh, then I would be accepted. I would be embraced and admired. I harbored some anxiety, though, that this ambition might clash with another secret resolve of mine, which was to master the English language until I could wield it like a shield against any prejudice. I would read the thesaurus, learn big words, coax my tongue into projecting an aura of intellect around my person. Could one be considered funny and erudite at the same time? After observing some typical banter that took place in the dorm halls, I decided that I would pursue both strategies, but prioritize laughter.

That was how my friendship with Katie SooHoo started. One day near the tail end of freshman year, she happened to sit down next to me in the dining hall. I had an open book pressed flat against the table. I was so immersed in the story that I didn't take my roving eyes off its pages as I ate. Absentmindedly, I shoved a cold french fry into my nose.

"Wow, must be a really good book," Katie said. "What is it?"

I was embarrassed, but also pleased. Closing the book on a greasy placeholder finger, I showed her the cover.

"*Hangsaman*? What the hell does that mean?"

"I don't know," I admitted. Then I added, a little desperately: "Maybe a new superhero? Something erotic?"

This set her off into boisterous laughter. When she finally stopped, my ears rang full of the soft-serve machine's rattle and hum.

"You're so into this book, and you don't even know what the title means?"

"It's an accurate depiction of how college feels if you can get past the title."

"But it's by Shirley Jackson. Doesn't she write horror?"

"Exactly?" I replied.

She laughed again, and a warmth flowed across my chest like a cape. I was doing it; I was succeeding.

You can understand why I was so eager to work at AInstein. A robot that could intelligently tell jokes! A selfless companion that would lift spirits, albeit in the form of a crude metal head attached to a (so far) immobile body. When I first started looking into tech jobs, it was solely because I knew that the industry was the biggest sponsor of green cards, and I needed one. Imagine, then, how lucky I felt to land a job that aligned with my more secret ambitions.

But now I was shuffling into the office with my head bowed, avoiding everyone's eyes. For the day after a steam pipe explosion, the bullpen was pretty packed. That's what our open-floor work-space was called—the bullpen. Very moralizing stuff.

"Hey, tester," Josh greeted me as soon as I slid into my ergonomic chair.

"Hi," I mumbled. I busied my hands aligning my trackpad such that it would be perfectly parallel with my keyboard, but he didn't take the hint.

"So what do you think? Ready for the next installment of *Gone with the Galactic Superwind*?"

I winced. Like AInstein itself, Josh had seemed so promising in the beginning. I had arrived for my first day of work full of opti-mism. My manager Lucas ("not Luke") took me around the bull-pen, introducing me to everyone. When we reached Josh's desk, he shook my hand and said, "Nice to finally have a female in here."

Before I could respond, he continued: "I saw your résumé. You majored in literature?"

I nodded. "Yes, but I took a programming class in senior year, so I have a little bit of experience." Confident but with the right touch of modesty, or so I thought.

"Uh-huh, cool. I'm writing a novel." He leaned back expectantly, arms crossed.

This caught me off guard. I'd spent the previous night reading up on AInstein so I could be prepared for intelligent work conversations from the get-go. Novels were far from my mind. "What kind of novel?" I asked, just to be polite.

"I see you two have a lot to discuss," Lucas said as he walked away. "I'll leave you to it."

"Here, sit." Josh patted the edge of his desk.

"Oh, I'm okay, I'll stand."

"What I'm about to tell you is confidential." He patted his desk again, his gestures weighty. I relented and perched. I didn't want to annoy a coworker on my first day.

"I had this genius idea," he began, leaning forward. His loosely clasped hands hung an inch from my knees. "I'm going to write a combination of all the best-selling genres: sci-fi, fantasy, mystery, romance. That way it's guaranteed to be a hit."

"How would you do that?"

He looked at me with a sly expression. "See, you're already hooked."

I said nothing.

"I'll tell you, but remember it's confidential, okay? You can't go and steal my ideas."

I wondered if he was about to ask me to sign an NDA. His expression was that somber.

"It's about a group of astronauts sent on a mission to investigate reports of life on Mars. After liftoff, one of them is killed. The main character has to find the murderer. It could be anyone, even the scientist he's falling in love with. It's a locked room mystery, but in space! The scientist is a girl, by the way."

Good for her. I didn't know what to say, so I asked a question. "What about the fantasy part?"

He looked momentarily taken aback. Then an idea seemed to strike him. He waved his hands in the air, slamming one against my leg.

"The victim haunts the spaceship as a ghost."

At least I had interesting coworkers, I thought, trying to keep my first-day enthusiasm going. Josh barreled on.

"The problem is, I've spoken to a few publishing people, and there's a pattern. They all get excited when they find out I'm an engineer. *Write about that!* they say. Apparently the only way for me to break through is to write a book about coding and startups. They want a takedown, of course, since the elite literati like to feel superior to us soulless STEM drones." A roll of eyes. "Satire might work. I've gotta have just enough jargon for them to believe they've been given a behind-the-scenes. But not so much jargon that it's off-putting, like I'm lording it over them with deets that're gonna fly over their heads. The target audience is people who say 'I've done a bit of coding myself,' and then you find out they meant HTML or CSS."

He stopped there and stared at me, eyes full of something like challenge.

"Right, HTML? What is this, GeoCities?" I said. He turned away, satisfied.

I began to regret my initial interaction with Josh almost immediately. That first encounter turned into a lunch invite the very next day, so he could "bounce ideas" about his novel off me.

"Why don't we book a meeting room?" I asked. I had brought

my own lunch, and was also wary of wasting time on something not directly work-related when I really wanted to make a good first impression.

"Come on, my treat," he cajoled. Was it smugness I saw in his expression?

"I'm not very hungry, actually. We could do coffee?"

"Oh, so you're okay making me starve?"

"No, no, of course not!" I shook my head. I could feel my face start to burn.

We barely talked about writing during that lunch. Most of the time was taken up by Josh explaining what each word meant on the Italian menu, and then, after we ordered, by effusive accounts of his previous and future planned trips to Tuscany, Naples, the Amalfi Coast. As he was signing the check, he said: "Well, that went by fast. We didn't even get to talk about my book. Wanna do this again next week?"

So it began, the semiregular lunch "meetings" accompanied by requests to read the manuscript-in-progress for his sci-fi-fantasy-mystery-romance mashup. The idea was that I could give him honest feedback face-to-face.

"I thought you were writing a startup tell-all?" I asked.

"I am, I am. I'm working on *Gone with the Galactic Superwind* on the side, though, so that by the time I sell the startup bullshit I'll have my *real* book ready to go."

I wanted to get along with people at work, so I agreed. Out of all the men, Josh was the only one who regularly said more than "Hi" to me.

Now, preoccupied with thoughts of where Marlin might be, I found my heart sinking as Josh gave me the "heads-up" about a third installment of his manuscript ready for my "reading pleasure."

Having already read the first two, I was pretty sure I had run out of nice ways to say "drivel." Not that he ever seemed to catch on.

"I'm sorry, Josh, things are a little hectic right now. Maybe I can read it later?"

He frowned. "What are you so busy with?"

From the corner of my eye I saw the tech recruiter Phil ("Philip is my father") stroll in. My eyes must have widened in excitement, because Josh said, unkindly: "Got a crush on Phil?"

"No! Of course not!"

"Okay, then why do you look so happy to see him?"

Because Phil was a recruiter, and recruiters were supposed to be familiar with other tech startups in the area, companies from which an engineer or two might be poached. He would know about Marlin's workplace. Most startups of the size that employed Marlin and me didn't have receptionists on staff, so I'd have to get creative to gain info on an employee or access to the office.

As I thought through how to approach Phil for help, I deflated. I obviously couldn't share with him the actual reason I wanted to snoop around Cachi I/O. But there were no other plausible excuses that I could think of either. Whatever I said, Phil would likely assume I was itching for another job. Then word would get to Lucas, and there would go my one shot at a green card. I squeezed my knuckles, one after another. It wasn't supposed to go like this. Marlin and I had discussed a plan, before he became unrecognizable. We were to be on our best behavior at work and then both ask for green card sponsorship around this time, July, nine months before our visas expired. Was it still a goal worth working toward? Right at that moment, wasn't it possible Marlin was sitting down with his manager and executing on the plan without me?

"Do you know anyone who works at Cachi I/O?" I asked Josh

suddenly, desperate. He wasn't Phil or my manager, and that seemed good enough given the situation.

"Why?" His eyebrows shot up, wary.

"I just, I heard they have a meetup there once a month? For female engineers?"

"Oooo." He visibly relaxed. "I thought you'd heard some rumor about me."

"What rumor?"

He shrugged. "I guess there's no harm telling you. I used to date a girl there. It ended badly. *Not* my fault."

I didn't want to wade deeper into this line of conversation, but I had no choice. "Does she still work there? Can you connect me?"

"Why? You're not a female engineer." He laughed and lifted a gigantic set of headphones over his head.

"I'll read your next installment."

Still laughing, he aimed an index finger at me. "*There* we go. I'll see what I can do."

BEFORE

2016—?

I don't know if you've ever been married. The app doesn't let you specify, does it? All we can advertise on our profiles are our current statuses and what we're looking for. Nothing about our pasts.

The Marlin I fell in love with was intelligent, logical, and curious. If I'd been asked to list the attributes of my ideal partner before I met Marlin, I never would have mentioned those qualities. I suppose I had no idea what I wanted. After I met him, I was charmed by his methodical care when interacting with the world, from researching the best way to unclog stubborn drains—"Never Drano, it hurts older pipes"—to understanding the minutiae of space travel. None of this made him wooden or boring. What I mean is, he liked understanding how things *could* work as much as he liked actually making them work. A representative tome on his side of our bookshelf was *Conceptual Mathematics: A First Introduction to Categories*.

Categories. We used to proudly tell everyone how well we, an engineer and a liberal arts major, complemented each other. "I bring the order and she brings the chaos," Marlin joked. "It's called spontaneity," I retorted.

Now there was no more order. My last memories of my husband are of him shouting accusations at me and going on about ghouls from an unseen world, an occult-looking crystal in his hands. Supposedly it let him communicate with spirits, and supposedly those spirits warned that he must distance himself from me. In short, Marlin had started to believe in ghosts, and not just in a passive, hands-off way. His ghosts gave him instructions and advice.

In the beginning it had seemed harmless enough. One day he called out across the living room, asking if I'd seen his phone. Before I could answer, he said: "Never mind, I'll try the rod. See if it works."

"Try the what?" I thought I'd misheard.

He waved me off, disappearing into the bedroom and closing the door.

Another time, when I complained of a case of the blues for no reason I could think of, he offered to "read the charts" for me to understand why.

"Like star charts?" I was confused. Marlin had nothing but disdain for astrology.

"No," he scoffed. "This is way more sophisticated."

He wouldn't clarify beyond that. "I'm still figuring it out. Once I get the hang of it, I'll teach you. For now it's better for me to practice and get better by myself."

I let it go. I left him alone at the slightest signal from him those days, assuming that what he wanted was space to grieve. Had that been a misstep? Maybe I should have been watching him closely for signs of—what, exactly? Was it or was it not normal for people to behave differently after the death of a parent?

Perhaps it'd started even earlier than the examples I just gave. It might have been the day we walked by a big furniture chain store, and he stopped to closely examine a taxidermied downy woodpecker mounted on a low stand.

"I wonder what Daddy thinks of that," Marlin mused.

I didn't think much of it at the time, but looking back now, the present tense seems ominous. His father had been dead two months.

So you see, it's hard to pinpoint an exact beginning to the end. You know, scientists have still not managed to figure out how life began. Yet some researchers claim to have solved certain mysteries of death. The speed of it, for example. The rate of dying has been measured as one-thousandth of an inch per minute.

Day Two (Thursday)

On my lunch break, I stood in line at a Pret a Manger near the office and dialed Eamon's number. I tried to remember the last time I had seen him. It must have been before the funeral. Afterward, Marlin had preferred to be alone. At first it'd seemed expected, maybe even beneficial. I thought Marlin just needed to grieve in solitude. Then a couple of months passed, and I started dropping hints that he should hang out with Katie and me, or at least spend time with his own best friend. But Marlin never did meet up with Eamon, as far as I could tell.

"Help me brainstorm something fun for a double date," I had begged Katie a few weeks into Marlin's self-imposed isolation. I was over at her apartment to meet her baby, but I couldn't help unloading my troubles on her.

"Marlin doesn't like the kind of stuff we do, though. Like paint and sip? Remember last year when we invited you, and he didn't want to come? He only likes boring shit, right?"

"Wow." The hurt I felt was personal. "You sound like you almost hate him."

"No, no!" She waved her hands emphatically. "When you two started going out, I thought he was perfect for you. Solid, dependable, you know? I've known you what, nine years? You definitely started coming out of your shell much more after you met him. Like you could be more fun and wild because you had him in the background. I thought it was great that he's so boring!"

I didn't know what to say. I hadn't known that was how Katie saw the dynamic between me and Marlin. It was clear she meant no insult, but still I struggled to accept what she said as complimentary. I set it aside, though, to focus on my mission.

"How about a compromise? A medium-boring activity."

Katie started smoothing down her eyebrows with the tips of her middle fingers, something she did when tipsy, uncomfortable, or pensive. I couldn't tell which one it was that day. Thinking back, maybe she had her own troubles too. Maybe I haven't been the best friend, since everything happened.

"Okay." She played along. "Trivia night? It's real serious and competitive, and you have to know stuff."

In the end it was all for nothing, because Marlin told me to stop pestering him about being on his own.

"I'm fine. I'm focusing on my own things," he said, carrying a tray of Amy's Vegan Organic Rice Mac & Cheeze into the bedroom.

"Can I join you?" I asked, twisting my hands together.

"Hmm. I don't think you'd be interested," he said coolly.

I WAS SWAPPING OUT MY PRET EGG SALAD SANDWICH FOR A CHEDDAR and tomato one when Eamon finally picked up. I shuffled in line to pay and cleared my throat.

"Hey, have you seen Marlin?" I tried my best to imitate a casual tone.

"No. What happened? Is he okay?"

I hesitated. "So you haven't seen him?"

"No, I haven't seen him."

"Okay, no big deal," I said, trying to keep my tone breezy, upbeat even. "Will you let me know if he shows up? Or if he gets in contact with you?"

"What's going on? Did you guys fight or something?"

"No. I mean, not today."

"So, what, you fought yesterday? The day before?"

Why did he sound so accusatory? It was true that Eamon and I had never quite hit it off. I found him awkward, his sense of humor juvenile. When I used to tag along to board game nights he hosted, he did nothing to make me feel included. Eventually I started making excuses not to go.

I really could not remember the last time I had seen him.

"You should tell me if there's something going on," Eamon pressed.

"I have to go," I said. I was almost at the front of the line.

I wandered around Madison Square Park after leaving Pret, wending between tourists with cameras and dog walkers wrangling six leashes at a time. Now and then I slowed to tip lentil soup into my mouth straight from the cup. Talking to Eamon had made me feel vaguely guilty. Why was it? Because I wasn't crying hysterically, wasn't at my wit's end?

I'd never been accused of being coldhearted. When we first started dating, Marlin said it was my "emotional generosity" that had drawn him.

"What does that mean? I give you handouts of emotions?" I laughed.

"That's right. You wear them on your sleeves, and I just pluck them like ripe fruit." He really did start tugging on my sleeves. Then he leaned in and nibbled my shoulder.

A lone streak of tears. I'd managed that at least. I let it slide into the soup tilted against my face.

Besides the rate of dying, another thing scientists discovered about death is that it can be stopped. Or at least one cause of it, aging, can be. Already certain researchers are making blustery predictions that within our lifetime, science will conquer aging and disrupt dying, rendering it obsolete—barring gunshot, opioid overdose, self-driving car crash, etc. All this points to the possibility of deciphering endings without really understanding their beginnings.

Who was Eamon to judge me? The deterioration of my marriage had happened not all at once, but instead at a rate so slow, it was something like the speed of death.

Some brain damage or stroke patients wake up with their personalities completely changed. Some have even been reported to start speaking like completely different people. For example, a woman who had never left the UK woke up from a stroke with a strong Chinese accent. This is called foreign accent syndrome, as if the patients had emigrated while traveling within their own unconsciousness. What I'm trying to say is, if a huge personality shift seems to happen "all at once," as after a stroke, then doctors take it seriously. There is a diagnosis and even an acronym (FAS) for it. But if it happens gradually, like Marlin at first just printing out articles about the spirit world, then apparently I'm overreacting if I think he might need help.

It's the same at the other end of the scientific research spectrum. For believers in demonic possession, a sudden, complete personality change would also be much cause for alarm. There'd be fanfare, religious experts brought in, candles lit, symbols drawn, incantations incanted, and so on. Out, ye devil! Satan, we drive you from us!

So where did that leave us? Marlin's personality shift was so gradual, there seemed to be no medical or spiritual cause for concern. What is the phrase people like to toss smugly in the face of those with opposing views? "Just because you don't believe in something doesn't mean it isn't true." Cuts both ways, doesn't it?

BEFORE

January 2018

We flew back to Malaysia at the end of January, six or so months before the steam pipe explosion. Usually when we go home it's a minor cause for celebration, our families having shored up warm feelings toward us in our absence. We usually manage to deplete those feelings over the course of a two-week stay, but during the first few days at least, we're feted like royalty. Sometimes I think our visits have become, like certain less significant holidays, just another reason for people to overindulge in alcohol and food, and they're not so much overjoyed to see us as they're happy for an excuse to depart from daily mundanities. They dress this up as accommodation for us, saying things like "Oh, Americans eat a lot, right, so we can't let you go hungry."

In January there was no celebration. Marlin's father had suddenly passed away from a heart attack, and we paid thousands of dollars each for last-minute tickets to fly back for the funeral.

During the flight, Marlin talked about a version of his dad that would never be. As I held his hand, he circled repeatedly over the plans he'd harbored, secret wishes never before shared with me. In these plans, he had it all figured out. Marlin would get a green card, become a permanent resident, wait the requisite five years before applying for citizenship, study hard and get naturalized, and then sponsor his parents to live with us in America. His dad would have especially enjoyed life there (sometimes Marlin said "here"). With a love of chess both Chinese and Western, he could have whiled away many happy hours at Union Square, challenging other seasoned players sitting on upturned crates. On weekends, we'd all go to Central Park, and Marlin would buy his dad binoculars because he liked to watch birds, even though he also had deteriorating eyesight, unfortunately coupled with a vanity that meant he refused to wear glasses most of the time.

Marlin went on like this while we were airborne. I murmured to let him know I was listening, my heart aching for him. A small part of me selfishly wondered: Why hadn't I heard him talk about these plans before?

I had few memories of my own father. When I was seven, he gave me a music box that housed a ballerina who would spin in slow circles when I lifted the lid. I cherished that box more than anything in the world. One day the ballerina stopped spinning, and I went crying to my father. He dissected the box, revealing gears and parts hidden under the platform on which the ballerina posed. The discovery of that inner intricacy increased my love for the toy a thousandfold, even as he gently broke it to me that the box was beyond repair; the ballerina would never dance again.

On the plane, thinking about the music box, I felt a surge of love for Marlin. It was as if I'd sewn a piece of my childhood and my own loss directly onto Marlin's present-day sorrow, connecting our griefs into something shared. Tears in my eyes, I squeezed his hand, and he in turn crushed my fingers. I bit down on the pain.

At the cemetery, I didn't know what to do with myself. It had been given an auspicious name, the Mountain Villa of Riches and Prosperity. Mummy draped herself over Marlin and wept in front of the fresh grave. With each jagged cry, she deflated a bit more, until she seemed like a shoulder wrap Marlin was wearing. I looked around. No sign of my mother, even though she'd said she'd be there as part of the family. The sun beat down and set everything subtly vibrating in the humidity. I tiptoed toward Marlin, asking with my eyes whether he needed me to help support Mummy. He was slouching only a little, his eyes tired and awash in red. His return gaze was blank.

In the distance, a patch of heat shimmered like a portal. I imagined it leading not to another place but to the past. Already it had happened, as people said it would—my country of birth had begun to feel unfamiliar after a decade away.

My mother finally walked up, swiping fingers away from the corners of her eyes.

"I thought I'd go see your Ba as well." She gestured vaguely at a different section of the cemetery. "Has your father-in-law visited Marlin yet? Visited in his dreams," she clarified. "It's a very important sign, especially in the first three days. It's like this: that is the spirit's way of letting us know they are at peace."

"Not now." I sighed. She had always been a staunch Folk Taoist/Buddhist combination, with emphasis on the Folk part. At home, she had altars perched high up for the Heavenly Grandfather and corresponding floor-level ones for the Lord of the Soil and the Ground, which I was pretty sure didn't belong in Buddhist canon.

This hadn't bothered me so much when I was young and thought, in the way typical of adolescents, that my mother's beliefs would never affect me. How wrong I was.

The karmic reincarnation part of Folk Buddhism had a particularly strong hold on my mother's imagination. Standing right there in front of my father-in-law's body, she started to speculate what fate awaited him in his next life.

"Maybe he'll be a rich and successful import/export businessman?" she pondered, lifting her ionic-straightened hair off her shoulders to expose her prominent collarbones. "He was so kind to beggars, and he loved to watch those travel shows on TV."

She went on with a string more of occupational guesses, which I tuned out. She'd been spinning past life stories as long as I could remember, many of them constructed to explain away aspects of my personality that she disliked. For example, she once told me I had been a cruel tormentor of animals in one of my past lives. I started small, she said, nothing more serious than a few well-placed kicks to the heads of passing stray dogs and cats, but as I got older I developed into a full-blown psychopath who impaled birds on tree trunks and skinned rabbits alive, and so on—I'll spare you. The gist is that the animal cruelty story helps her come to grips with the fact that, in this life, I decided to be a vegetarian. Under the rules of karmic reincarnation, if you do bad things in your past lives, you have to atone or suffer for them in later lives. To her, not eating meat is definitely a form of suffering.

Storm clouds passed above the Mountain Villa of Riches and Prosperity, collapsing the shimmering portal of heat. I blinked. My mother was telling yet another past life story now, seemingly about me, which she called the banana tree spirit story. I readied my eyes for rolling, but the more I listened, the more my scalp tingled as awe and pity flooded through me. The story was about a beautiful teen-age girl, promised in marriage by her parents to the highest bidder but secretly seeing a different boy on the side. As my mother described the girl's ultimate fate, I blinked back tears. I turned away to wipe them when my mother finally paused for breath.

I chalked it up to understandable emotional vulnerability at the funeral, though I would change my mind. Later, I would come to believe that there was something about the banana tree spirit story itself, something about the shame it held up to the light.

Day Two (Thursday)

"Hey, just emailed you part three of *Gone with the Galactic Super-wind*," Josh said when I returned from lunch. He had a half-eaten prime rib sandwich next to him, balanced on top of a decorative ashtray printed with the words ATLANTIC CITY.

"Why do you want to be a writer anyway?" I asked. The phone call to Eamon had agitated me.

"Because it's dope, yo! I wanna be like George R. R. Martin. Except not fat, obviously."

Was it me, or did he give my figure a meaningful look? I knew I shouldn't have worn the ill-fitting purple sweaterdress. It was simply the first thing I'd grabbed in the morning, groggy from lack of sleep.

The first time I realized I was fat was at Buddhist camp. I was twelve, and the list of items forbidden to me by my mother included bras with underwire, motorcycles, makeup, and coffee. My father was dead by then, and so unable to take my side.

At camp during mealtimes, we sat at long picnic-style tables and thanked Buddha for the food and drinks arrayed neatly in front of us. Eyes closed, head bowed, lips chanting an old language in rhyme, I got my first taste of complicated, grown-up desire. The breaths I took in as we circulated our gratitude to Buddha, up high and hidden from view by sloping roofs, carried with its atoms the gritty aroma of coffee. The whole time I was verbally being thankful for the plenitude before me, an internal struggle was raging. Was it so wrong to drink coffee with Buddha's blessing, against my parent's wishes? Surely, in the hierarchy of authority, Buddha was top dog?

The last echoes of the whole camp chanting in unison died away. I opened my eyes. There it was right in front of me, the contraband: black coffee that looked thick and solid somehow, filling up a translucent plastic jug that did nothing to lessen its serious, adult allure. I formed a fist around the jug handle and jerked upward as if the coffee was weightless. I was expecting something ethereal because I'd never had a wish come true before. But of course that jug of black liquid had mass in the real world. My grip wavered under the unexpected weight, and the jug swayed, splashing puddles of coffee around my section of the long mess table. A few drops landed in my tin mug, pooling against one edge.

"Watch it, fatty! No brains, is it!" a boy yelled.

I hastily banged the jug back on the table. More coffee sloshed over.

"Wow, ugly bitch is so useless she's going to waste all our food!"

I looked up at the boy who had hissed at me from across the table. "You're not supposed to be mean at Buddhist camp," I said.

"And you're not supposed to be fat," he jeered. "Buddha achieved nirvana by fasting to death, so you how?"

I had no retort for that. I held up the tin mug, its lip against my lip, and waited. Forever later, a droplet washed onto my tongue, and it was bitter.

Perhaps you can see why I developed a resistance to Buddhism and, with it, my mother's beliefs about karmic reincarnation. And I bet you thought Buddhist camp would be an oasis of peace and Zen, right?

But still, sometimes, early on quiet spring mornings, the radiator in our New York apartment dings just once, and it sounds exactly like the tock of a wooden fish in the hands of a monk.

I SLOGGED THROUGH THE REST OF THE WORKDAY, SPENDING MOST OF my time on Google Street View inspecting all available angles of the building housing Cachi I/O. As far as Manhattan coworking spaces went, it was standard fare. The facade was grand but bland, featuring weathered gargoyles and a lintel that would be impressive, were it not mostly obscured by scaffolding. I peered one by one at the faces blurred into gray smudges, even though I knew very well that it was pointless; any unlikely photographic evidence I found of Marlin here would be from months, if not years, ago.

Pushing back slightly from my desk, I called Marlin again, and emailed, and texted. Perhaps it was a sign of my pessimism that I didn't go somewhere more private to call. I wasn't expecting his voice mailbox to be restored, and I was correct.

Phil stopped by at some point in the afternoon, much to my alarm, while I gazed unseeing at my computer. "Hey, tester. I heard you wanted to talk to me?"

I stared at his shiny forehead, his scraggly beard, unable to speak. Sputters of laughter rose from behind Josh's tower of monitors.

"What's so funny?" Phil smiled.

"Oh, nothing, just the look on her face." Josh stood up, grinning right at me.

"Whose face?" Phil asked. "Edwina?"

Josh coughed. "Some girl in a video I was watching."

"Something wrong?" Phil turned to me.

"I was actually about to leave," I said. "I need to take care of something at home."

"All right, see you later," he said, rapping a knuckle against my desk.

October 2017

Thanks for saying I'm not ugly. Marlin used to tell me that too. He said kids are cruel and childhood bullies should not have such an outsize impact on the rest of my life. Then again, you've seen me only on the app and not in person, so maybe you should withhold judgment for now.

After we came back from our honeymoon, Marlin and I wondered whether to get a cat. Marlin is (was?) more of a dog person; he's charmed by bigger, fluffier breeds like huskies and Samoyeds. I took advantage of this preference to persuade him that a cat was the more ethical choice, because our apartment was small and a big dog would quickly become restless and feel fenced in.

He admitted that he could find no fault with my logic, but I could tell that the emotional resonance wasn't there. He had one hand lifted, absentmindedly fluffing the back of his hair, like he was fantasizing about petting a goofball dog. As a joke, I grabbed a pair of scissors and made a life-size cutout of a cat from construction paper. I posed the jagged-edged cat next to him on our couch, telling him to try imagining having a cat around the place.

"Maybe this will change your mind. You'll get so used to her presence that she'll become real to you," I said, pleased with my crude work.

Marlin seemed unimpressed. But the next morning, as I stumbled bleary-eyed into the bathroom, I nearly sat on the cat cutout posed on the toilet seat. I huffed out belly laughs so big I could smell my own stink of unbrushed morning breath.

After that it was game on. Sometimes our paper cat would be perched right in front of Marlin's computer, obscuring the screen. Other times she snuck under my pillow, with only a little nub of a paw or tail tip sticking out to let me know she was there. Occasionally she went missing, and I would almost even forget about her, until she surprised me, waiting in the freezer.

One evening after work, standing in the dim hallway outside our apartment door, my keys jutting out from one tight fist, I had a sudden feeling that something was wrong. There was a persistent scratching sound coming from the other side of my own front door. I kept my eyes on the keyhole, which seemed to be shining, dully. The scratches became more insistent, almost like a saw's whine. I checked again; yes, it appeared to be the right door, the one that would open to our mess of partially dry umbrellas sagging against cardboard boxes waiting to be collapsed and twined, a dying potted plant lurking in the background. What was there? What had gotten in while we were at work?

I must have stood there for minutes. I would have stayed even longer, were it not for the ding of the elevator down the hall. That broke the spell. I didn't want my neighbors to catch me standing frozen in front of my own home.

I hunched over the doorknob and twisted it, degree by degree. Then, just as carefully, I leaned against the door until it opened a crack. The scratching stopped. I thought I felt resistance on the other side of the door, so barely perceptible that I couldn't be sure it wasn't my mind, conjuring.

The elevator dinged again as I pushed open the door more, peering around it. I saw a tangled mess of black geometric shapes, like someone had spilled a monochrome Lego kit on the floor. Then the mess juddered, and I realized I was looking at four straight locked limbs connected to a glinting carapace, topped off with a passably globular head. The creature was on its back, shuddering in a frantic rhythm and whirring mechanically. It was trying to sit upright on its metal haunches.

"What the heck?" I muttered.

Laughter erupted from somewhere behind me. I jumped, kicking the creature and accidentally righting it, setting it roaming into Marlin's ankles. He was doubled over, his laughter a seesaw pitch.

"Best day of my life," he said, when he could speak again. Wiping tears from his eyes, he explained how he'd built a robot cat out of 3D-printed frames, springs, and rivets, then given it a Raspberry Pi for a brain.

"Raspberry Pie? That's an odd name for a computer."

The cat lurched alarmingly from side to side as it came toward me.

"So what is it called? Marlin's Monster?"

"You were the one who wanted a cat." Marlin widened his eyes, long lashes underscoring put-on innocence. "You name it."

"I'll think about it," I said, delighted. He'd taken my desire and crafted it into corporeal reality. How could I be unmoved?

The next day he came home to a surprise of his own. I'd picked up a stuffed dog the color of a radioactive eggplant and the same size as the robot. I gutted the dog, skinned it, and fitted its fur around Marlin's robot cat. My turn for a good laugh.

It went on like this, Marlin incrementally improving the robot's balancing skills, giving it a speaker for grotesque meows, installing a fish-eye camera, while I added a mismatched blue tail, ears torn off a toy bear, stirrers nabbed from a coffee shop for whiskers. The robot was truly a sight to behold. Eventually I named it Buster, because it was the most American name I had ever heard—surely no one outside America could be called Buster. It seemed apt, too, as it often walked itself into walls and chairs, busting its own delicate setup, requiring tinkering.

When Marlin fired it up and tried out new tricks, I'd look on with pride and imagine that this was what parents of human babies felt. No matter how hideous or ungainly, it was something that we, and only we, could have created. There was no entity like it anywhere else in the world. And tenderness would well up in me, something that seemed very much like bliss floating to the top.

It makes me feel like a fool now. Zoomed out, you can see how ludicrous it is, the way everybody un-uniquely fixates upon how unique their creations are. Really, we are just marveling at chance. Babies switched at birth inspire the same misplaced warm feelings in both sets of parents. That alone should tell us how mistaken we are. Interchangeable uniqueness? What a concept.

Marlin had taken Buster with him. I wasn't delusional—I knew it wasn't really alive—but it still hurt. He hadn't explicitly presented Buster as a gift to me per se, but I'd always thought about it that way. Hadn't he made it to impress me?

Day Two (Thursday)

At home, I snatched up the list of possible places where Marlin could be. Setting aside hotels and vacation spots, there were eight leads to follow. I'd spoken to Eamon at lunch, so I crossed him off, which left me with seven avenues of investigation.

- Home with Mummy (unlikely, based on phone call yesterday)
- His office (possible, though need an in to get past building security)
- Crashing with someone?
  - ~~Best friend Eamon (possible, all the way out in College Point)~~
  - Friends from work (possible, could verify by visiting office—see above)
  - Climbing gym partners? (can't remember names other than Eamon)

- Climbing gym (possible, given three-times-a-week routine)
- Favorite restaurant (too close to apartment? worth a try anyway)

I lifted a pen to cross out item 1 as well, but my hand hovered over the word *Home*. A trip from New York to Malaysia took at least a full day; there were no direct flights. Marlin couldn't have been at Mummy's when I'd called her yesterday, but who was to say he hadn't been on his way? The discovery that he'd taken Buster with him meant it was likelier Marlin hadn't gone far, but I had to be sure. I dropped onto our couch and called Mummy again.

When she picked up, I strained my ears for any sound that might give Marlin away. Was the tinny noise in the background him, stirring condensed milk into Milo? That rustling—it could be him lifting the tudung saji for a bite of kuih.

"Edwina?"

She sounded tired. It was not even six in the morning for her, after all.

"Sorry, did I wake you?"

"No, no. I was just scrubbing some clothes."

"Did Marlin mention we might want to visit soon?" I held my breath. Why was she taking so long to answer?

"No," she finally said. "But that's nice. He called me the other day and asked some strange questions."

"What questions?"

"It's probably nothing. I was just a bit surprised. How is he doing?"

"He's good. Still at work. You said he sounded strange when he called you?"

"He was asking about the cemetery . . . how much it would cost."

"I don't understand. We already settled payment for—for—," I stumbled. I was hunched over, my neck sticking out like a turtle's. It felt cruel to remind her so baldly of her husband's death.

"He actually asked how much it would cost for himself."

"What? You mean Marlin was trying to buy his own funeral plot?"

"He wanted the place next to his daddy, you know."

"In *Malaysia*?"

She fell silent.

"Shouldn't you be the one next to his dad?" I was desperate to refute, in some way, what I'd just heard.

"Oh, forget I said anything. Obviously I'm being silly. It's wise to plan ahead."

"Wait. Did he ask for one plot? Or two?"

Mummy begged off, saying she needed to get back to her clothes. Right before she hung up, I heard the call of azan swell through the phone.

SIX MORE LEADS TO PURSUE. I COULDN'T FOCUS ON THEM. MARLIN HAD called about a final resting place. He was thinking about death, perhaps obsessing over it. I tried to convince myself it was a touching gesture, born out of straightforward love for his father and a keen sense of loss. But I couldn't help returning to the number of plots in question. It wasn't just that I wanted to feel included in his plans. Two plots implied he was thinking of me, yes, but also that he was preparing for something far in the future. One, going solo, hinted at something much darker.

I clutched my head and rode it out, the carousel of gore presented by my mind. Marlin lying in a pool of his own blood, one edge of his suicide note scalloped red. Marlin sprawled half in and half out of a shattered windshield, splinters of glass wedged into a broad tree trunk. Marlin gone, replaced by a dull mound of brown earth.

I gripped my upper arms and kneaded them with crossed hands. If I didn't find Marlin soon, my nightmarish visions would either come true or drive me to a breakdown. The sun had set sometime during my brooding. I got up from the couch to turn on a floor lamp. It had been approximately a whole day now since Marlin left. Not enough time had passed for a missing person's report. Besides, it was obvious what conclusions the authorities would draw. Husbands vacated marriages all the time, after all. Not to mention I couldn't get him in trouble with the law, not when he was an immigrant on a work visa. I wouldn't make the same mistake again.

I'll explain. In sophomore year of college, I was assigned a single room next to a student from Germany. The dorm walls were thin. Night after night, the sounds of vomiting and weeping drifted into my room. At first I tried to ignore them, stuffing earbuds deep into my ear canals. Then one morning I walked in on the German in our shared bathroom down the hall. She was wearing a tank top, her spine protruding through the thin material as she brushed her hair. It wasn't that cold, but her scapulae vibrated like violin bows. When her comb ran through, it came away with a tangled fistful of blond hair.

I reported what I'd heard and saw to our RA. That same afternoon, campus police showed up. She cried as she picked up her shoes by their laces, two men hulking over her tiny frame. Later, I learned she'd been considered a "threat to herself or others" and kicked off campus housing. She lost her scholarship. Had to leave the country.

I couldn't do it again, put someone's fate into the hands of un-compromising men in uniforms. Marlin had so much to lose, and I wasn't ready to give up on us. I could still find him and make him see sense, persuade him to come back to me.

I sat down at the kitchen table with my laptop, thinking I'd give Josh's novel installment a thirty-second skim. That way I could strategically drop in the right keywords when I saw him the next day. Maybe then he would get in touch faster with his ex, or whom-ever it was he knew at Cachi I/O.

Radmonsius balls his fists in anger as the space alien raises its laser gun cockily. The enemy's face is covered with strange markings. A nearby dying planet lets off a burst of illumination. The alien's blue skin seems to darken as he takes a threatening step forward. From behind Radmonsius the ghost of his friend Space Lt Col Coiler whispers: "Kill it, before it takes away everything you love."

I thought Josh's novel couldn't get any worse, but he had ven-tured into racist territory with his latest. I debated reading further. Clearly Radmonsius would emerge victorious. I could tell Josh I appreciated the nail-biting suspense of the duel, or some such. But did I also have a moral duty to call out the problems in his text?

My mother's face popped up, obscuring Josh's masterpiece. If I were the fist-balling type, I would have done just that—curled my hands and dug in my nails. Instead I sighed and clicked to accept the incoming Skype call.

"Wow, what happened?" my mother said immediately. "You look terrible!"

"I didn't sleep well."

"Your face so fat! Are you eating too much again? Better stop doing that."

It was a familiar routine, enacted and reenacted since I was a child. At least she couldn't see me from the neck down, now that I'd moved halfway across the world.

When I was thirteen or fourteen, my mother obtained a life-size poster of a local beauty queen from my uncle, who ran a coffee shop in town. The beauty queen advertised a brand of cheap beer that was popular at my uncle's establishment. My mother taped the beauty queen's head to a pillow, showcasing the touched-up face of pearly radiance and hair of new-car sheen. The rest of her body was affixed to a mop handle that was about the right height. Thus given heft, the beauty queen was lovingly carried into my room, where I was sleeping way past the time my mother would have liked for me to wake up. Gently, my mother laid the embodied beauty queen next to me, her head-pillow flush against mine. Then my mother left the room. She didn't return until she heard my screams.

"What is this?" I shouted at her. I'd woken up and shrieked in terror, believing for a moment that a stranger had invaded my bed.

"It's your motivation," my mother said.

"My what?"

"She can help you lose weight."

"What is this piece of paper supposed to do?"

"It's like this: auntie next door said she listened to classical music when she was carrying her baby, and now look how smart Ah Bee is. So if you look at skinny beautiful girls every day, then you can imagine yourself one day looking just like them. It will inspire you!" She spread her palms, a ta-da gesture.

I made her leave and banged the door shut. Then I sat down on my bed and focused on the unnaturally beautiful woman beside me. Would it work? I concentrated, beaming my wishes at the prone figure. Yes, my eyes would widen to take in all the appraising gazes of my admirers. My two cheeks would smash into each other like earth plates, giving rise to a tall, proud ridge that was my nose. My eyebrows would arch, well, archly, my jaw would taper, my chin would complete the gentle tip of my pumpkin-seed-shaped face. And my lips, oh, my lips would be like the softest flower petals, never cracking, no matter how wide I stretched them to smile or to fit them over a pineapple bun, the crust flaking off as I bit in with cute yaeba teeth.

Who was I kidding? I turned away, feeling humiliated. With one kick the beauty queen flopped to the ground and lay there facedown.

On Skype, my mother was telling me to start every morning with a quarter of an apple and as many celery sticks as I wanted, because they had "negative calories."

"That makes no sense," I said. "Can we talk later? I'm busy."

"Oh, right. Actually, I have something to tell you." As she said this, her image on-screen froze, so I couldn't see her expression.

"You're not moving. I can't see you."

"Hello? Hello? Can you hear me?"

I went with it. I played the "Hello?" game for a few seconds, and then I ended the call.

I hate talking about my mother this way. Though maybe you see it as a gold mine for therapy. I see how my depictions reduce her to a kind of movie stereotype: that harsh, unfeeling, tactless Asian mother who criticizes constantly and expresses love never, or at least not until the very last scene of the movie. And what if, in my case, it is a truthful depiction? Does that mean (a) my mother molded herself in accordance to a stereotype, which is to say a societal expectation; or (b) I can view my mother only through this mediated lens of caricature imposed by entertainment?

It is so hard to trust our own thoughts.

March 2018

You remember what the snow was like that winter? People were throwing out words like "bomb cyclone." Sometimes I wonder how things would have turned out if the weather had been less brutal, at least from the perspective of two immigrants who'd moved from a tropical country. If the world outside hadn't loomed ominous and gray, would that have made a difference? Would Marlin have felt any better?

I, at least, was not immune to the forbidding look of the city outside. I'd just gotten off a call with my mother. It was only ten in the morning, but already our living room was awash in shadows. I walked toward a window, wanting more light, and suddenly found myself sobbing.

"What's wrong?" Marlin looked up from his computer, concerned.

"Oh, it's nothing." I scrubbed my face. "The usual. Why is my mother *like that*?"

I wasn't expecting an answer to my offhand rant. To my surprise, Marlin stood up, looked me in the eye, and said gently: "Maybe we can find out."

"What do you mean?"

"Wait here." He retreated into the bedroom. When he returned, I'd managed to dry my eyes and was feeling embarrassed about my earlier outburst.

"You'd think I'd be used to talking to my own mother after all this time," I said, attempting a laugh. I didn't want to burden Marlin with my petty frustrations. It was still so soon after his father's death; if anything, I should be the one to offer comfort.

He didn't react to my inane joke. Instead he busied himself with something on the dining table, his back to me. Then he came and told me to close my eyes, his expression tender and serious at the same time.

"Why?" I resisted at first when he tugged on my right hand. I didn't want a mountain made out of my molehill of a crying session.

In the end, it was his warm touch on my wrist that did it. I'd missed that. His skin, the bulging veins you could actually feel on his arms. We hadn't been intimate for a while, for good and obvious reason. And so I lowered my eyelids and trusted his grasp, and we shuffled forward until my feet tapped something solid.

"Sit," he said, lightly guiding me by my shoulders. I braced myself against an edge right in front of me—the dining table, I assumed.

"Empty your mind," he instructed, once I'd stopped fidgeting.

I wanted to toss out a wisecrack, something about how my thoughts were already devoid of substance. Instead I shut up and tried to do as he said. I did my best to imagine a white screen, willing my brain to collapse into something two-dimensional.

I was just starting to think, against my will, about a bodega cat I'd seen the other day, when he lifted my hand and pinched my fingers around a thin, supple object.

"A noodle?" I asked, confused.

"Please." After a while, I heard a sigh. "Try to take this seriously."

I wanted to object, say that serious business was not usually conducted with eyes closed. But I also wanted him to keep curling his palm around my fingers. I stayed quiet.

"Now think about your mother."

I made a face.

"Just follow the instructions for now. It'll make sense later. That's how it worked for me. I kept an open mind and went step by step."

His words were vague, almost meaningless, but I wanted to please him. So I tried. At first there was nothing. Then I did picture her. Not as she'd last appeared—chin forward, tattooed eyebrows so sharp they defied the blurry quality of our video chat—but as she must have seemed to me in my childhood, a towering figure.

"What do you want?" She bent over me, smiling. Overhead, a gecko crawled across the ceiling. "Honey Stars or Koko Krunch?"

I stared, fascinated, wondering if the gecko would fall on her beautiful head. What would she do then? I couldn't imagine.

"You don't know what you want?" Her smile contracted. Her hands rose from her knees to settle, braced, against her waist.

"You can ask your question now. About your mother, why she's like that." Marlin's voice cut through my memory. I suddenly noticed that his grasp was much tighter. He was guiding my balled-up hand to swing the noodle-like object, at first in a hypnotic left-right arc, then in a more complicated rhythm that eluded me.

"Who's answering the question?" I asked. "You?" Marlin was

acting like some kind of strange, authoritative therapist. It made me uneasy.

"No." A pause. "Think of it as . . . a presence that has higher insight."

"What do you mean?" I opened my eyes to search his face. "Like a god?"

"Keep your eyes closed!" Marlin looked as dismayed as I felt. For a moment, I thought this was good, a sign that we were in sync. Then my hand dropped and thudded against the dining table. He'd abruptly let go.

"Ow." I rubbed my hand, pouting.

"I can't continue if you don't take this seriously."

"It's hard to do that when you're being all mysterious! What is this, some kind of religious thing?"

Marlin said nothing, his expression rigid. I turned to see what my hand had been holding and swinging. I just wanted to understand. But Marlin leapt into action, sweeping items off the table in big, exaggerated motions, cradling them so I couldn't get a clear view.

"You don't get it. And it's okay, that's fine, but you could at least not make fun of me," he said, his voice cold and clear.

"I wasn't—"

He was already halfway across the room, arms full of knick-knacks, determined not to listen.

Day Two (Thursday)

My mother's talk about apple and celery on Skype made me hungry. I hadn't had dinner. The old resentment surged again, annoyance at the power she seemed to hold over my body with mere words. *I did as you asked in the past*, I wanted to say to the laptop, now asleep with a blank screen. *I worshipped at the feet of a paper beauty queen and lost not an inch of fat. I did your calisthenics and toning exercises, and all I got out of those were "calves thick as tree trunks" (your words).*

I left the apartment for food. The Financial District at night was a dead zone, rows of shuttered shops squeezing narrow lanes into haphazard, triangular dead ends. I walked past a hardware store established in the 1950s. A sign read KEYS MADE. I started sobbing on the quiet street. When I confirmed no one was looking, I pressed my palms into my face and continued on unseeing.

A motorcycle gunned somewhere behind me. I started and

gripped my wallet tighter. The streetlamps were so dim I couldn't see all the way down the block, but when I peered up at the faded awnings around me I recognized Leo's Bagels, a small deli-like space with bagels hailed as FiDi's best, though that was mostly from a lack of competition.

So many bagels we'd had from here. Marlin and I had stumbled upon it early on in our relationship, one day when we'd spontaneously decided to play hooky and both call in sick so we could spend time together. There was no line on a workday, just a couple of tourists ahead of us. When they asked for their bagels toasted, much to the irritation of the mustachioed man we christened the Bagellier, we scoffed at them. No, we knew better than that. We ordered our breakfast untoasted like real New Yorkers, and we took our everything bagels to a tiny public garden around the corner. There, we spread the bagels' paper clothes on our laps and listened close as we bit into yielding bread, scattering everything onto paper, sesames pinging, making it sound like spring rain that was just starting to pick up.

I could almost taste that runny tofu cream cheese. I'd opted for it out of an early-romance eagerness to please, as if I could charm Marlin further simply by trying vegan cream cheese once. Then again, we'd first been drawn to each other precisely because of our dietary choices, bonding over how veg*ism drove our meat-obsessed friends and families up the wall. We had betrayed our culture, some of them thought, offended that we would not eat their beloved char siu and satay. Right off the bat there had been something that united Marlin and me against the world, a stake on which our love, orchidlike, could twine and grow.

A shadow wavered behind a clump of short bushes in the garden ahead of me. I'd thought I was alone on this dark corner, but

I could hear coughing now, coming from the stirring shadow. I lurched forward, irrationally thinking: *Marlin?*

It was a stranger, a man kneeling with one hand thrust into a bush. His head lolled from side to side, like he was trying to look up at me but couldn't.

"Sir, are you all right?"

A long pause, and then: "Leave me the fa' alone!"

So debilitated he couldn't say "fuck." I stared at the bush swallowing his hand and felt a sudden, perverse longing. I wanted to be lost like that too, drifting in a place that was not exactly my own life. I wanted to be messed up. I backed away from the man, knowing exactly where to go.

As I walked, I wondered for the hundredth time what Marlin might be doing now. What did it feel like for him, having changed so much? Was it a process that was discernible to the person caught within its throes?

Voltaire asked and answered: "Can one change one's character? Yes, if one changes one's body."

Was that what had happened? I'd read that you could get a brain injury from simply falling off your bed. What if Marlin had taken a tumble somewhere—in the shower, riding a colleague's hoverboard at work, while bouldering—then simply picked himself up and brushed it off, never bothering to tell me about it? He could have bumped his head and damaged it while being none the wiser.

I made a note to append this line of investigation to my list when I got home. Ahead of me, McDonald's golden arches shone against a starless sky. This was it, what would fuck me up. If I changed my body, then perhaps I could change my character. Marlin had abandoned the things that made him himself. Maybe I could too, and maybe that would bring me closer to him somehow.

Inside, it was not like what I had imagined. The smell of industrial cleaners soured my nose. I walked up to the counter, trying to keep my breathing shallow. When the cashier cheerlessly greeted me, I was unprepared. I glanced up and ordered what was advertised directly above her head, which happened to be ten pieces of McNuggets.

"Would you like an order of twenty instead? It's the same price," she said.

I stared at her, stupefied. She repeated herself and tacked on the analysis that it was a good deal.

"Why is it the same price?"

She shrugged. "You can get ten nuggets for five bucks, or you can get twenty. It's up to you."

Odd to say, but it was then that I finally experienced the full weight of my panic. For a few long, confusing seconds, I believed that the stitches of the world had finally come undone. Marlin's deviation from his original self had been the first sign, which was now joined by the malfunctioning of basic nugget math. Everything would soon be utter chaos. That was how I felt.

I left shaken, cradling the twenty McNuggets in my hands. Back in our apartment, I peeled the lid off a sauce pack and carefully sniffed its insides. Then I decided it would be literally sugarcoating and so set it aside. If I was going to sabotage my vegetarianism, for so long a core part of my identity, then I would do it without some chemically yellow sauce masking that decision. I readied paper and pen next to the nuggets, intending to write down every minute sensation of my transformation.

But there was to be no detailed analysis in writing. I gagged my way through the first half of a nugget. The second half I spit out as a macerated mound. Feeling like a failure, I tried to compensate by rushing through the next half dozen meat chunks with a bare minimum of chewing, after which my jaw began to burn, followed by my stomach. My body, having long forgotten the existence of meat, was rejecting the nuggets as an alien substance that needed to be purged. I rushed to the bathroom. Out, ye devil! We drive you from us!

BEFORE

January 2018

On our way back to New York from my father-in-law's funeral, we had a four-hour layover in Hong Kong. We were alone with each other at last. Marlin was understandably not quite in the mood to talk, but he leaned his head into mine and huddled against me for what little comfort an international airport could provide. We sat in a din of suitcase-wheel squeaks and repetitive airport announcements, punctuated by the occasional golf-cart-type vehicle beeping past. I kept up a stream of patter, hoping to take Marlin's mind off things a little. As usual I fretted about time running out on our visas and the hope or lack thereof of getting green cards, what with mounting difficulties thrown up by the current administration.

I knew Marlin was listening, because at this point he wordlessly handed over his phone. I glanced down at the headline centered on the screen: "Supreme Court to Take Muslim Ban Case." I glanced at Marlin.

"You think we'll be affected?"

Marlin yanked the phone back. "I wouldn't be too optimistic. The court's conservatives outnumber the liberals."

"Malaysia is majority Muslim," I said stupidly, as if he didn't already know.

"We could be next on the ban list." He completed my thought. "Unlikely, but you never know. How's work?"

I looked at his profile. Was the abrupt question meant to gauge how close I was to a green card? Or was the phrase a mindless change of topic, the way Katie regularly used it?

"Not bad," I said.

"Do you have Presidents' Day off?"

"No, do you?"

"Yeah. Maybe I'll come visit you at your office."

"No!"

I'd startled both of us. Marlin gave me a questioning look. I froze my face, trying to figure out why a coil of uneasiness was stretching out in me.

"Something wrong?"

It was Josh and the guys, I realized. I didn't want Marlin to see the way Josh patted the edge of his desk whenever I needed to talk to him, something he did to absolutely no one else. And what if he challenged me again about having a crush on so-and-so at work? He had a strange habit of trying to link me with various coworkers in the office, including my manager Lucas, much to my mortification. I also didn't want Marlin to hear the kinds of jokes that flew around the office, or the jokes that came out of our product AInstein's mouth, for that matter. Worst of all, I didn't want him to see me force a smile or even a chuckle.

I cast around for a subject distracting enough to banish Marlin's idea of an office visit. My mother's past life story about the banana tree spirit was fresh in my mind, and so, unfortunately, that was what I chose to retell, there on the terminal's scuffed and rigid chairs.

Before I tell you the story, I have something to confess. I shouldn't have twisted the truth earlier. You are my therapist, after all.

Remember how I told you about the girl in my dorm that I reported to my TA for frequent vomiting and weeping? That was me. It was the other way around; she ratted on me and got me in trouble with the school. The prominent scapulae and bony limbs, that was all wishful thinking, what I yearned to actually look like.

I was the one whose hands shook as I put on my shoes to be escorted out of my room. In the end they didn't kick me out of the dorm, though they came close. I was allowed to stay, on the condition that I attend mandatory therapy sessions and make the therapist's notes available to whichever school official deemed it necessary to check on me. For my own welfare, they said solemnly, though I got the impression that they were mostly concerned about the location of my "episodes." As long as I didn't pose a threat to myself on campus, there would be no scandal.

Knowing I deceived you, do you still want to continue emailing and talking on the phone? I understand if you want to cease communications. I shouldn't have told a lie. But if you're sure you want to continue, I'll go on. It means so much, to have someone willing to listen without judgment.

I've spent so much time turning this following story over in my head that I've given it flesh and blood. Don't get me wrong, my mother is a gifted storyteller. Yet since I first heard the story at my father-in-law's funeral, I've tried so hard to inhabit it, immersing myself in the character and the world, I can't promise I haven't embellished some details.

It starts with the delivery of bad news.

THE BANANA TREE SPIRIT (A PAST LIFE STORY)

The most beautiful girl in the village limps home with a bucket of water balanced on her head. Her pulse quickens when she reaches the odd-shaped boulder twenty paces from where the river bends. She parts the blades of grass around the boulder, careful not to upset the bucket. There is no note. Disappointment furrows her brows. She peers around at the trees and bushes nearby, hoping to catch the playful glint of Ah Gu's smile. But there is only the calm hurry of ants, carrying their own load.

When she gets home, her parents are waiting at the small table they use for everything: eating, sewing, air-drying harvests. Seeing her, her mother begins doling out portions of rice, her expression grim and her motions a little forceful. Her father eyes her movements and jiggles his knee.

The most beautiful girl sets the water down in the kitchen and joins them at the table, her bad leg dragging. Sure enough, her father clears his throat as soon as she sits.

"Daughter," he says. "The engagement has been called off."

She tries to hide her pleasure. Immediately her thoughts fly to Ah Gu, the way his eyelids tremble lower and lower as he climaxes on top of her, wreathed in the shadows of banana trees at dusk.

"Don't you understand what this means?" Her mother wrings her hands.

"It means I can be with the one I love," the girl says, lifting her chin.

"Stupid girl! Ah Gu won't be marrying you either, not after what's happened." Her father bangs a fist on the table. A few grains of rice hop onto the dirt floor.

"What's happened?" She looks defiantly into her parents' eyes in turn. Dark shapes loom through the window behind her. The day's last light sketches only the faintest edge of things, like the shape of the fence around their house. When a gust blows, with effort the light picks out the fronds of banana trees swaying, conjuring the waving of giant hands or the tossing of thick hair. Every morning clumps of these trees greet her, and she touches them where they are no longer whole—a bald patch here, an enervated limb there.

"She doesn't know." Her mother sighs. "You can't blame her for not knowing."

"Know what?"

"That we are ruined," her father says heavily. "Ruined."

"Why did you have to go running around with Ah Gu behind the back of your betrothed?"

"That's not why he called off the engagement, though, is it?"

"We had our pick," her father mutters. "So many promises of proposals, good families all of them. You know what some of them said? They told me they started saving up for you since you were thirteen, so they could compete with other families' bride prices. Now it's all gone. Not even Ah Gu wants you."

The most beautiful girl swivels to look out into the night. Is it truly her fault, or is it something that lurks out there, beyond the candlelight?

"My Ba planted those," her father continues, waving a shaky hand at the window.

Yes, she has heard the story countless times. Her grandfather started with a handful of saplings, which bore fruit that he then piled onto a handcart wheeled from door to door. But his hardy bananas were not like their cousins with sweet, pliant flesh that the villagers loved to eat. He barely made ends meet. His luck finally turned when he married. His wife worked magic by extracting fiber from the hardy bananas to become mats, curtains, and even clothes. They started scraping by, though they never did quite become comfortable. Then the most beautiful girl in the village was born, and her parents began to hope.

"All gone now," her father repeats, staring at the table.

None of them will say it out loud, but they all know their predicament is really because of what happened to the fishmonger's third son, who smelled, naturally, always of fish, and seemed excessively courteous because of this. The girl remembers the way his hands glistened as he deftly pinned down the wriggling fish she'd selected from a shallow basin. Watching him in action, she thought it looked like the fish's bright, silver life was transferring over to those hands that brought the knife slamming down. He seemed so hale.

The day after she bought the fish from him, the boy woke up listless, his skin the color of spent rice hulls. The fishmonger gave him a tongue-lashing when customers grew impatient with his slow movements, but the boy barely responded to his own name. The next day he grew worse, and in just three days he had lost a quarter of his body weight. His bones seemed to be planning an attack, floating slowly but surely to the surface like preying crocodiles. By the fifth day, he was confined to his bed.

That night, the fishmonger was roused from sleep by what sounded like supplications from his son's room. He hurried over with a pitcher of water, concerned. Standing right outside the boy's door, he heard a sound that almost made him drop the water. It was laughter, unmistakably his son's. The fishmonger was so surprised that he stood rooted to the spot, and he might have kept on standing there were it not for the next sound he heard—a woman's giggle.

When the fishmonger burst into the room, everything flew into chaotic motion. Papers spiraled, brushes and ink stands flew. The shit bucket overturned. One hand shielding his face, the fishmonger saw a woman with translucent skin astride his giggling son. The woman, radiantly beautiful, gusted out of the open window in a brilliance of green streaks. She shot the fishmonger a look of pure malice right before she disappeared from view.

The fishmonger rushed to the window. His hands gripped the sill so hard that they bore marks for days, something he kept showing to the villagers later. Outside, it was a breeze-less night. There was no wind—he would stress this repeatedly. Leaning into the stillness, the fishmonger was drawn to a movement across the pond next to his house. He squinted. The only thing moving in the world was a lone hardy banana tree that had sprung up mysteriously during the past year.

There, perched on the very top, was the translucent woman. She sat cross-legged, her long hair splayed out into space as if held up by invisible, floating demons. Yet the tree showed no signs of bearing weight, its broad leaves unruffled, without a dent or dip. How could it be? Spooked, the fishmonger leaned farther out the window, neck jutting. The alluring curves of that waist, the elegant slopes of those shoulders, and the beautiful silk of that eerie hair . . . It was, without question, the most beautiful girl in the village. The fishmonger raced out of the house in pursuit, but the girl had vanished.

By the time he returned to check on his son, the boy had perished. Sucked dry of his yang vitality, concluded the village medicine man. Sapped of his male life force.

By morning, a crowd had gathered outside the most beautiful girl's home. The girl and her parents were forced to greet the medicine man, sent as a representative to confront the hardy banana tree spirit.

"Any dreams of flying last night?" He prodded. "Any floating sensations?" He looked at her face. He looked at her breasts. He even tried to touch her hair.

The girl fled. She pushed past her gasping parents and shot out the door into the surrounding grove of hardy banana trees. The medicine man and a few villagers chased after her, but the girl was fleet-footed. She had the advantage, too, of knowing that maze of trunks and leaves like the back of her hand. Panting, her pursuers soon lost sight of her. They swiveled their heads and looked up into the blue sky, their mouths open.

"Here!" A shout suddenly rang out. The girl's own voice. Her accusers hurried to the source and found her crouched precariously in the branches of a tall, old tree. The tree listed to one side under its burden, a spot of blood marking its rough bark where the girl had cut up her palms.

"Get down at once," one of the villagers ordered. "You—"

The medicine man extended a silencing hand. A hush fell

over the grove. Then, with a flourish of his sleeves, he began to chant, melodic phrases intermingled with guttural yawps that no one else could comprehend.

"No! I'm not a monster!"

Even in her fury, the girl in the tree was beautiful. The men watched, paralyzed. She stood and plunged. As she rushed toward the ground, the air seemed to ripple around them, raising the hairs on their arms on end.

The girl landed on her side. One foot arrived last, trailing the rest of her. When the foot made contact with the soil, it bounced high, then smashed down once more. From the foot's odd bent angle, they could all tell that something precious had departed, never to return again.

"Do you believe me now?" the girl said through gritted teeth. "I can't fly, see? Not at all. Look, my hands are bleeding. Is that proof enough? Or do you want me to fart in your face? Ghosts don't fart, do they? How about watching me take a shit?"

A bizarre and unrealistic tale, isn't it? A young girl trying to convince an entire village of her innocence by maiming herself. And yet I was moved by the pointless bravado.

That doesn't mean I didn't catch on to the central barb in my mother's story. In that supposed past life of mine, I possessed great beauty but acted rashly and dishonorably. As punishment, I am doomed in my present life to be homely. For most of my life my mother had urged me to not "eat like a pig," later amended to be "like an American" after I escaped to New York. She herself was svelte and youthful, and she relished nothing more than to be mistaken for my sister.

Katie's take on this was that I should play up what I had, and draw attention away from what I didn't. "Get to know your own face and body," she told me. I tried, leaning right up against mirrors to pore over my, well, pores. Which of my features were strengths, and which weaknesses? In the end, I realized that the game was rigged. "Strengths" and "weaknesses" were evaluated in comparison to all the other faces out there in the world. In that way, the scrutiny of my face could never be on its own terms, but always measured against an unspoken standard of beauty, a double always projected over my own inadequate mien.

And yet Marlin found me desirable once. When he looked at me, he glimpsed something different from what my mother saw, what I myself couldn't bear to scrutinize in my reflection. (Please, no need to comfort me. I'm just sharing my honest feelings.)

My mother probably meant the banana tree spirit story as yet another source of motivation for me to get my act together and lose some weight. I interpreted it simultaneously as what people called "negging" (am I using that correctly?), and also an oddly moving account of defiance. Whereas Marlin, his takeaway was something else entirely.

Day Two (Thursday)

Around four in the morning, the McDonald's nuggets' destructive effect on my bowels finally subsided. I slumped against the cold bathtub we never used for its intended purpose, preferring instead to stand right under the showerhead. Both of us had grown up with a tank and a pail from which we scooped water onto our bodies. Lying down to get clean seemed unnatural.

It wasn't the first time I'd hoped for psychic transformation and ended with diarrhea. The previous time was over a decade before, when I'd just gotten my acceptance letter to an American college. I was terrified at the prospect of leaving the country for the first time to be in a place where I knew nobody, and also paradoxically terrified of staying, now that I knew leaving was possible. I was afraid of incurring future regret, if that makes any sense.

I read and reread the letter, hiding it from my mother. On one hand, I was eager to flee my mother's judgment and her incessant attempts to mold me. On the other, what did I know about America, except what I'd seen in movies?

For a week I barely slept. I was convinced this was a major fork in my life, and the wrong decision would doom the rest of my days. I walked around squeezing my temples with the heel of my palms, and soon I started having vaguely suicidal impulses, like wanting to step into traffic or wondering what garden shears would feel like against the skin of my stomach. Just little blips of irrational curiosity, nothing more. I was young, though, and scared. I wanted help.

I was familiar with the concept of psychiatrists, but had never seen one advertising services in my small town. For lack of a better choice, I went to a Western family medicine clinic, where I sat down in front of a gruff male doctor and very earnestly said that I would like to be prescribed antidepressants. The doctor grunted and asked if I had any thoughts of self-harm. I hung my head and confessed the little blips. He wrote something down on his pad, and then I was on my way to collect pills from the dispensary. I walked away already feeling a little better, believing that I would soon be relieved of those unwanted thoughts.

At home, I hid in the bathroom and looked at the pills. I decided to take one more than the prescribed number, wanting to get better faster so that I could finally make a clearheaded decision about whether to leave for America.

After swallowing the pills I hugged my knees and waited, the American college acceptance letter half rising from its accordioned pleats at my feet. For a while I wasn't sure anything was happening; I wavered between conviction that the pills were working and suspicions about placebo effect. I was about to go find the kitchen shears as an experiment when it hit me, a grinding pain in my gut like someone was mincing my insides for wonton filler. I collapsed back into my chair and then almost immediately jumped back up. I rushed to the bathroom and groped to raise the toilet seat, hunched over like a shrimp.

Many agonizing hours later, when I had the sense to read the fine print on the pill packaging, I saw that my prescription anti-depressants were nothing more than common laxatives. Perhaps the doctor believed that emptying my bowels would rid me of my more alarming feelings, the way leeches were once used to drain patients of bad blood.

THERE WERE STILL A HANDFUL OF NUGGETS LEFT WHEN I JUDGED IT SAFE to leave the bathroom. I touched their cold crusts, my finger pads brushing back and forth like an archaeologist demanding a story from an inert shard. The experiment had not been a success. I felt no closer to understanding how Marlin had changed. I looked around the apartment, hoping for some other inspiration.

My gaze landed on the TV. Marlin had loved watching nature documentaries. They weren't quite my cup of tea; I found them dry. When Marlin streamed them, I'd sit next to him but busy myself with something else, like studying programming for interviews. Now I regretted not paying more attention. Marlin had derived pleasure from those panning high-definition shots, just like he had once found joy in my company. Was there any magic left in either for him?

Cold nuggets in my lap, I turned the TV on and pulled up one of the documentaries Marlin had been watching. It was about ants. The deep-voiced narrator talked about the ants' mysterious hive mind, which regulates the makeup of the colony's occupants. Based on the colony's needs, the hive mind might determine that 50 percent of the worker ants need to gather food, while 25 percent should be soldiers, with the rest staying close by the queen to serve her whims.

Say the half of food-gathering ants are out in the open, doing their job. Say it is a sunny, scorching day. Suddenly a shadow obscures. From the sky, a shoe plummets onto the trail of ants winding its way between food source (dead gnat) and home. In a twitch of an antenna, a large number of ants are snuffed out. Their bodies lie in a kind of squashed, semi-solid puddle. The ants snaking up from behind crawl around the puddle like it's just another obstruction. They're bearing precious gnat cargo; they cannot stop. Because the ant in front of them has not stopped, and the ant behind them hasn't either.

The vanguard approaches home. Some distance away from the nest, they run into soldier ants from their colony. They exchange information via pheromones with their nest mates. Chemicals rise and waft from the shiny bodies of the ants that have survived a massacre. The soldier ants twitch, receptive. Then in them a switch flips, without need for conscious, individual thought. They are instantly reprogrammed because the colony is now imbalanced: the ratio of food gatherers to soldiers is off, and at this rate the queen won't have enough to eat. A very precise number of ex-soldiers fall seamlessly into step with the food gatherers, transformed. They have now assumed whole new identities for the greater good.

That's what the change in Marlin felt like. Total, and absent deliberate decisioning. Brainwashed, I'd thought at first. Or, in Chinese: "taming of the head." Voodoo. Black magic. Here it was, a scientific equivalent found in ants. What if humanity was similarly connected and orchestrated into achieving some kind of balance? Maybe, somewhere, there'd been a cliff fall in the number of people who believed in spirits. Then the smell of the world changed: oilier, more like cacti and less like hibiscus. Marlin lifted his beautiful head of curls and sniffed, nostrils flaring.

May 2018

I forget what I was dreaming about that night. It might even have been the beautiful girl and her hardy banana trees. Whatever the dream was, it was harrowing or strange enough that I did not immediately realize I was awake when Marlin startled me from sleep. He was sitting up in bed, back ruler-straight, shouting. He yelled without forming words, the unfamiliar sounds coming as if from the deepest reserves of his throat.

After a moment, I understood I was no longer dreaming. I groped for his arm.

"Wake up, Marlin."

His face was turned slightly away from me. I couldn't see them, but I imagined his eyes squeezed shut in terror. I was utterly unprepared when his wild screams stopped and he turned to look right at me. His eyes were wide, clear, and lucid when he asked: "Why did you cheat on me?"

I stammered in surprise, every sentence imbued with uptalk. I had never? I would never? Why would he think? I can't believe?

"Not never. You've done it before," he said. "With Ah Gu." He threw the name down on our bedsheets with finality and conviction.

"Ah Gu? From the banana tree spirit story? Are you serious?" He simply stared at me.

"It's just a *story*! You know how my mom is, she's superstitious and she has an overactive imagination. Also she makes up these stories to judge me on the way I live, you know all that. I've told you!"

"So you're saying she has nothing better to do than sit around all day coming up with stories to annoy you?"

I felt slashed. It hurt, having to defend myself against the charge of cheating in particular. Years and years ago, I'd closed my eyes and made a wish to no entity in particular that if I could please, please just get a boyfriend or girlfriend, I would treasure them forever. I would never cheat on them. I'd told Marlin this silly anecdote, just as I'd shared my feelings about my mother's past life stories with him, and now he was using both against me?

"Even if that *did* happen in a so-called past life, I don't remember any of it, so it has no bearing on our situation now," I said, trying to sprinkle some logic into the argument. But that turned out to be my grave misstep. Marlin pounced, seizing upon what I'd just said like it was a confession.

"Even though you can't directly reason about it, things buried deep in your subconscious can still influence your behavior. Your past life memories are one of those things."

"Where did you learn all this? From your 'spiritual advisers'?"

"Now you're just deflecting. Tell me, who is it? Your yoga teacher? A barista? Someone at work?"

For some reason I thought of Josh then, the way he kept embarrassing me by claiming I had crushes on a rotating cast of colleagues. I could feel my face start to heat up.

"I barely go to yoga," I said weakly.

"You're clearly hiding something. Why do you never tell me anything about your job? You're just like the banana girl, lying to Li Shen."

"Li Shen?"

"You don't even remember! The fiancé, the one she cheated on!"

"Okay, the point is, *I'm* not cheating on *you*." I was crying now, worn down.

He swung his legs off the bed, turning his back to me. I wanted to hug him from behind, the way I used to early on in our relationship. I'd press my face into his back and soak up his warmth without letting him see my expression. I was sure then that my happiness couldn't last; it felt so undeserved.

I didn't hug Marlin that night we fought. I wiped my tears and convinced myself that Marlin was still half asleep, his outburst a temporary by-product of nightmares. I curled up on my side of the bed, thinking that in the morning he would be back to normal, a dependable Myers-Briggs T if ever there was one.

YOU DON'T HAVE TO SAY IT. KATIE BEAT YOU TO IT. WHEN I TOLD HER what had happened, she gasped so loud that heads turned in the busy café we were in. I stopped talking and tugged on her sleeve, hoping the motion would make her lower the coffee cup she was holding dramatically aloft. She did, but chose to keep her mouth stretched wide in imitation of the famous Munch painting.

"That's, like, verbal abuse," she eventually said.

"What? No." I frowned.

"He's gaslighting you! He's making you feel guilty for something you didn't do."

"He's going through a lot. Maybe he just woke up from a dream and was still confused."

"You don't take it out on your wife like that, though!"

"Can you speak a little softer? Also, who's he supposed to turn to?" I grabbed her again, trying to pull her closer. "I've met his dad. I was there at the funeral. Who else even remotely understands what he's going through?"

"So that's your plan? Grin and bear it because there's no one else?"

"You don't abandon your spouse when he's in pain."

She had no immediate comeback for this. I don't know what she was thinking about, but I hoped it was of the time she called me a bitch, in an earnest way, after I hid her phone to prevent her from calling her ex's new girlfriend.

"You're better than this," I had said to her, over and over, while she continued calling me names.

Katie lifted her coffee cup and drained it like it was sloshing with vodka. "Well, as long as it's a onetime thing. He should be snapping out of it soon, right? What's it been, six months?"

"More like four. Both your parents are alive, though. Maybe you don't know what it feels like."

"You lost your dad," she pointed out.

"Yeah. But I don't remember that much." I put my cup back in its saucer too hard and winced at the inelegant clang. I stared at my lap. With my head down, I could feel Katie's eyes on me. A while later she asked if I was ready to go.

Day Three (Friday)

I woke up convinced Marlin was back. There was no reason to think so, no sound from another part of the apartment. I simply sat up on the couch and blinked, waiting for him to sit down next to me. My delusion went beyond just believing he had physically returned. I had somehow been sure, for a moment, that he was his old self again, logical and unflappable. I checked my phone, heart pounding impatiently, but there was nothing there from him either.

Where had these false feelings come from? I stared at the ceiling. Maybe he'd been such a grounding force of pragmatism for me that I didn't know how to be rational on my own.

We had a conversation about intelligence once. Marlin, to my amused annoyance, was being falsely modest. He waved off my insistence that he was extremely intelligent and said he was merely smart enough to realize he wasn't *that* smart.

"Isn't that like saying 'I'm a good person because I don't claim to be a good person?'" I asked.

Marlin frowned very seriously and kept saying no, no, there's a difference. I wish I could remember what his arguments were. In my memory, I gave myself the last word.

ON THE SUBWAY, I LEANED AS FAR AWAY AS I COULD FROM A BRIEFCASE poking into my butt. I scrolled through my smartphone with one hand. Lucas had canceled our meeting today. As the train lurched around a corner, I brought up Josh's latest novel installment and picked a section at random.

Radmonsius leans into her face. "You don't mind if I call you Kathleen, do you, doctor?"

Kathleen lets out a breath she hadn't known she was holding. Yes, she is a scientist, but she is also a sensitive, romantic woman! She has been waiting for this moment for so long, and now it has finally arrived.

"You can call me anything you want," she murmurs as she stands on her tiptoes to press her lips against his. In the background, the ghost of Lt. Col. Coiler pumps his fist.

I figured I'd read enough to tell Josh what he wanted to hear. Hero slays alien, hero gets girl. I could probably extrapolate from that.

The stink of a fart blossomed in the train car. I looked around and unintentionally met the eye of a woman in a pencil skirt. She pinched her nose and grinned, so I did too, before glancing awkwardly into someone else's armpit. It felt unnatural to smile.

Once, Marlin and I were stuck on a stalled 7 train. We were on elevated tracks suspended high over Long Island City, on our way back from visiting Flushing for good food. Through the train's dirty

panes we could see the sun setting, a purplish pink that seemed innocent but also somehow gravely wrong, like a birthday party full
of zombie children.

A middle-aged man at the other end of the car stood up and
declared he could no longer hold it in; he was very sorry but he simply had to relieve himself. A commotion started, strangers uniting
in aggressively expressed admonishments for the man to sit back
down and "chill."

The man sulkily plopped back onto his hard, shiny seat. A minute later he sprang up and made again for a corner of the car, wagging his hands and head to show he was not listening, no, really, he
was going to do it. Two youngsters in sports jerseys stood up and
puffed their chests out imposingly, and for a moment I thought the
man would simply pee on them, but instead he turned around and
marched quickly toward our end of the car. Groans of alarm immediately took up our side of the train, and the passengers across
from us tried to dissuade the man, now red in the face, except his
body could no longer be stopped. It would do what it had to do.
As people started moving away from him, the man unzipped his
pants. In his hurry he yanked on his trousers too hard and they
fell to the ground, exposing his bare ass. The hems of his pant legs
darkened with the backsplash of pee.

Marlin grabbed my face and overlaid his on top, blocking the
man from my view. He could be old-fashioned sometimes when it
came to nudity, prudish almost, even though he was very liberal-
minded about everything else. I thought this was because he'd
grown up in a country that regularly censored nudity and sex scenes
from movies, if not outright banning them. Then again, I'd been
brought up in the same country and was not bothered by naked
body parts unless they happened to be my own. It was interesting

how the same forces of influence and pressure could produce something so dissimilar in different people. I thought about all this, and a tenderness for Marlin suddenly washed over me. I found him special, charming in the ways he diverged despite our many overlapping experiences. I nuzzled his neck and whispered into his ear: "It smells bad in here."

Then we were kissing, our lips furiously working. I felt his tongue spread like jam and our teeth bumped, while four feet away a man beset by his fellow New Yorkers let it all go.

I FLICKED MY COMPUTER TO LIFE IN THE OFFICE AND TYPED UP A PARAgraph of gushing "feedback" for Josh. I figured that by sending this to him digitally, I'd preempt another lunch invite. I'd also be saved from having to keep a straight face.

I hit send when I saw Josh walk toward his desk, messenger bag bouncing. I decided I'd give him until lunch before I asked after his ex at Cachi I/O.

"Exciting night?" Josh asked, eyes serious and trained on his screen, smirk mismatching.

"Me?" I looked up. The typing to my left stopped. Maybe he meant Ben, the quiet one who kept his head down and worked with a grimace of concentration.

"Aww, it's okay, I don't judge," Josh said.

"I don't know what you're talking about," I said.

Ben let out a squeaky, obviously fake cough. "Your hair, ah, is a little messy." His voice was even quieter than usual.

Had I forgotten to brush my hair? Were there nugget crumbs tangled in there? I pushed back from my desk, my ergonomic chair rolling into Ben's with a muffled crash. I was at the women's bathroom door as Josh's voice rang around the open-floor office: "Hey, Phil! What were you up to last night?"

I ran the tap so I wouldn't have to hear anything else. In the mirror, I did indeed look frightful. My hair was tousled on one side but flattened on the other, where I had fallen asleep on the couch learning about ants. I found just a single flake of desiccated nugget, a blessing I counted out loud in the empty bathroom: "One."

I combed wet fingers through my hair, my back to the oversize mirror. I could feel a scowl distorting my face. There had to be something I could do to Josh. Some way to hit back. But I still needed to get into Marlin's office. My nape burned as I mentally recited the obsequious praise I'd just sent Josh for his inane novel.

Pursuing a half thought, I took out my phone, navigating to Stack Overflow, the hub for programming-related dumb questions. "List of common edge cases," I typed in the query box. Edge cases are rare situations or use cases that engineers might miss when they write code, resulting in ugly bugs. It was simultaneously the engineers' responsibility to anticipate these edge cases and the bread and butter of my job as testing analyst to catch them. I scrolled through Stack Overflow posts, making note of potential gotchas to try on Josh's code. Some of them must trigger flaws in his work. I imagined filing virtual reams of bug reports, writing up taunting descriptions, and assigning them to Josh. I'd present it as a problem to Lucas, and maybe, just maybe, Josh would get a stern talking-to. It'd take him down a few pegs. After he connected me to Cachi I/O, of course.

JOSH DID COME THROUGH WITH A NAME AND A PHONE NUMBER, AFTER a lunch break from which he returned humming. I read his email and glanced at his serene expression from the corner of my eye, wondering if he felt bad about his innuendo-laced comments this morning. Since then I'd bought an I ♥ NY cap from a street vendor, hoping it would make me look less ragged.

I took a break from my hunt for Josh's coding errors to contact the Cachi I/O connection. He had provided only a first name, Meg. Outside our office building, two competing halal carts stood at opposite ends of the city block, spreading a smell of charred meat that nauseated me in my nugget hangover. I tried my best to stand equidistant between the carts, fingers hesitating over my phone's dial button. It was probably better to text, so Meg wouldn't detect my "foreign" accent. Who knew what she'd be like? She had some kind of relationship with Josh, after all. Then again, was it wise to leave evidence of my probing in writing?

I hit call before I could waffle further. I didn't think people still answered unknown numbers, but Meg picked up after a few rings. I introduced myself in my best movie-American twang, deepening my voice and thinking *Scarlett Johansson, Scarlett Johansson.*

"Oh, it's you," Meg said with a light laugh. "Josh told me you might call."

Next to me, someone lit up a cigarette. I moved away from it, past the P.C. Richard & Son somehow still in business in the age of Amazon.

"Thank you for taking the time."

"It's about the WIT meetup, right?"

"Wit?"

"Women in Tech?"

"Yes, I'm a woman in tech," I said woodenly, unsure how to steer the conversation to Marlin.

"Do you want the email to RSVP?"

"Actually, I was wondering if you know a coworker named Marlin." There was no good way to do it, I decided.

"Marlin? Yeah, why?"

"Is he—there?"

A white van with AMBULNZ emblazoned across its side approached, blaring its obnoxious horn. I watched passersby frown as they tried to puzzle out the ambulance that couldn't spell.

"I'm sorry, I couldn't hear you," I said.

"I said I just checked, and I don't see him. He's been coming in pretty late these days. Something about commuting all the way from Queens. Are you a friend? You're not, like, a stalker, right?"

"No, please don't worry." Queens? Eamon lived in College Point, but he hadn't seen Marlin. How many hotels were there in Queens? Probably fewer than Manhattan, so maybe a search was actually feasible?

"Then what is this about?"

"He was the one who told me about the WIT meetup," I said, pronouncing "WIT" carefully. This part was almost true. I'd seen the flyer for it, after all, tucked among the papers on his desk.

"That's nice of him."

"You said you had the email for RSVPs?"

She spelled out the address and I memorized it, pretending all the while that I was writing it down. I thanked her. Just before she hung up, I added quickly: "Please don't tell Josh about this."

She waited for me to say more.

"I don't want to give the wrong impression," I said.

"Look, I don't know what's going between you two. Just know that Josh can come across, eh, a bit of a dick? But once you get to know him, he's not that bad."

"Okay," I said. "Thank you again."

I bought some prosciutto from a deli before returning to work. Back at my desk, feeling somewhat grateful, I decided to stop scrutinizing Josh's code and work on the AInstein master test plan instead. The plan was a long document laying out every common scenario that a user could possibly encounter with the AInstein robot, with corresponding test cases to make sure AInstein behaved as expected in said scenarios. I checked my calendar. I was supposed to present a completed plan to engineers next week. Once they signed off, I would then actually write the tests and run them against both production and upcoming code. If I did my job right, my tests would catch errors and flag them for fixing before our September launch.

It was nearing the end of July, and I was behind on finishing the plan. The problem was the engineers kept veering off their specs, surprising me with modified implementation methods and new expected behaviors. Not to mention the biggest headache so far, stemming from the mass reneging of comedy writers.

You see, AInstein's artificial intelligence did not extend to writing original jokes. The plan had been to pay up-and-coming comedy writers a modest fee in exchange for material that would become part of AInstein's database. Then one of the contracted writers, who must not have read the nondisclosure fine print, tweeted about how he had been personally invited to contribute to AInstein because he was the "king of eggplant jokes." This drew ire from another writer who had also been approached by the company with the same compliment (I suppose). A Twitter war ensued, with other writers and completely unaffiliated parties leaping into the fray. Many emojis and gifs were abused. The company, also angered, sued the most high-profile instigators for breach of contract, which turned into a backlash against AInstein and led to almost all the comedy writers withdrawing their content. Which is how we came to be trawling Reddit and other online message boards for copyright-free jokes two months before launch.

I went to visit our AInstein prototype on a whim. It had its own dedicated room named Bond, after the English spy. As soon as I walked in, AInstein trained its facial recognition cameras on me. An engineer must have just been in here, talking to it, tweaking.

"Hey," I said.

"Hello! The time is: two oh four p.m."

"My husband left me."

The robot whirred its bulky head side to side, a motion meant to mask the delay in AInstein's response as it calculated the user's emotions based on facial expression, body language, and tone of voice.

"Congratulations!" it said. "I'm sure you don't mind getting divorced—"

I waited, watching the row of LED lights standing in for AInstein's mouth flash to the rhythm of its speech.

"—but I bet you'd much rather be widowed!"

WHEN I RETURNED TO MY DESK, I WAS TAKEN ABACK BY A WALL OF WHITE-on-black text scrolling rapidly down my terminal. I must have launched the tests I'd slapped together to find Josh's bugs, I realized, even though I didn't remember doing it. And there was a hit. I leaned in. In tech, the ability to understand where errors come from is called "introspection." This part never got old, the high of a detective finding a key clue.

The failure conditions showed that Josh had broken AInstein's ability to de-duplicate jokes. AInstein was never supposed to tell the same joke twice within a certain time parameter. Josh's latest branch in code review violated this constraint, serving up more-or-less identical jokes with only a couple of words swapped out. I stared, savoring the victory on-screen: "AssertionError: Expected false to equal true."

Then the rush receded. I stood up, shocked by a sudden realization. Marlin had been commuting from Queens, Meg said. I had assumed this meant he was staying at a hotel. But Eamon could have been lying, couldn't he?

I typed in Eamon's College Point address and watched Google draw colorful lines connecting him to me. The lines crossed water, Manhattan to Queens. One hour and fourteen minutes by train and bus combo. Four hours and twenty-six minutes by foot.

After work, I got on a rush-hour train and transferred at Grand Central, settling in for a long ride. A couple of stops in, a man walked on dangling a tiny child-size scooter by one handlebar. The scooter's lime-green deck sported a sticker of Dwayne "The Rock" Johnson. I stared at it, thinking about the Hollywood practice of giving male action heroes beautiful wives and sometimes adorable children, all so that these men can have something to fight for. Even without much (or any) time spent detailing how the couple met or what made their relationship work (it is always a given that they are blissfully in love), audiences instinctively understand and accept without question the motivations of these action heroes, who have to prove that they can single-handedly fight off twenty-five foes with nothing but a car key, yet who never have to demonstrate the authenticity of their picture-perfect love. How had these rough-and-tumble men all successfully maintained loving relationships, while mine had fallen apart?

It was night proper when I got off the bus closest to Eamon's place. I had no plan. A summer breeze dried my nervous sweat into a kind of casing, reminding me of the salt-baked chicken I used to watch my mother devour.

I'd grumbled about the trek out here to Marlin once, complaining that Eamon lived in the middle of nowhere. Marlin, kind, understanding Marlin, said Eamon had a very straightforward dream. He wanted to become a homeowner before thirty, and he'd achieved his dream. It was a big deal.

"Why does he want to be a homeowner before thirty?"

"He's American."

I pulled on Marlin's hand. I could always tell when he was leaving something out.

"What else?"

Marlin sighed and rubbed his chest with a palm, a sign that he was giving in with reluctance. "He had a fiancée in college. She was from the Midwest, I don't remember which state. They had this grand ten-year plan with major milestones all marked out, and the house thing was one of them. Then she left him after they graduated."

"I had no idea!" I gasped, feeling for Eamon.

"He told me not to tell anyone."

"But I'm your wife."

"That doesn't mean I don't keep secrets."

"Okay, so I *should* or *shouldn't* bring up his fiancée when we see him?"

"Don't be rude now."

I stuck my tongue out at Marlin, and he kissed it.

I'd been unimpressed by the fruition of Eamon's dream. The house was squat and boxy. Under streetlights, its washed-out baby blue looked like the color of childhood corrupted. Instead of a porch, four stone steps barely wider than the front door jutted onto a cement path that ran straight into the main road. The windows had grilles over them. Inside, not even a tiny skylight and antique ceiling fans could endear the house to me. My heart did lift when I glimpsed the clawed feet of his impressively large bookcase—a family heirloom, Eamon said. But then I curtsied to look at the spines on the lower shelves, and was dispirited to see neat rows of paperback Barnes & Noble classics, bought in bulk with no apparent wish other than to fill space.

On that first visit and on subsequent ones, I'd always brought whatever Instagram recommended as gifts (orange wine, succulents), but on this mission to find my husband I arrived empty-handed. When Eamon opened the door, I had to resist the urge to place my hands on his wrist and squeeze, hard.

"Tell me where he is." I tried to channel The Rock, Liam Neeson, Keanu Reeves.

He didn't close the door on my foot, which was at the ready to wedge against the frame. He simply stood tall, arms relaxed, surprisingly unfazed.

"Come in," he said. "Would you like to see him?"

I hung back, surprised. Somehow I had not allowed myself to believe that the answer was really so simple, that Marlin had been at Eamon's all along. The magnitude of loss had felt so much bigger than the solution; it didn't fit. I realized I was in fact expecting Marlin to have hitchhiked to the Appalachians, or be holed up in some elaborate underground labyrinth, which I would have to Mission Impossible my way through. But no, he was here. I looked helplessly at Eamon until he guided me in by my elbow.

Inside, the house was not the neat, if drab, space I remembered. Clothes sagged everywhere, draped over arms and backs of couches and chairs. I recognized a pair of joggers by a tear in its crotch. In the kitchen, a sock crowned a microwave. The abundance of clothing gave the house an oppressive padded feel, like the inside of an asylum cell.

"Excuse the mess," Eamon said. He was frowning, looking like he was struggling to contain his anger. A dot of hope smeared in me. Maybe he had now seen for himself how different Marlin had become. We understood each other, Eamon and I. We'd both been abandoned by the ones we loved. He would help me chip away at Marlin's unreasonable stubbornness.

"This way." Eamon gestured.

I followed him down the short hallway to the back of the house, where the master bedroom and guest room were laid out perpendicular to a small half bathroom. The doors on all three rooms were closed. A narrow bar of light marked the bottom of the guest-room door, making it look like a battery icon that was almost out of juice.

Eamon indicated the guest room with a finger. I stood at the mouth of the hallway, arrested by the strip of glow.

"Is he all right?" I whispered.

"See for yourself," Eamon said, shadows rendering his face harsh. *Don't be so hard on Marlin*, I wanted to say. *He's been through something difficult. Maybe he's not well.* I silently made plans to ask for Eamon's help with Marlin. If Eamon could convince him to answer just one email, or read one text . . .

Eamon swung the door inward. Some kind of chronostasis must have kicked in. I looked at the doorknob, then into the room, locating the human body seated on the bed. When I crossed the threshold, I twisted my body back to find the doorknob, a strange instinct to make sure I wasn't being locked in with my own husband. When I turned again to face Marlin on the bed, it appeared to be entire minutes before he moved to confirm my presence. A trick of the mind, neural antedating, my brain trying to be kind and magicking away unbearable images, for example the naked hatred in Marlin's eyes.

"Marlin, I just want to talk."

As soon as I said the words, he went from glaring round-eyed to pivoting his entire body away, shoulders hunched up. I stared at the back of his head, holding back tears.

"I'm glad to see you're okay. I was worried."

Nothing. No heaving, no trembling. Why was I saying such trite things? Couldn't I do better?

"Marlin, please talk to me."

I strode toward the head of the bed, which he was facing. I wanted to clench him by the shoulders like a UFO catcher and lift him up out of his funk.

Marlin sensed my approach and rotated so he could keep his back to me. Like a sunflower. No, like the reverse of one. My body irrationally followed what it saw as an imperative: dodge Marlin's back, chase his face, perform fake-outs like a basketball player to trick him into meeting my eyes. We were playing a schoolyard game like children.

"Marlin, this is ridiculous. Why can't we talk like two adults?"

No word, no sign. How funny. I'd found my husband, but we were deadlocked in a standoff that would bore nine-year-olds in ten seconds.

What could I do? I wasn't really The Rock. I couldn't drag Marlin out the door by his hair. He was physically stronger. Nothing I could do would compel him to acknowledge me, much less love me. Adulting 101: When someone doesn't love you anymore, you're supposed to walk away graciously and leave them alone. To do otherwise would be creepy, stalkerish.

I thought to bring up the banana tree spirit story, trying to get a rise out of him. Anything was better than him willing me into nonexistence.

"You want to talk about Ah Gu?" I cried. "My *lover*? Well, let's talk, then!"

"Lover? It's true?"

I'd forgotten Eamon was perched by the door. I whirled around.

"Are you pregnant?" he asked in a kind of fascinated horror.

"Go away, Eamon," I hissed. "This is none of your business."

"He told me you cheated on him." He stared, eyes boring into the mounded heap of fat on my stomach.

"That's not true," I said. "Well, maybe, in a past life, just according to him—"

I found myself unable to make the choice between falsely implicating myself and painting a picture of my husband as mentally unstable. I took a last look at Marlin's head, focusing on the whorl from which all his hair seemed to be flung out in circles the pattern of a galaxy. If only it were a portal into his mind.

"You should leave," Eamon said. I looked at his grim face and realized, finally, that he had not been on my side at all. His sympathies were with Marlin. I was the cheater, the wayward lying woman here to beg for forgiveness.

More than anything, I felt foolish. I'd propelled myself here out of fear that Marlin had stepped onto darker, possibly suicidal paths, and he'd proven to me that it was all in my head. His pain was directed outward, at me. My concern for his well-being made me seem like the one unbalanced and hysterical.

"He's the one who left me!" I choked out to Eamon before hurrying down his cement pathway, as quickly as I could manage.

Day Three (Friday)

There was a lot of crying. At first I did it on the living room couch, but then my nose became too clogged. I went to the bathroom, blew my nose, and talked to the mirror. "Crying is easy. Anyone can do it. Crying means you're not trying hard enough. You're not trying at all."

When my stomach grumbled, I plodded to the fridge and dug out the pack of prosciutto, its streaks of pink and white reminding me of scar tissue. I parted them gently from one another, lifting a slice at a time, the way I used to strip a flower bald petal by petal as a child. Alone, each prosciutto piece was filmy and suggestive, like a swatch of skin for a custom-tailored new body. I splayed one out across my knee, then another over my belly button. I tried my best to believe I was shedding skin, growing into a better being.

A fable told to me at Buddhist camp: An inquisitive python wanders into a carpenter's shop. The carpenter screams and dashes out, dropping a hand saw on the floor in his haste. The python, curious, slithers up to the saw. One of the saw's teeth snags on the snake and cuts it. Alarmed, the python goes on the offensive and binds itself around the threat. The harder the snake squeezes, the more pain it feels, and so the tighter it tries to choke the saw, desperate to extinguish its enemy. In the end, the python dies from its wounds.

I plucked the prosciutto off my stomach and chewed it. The Marlin I'd married had no use for fables. He scoffed at studies showing that most people responded more to emotional appeals than to logical presentation of facts.

"Too bad for humanity," he'd say. "We'd be far better off if everyone could reason without emotions clouding their judgment."

I used to wish Marlin would change, just a little, into someone who was half as moved as I was by fairy tales and parables. Now I just wanted him back, in whatever form.

I had another bout of intimacy with the toilet after eating the prosciutto, and then I couldn't sleep. I woke my laptop and looked up facts, hard data about things that were abstract and things that were untrue.

Datum: about 8 percent of American adults are vegetarian or vegan. Datum: one in three Americans believe in ghosts. I experienced a nonsensical flash of hope. Now that I was no longer vegetarian, I belonged to the 92 percent, far outnumbering Marlin's sect of ghost believers. That meant the country was on my side, didn't it?

I know, that logic makes no sense. I'm recounting it to you so you get a sense of my mental state at the time.

My belly button itched, and I scratched it. I'd undergone a drastic change to become an omnivore, but I still wanted Marlin back. Whereas Marlin had also undergone a drastic change, except in his case I was dead to him. Didn't this indicate that there was something wrong with Marlin's newfound belief itself, rather than with his transformation?

But then my mother believed devoutly in past lives, and I still saw her as sane. I had to assume, too, that the majority of the one-third of Americans who believed in ghosts were interpreted by society as well-functioning. That seemed to rule out mental illness when it came to Marlin's behavior. Yet—another hairpin turn—perhaps it was what one did with those beliefs that marked off the territory of illness? My mother nagged me with her past life stories, trying through them to influence my lifestyle. If she one day declared our mother-daughter relationship over because of some insight gleaned from a past life regression, then wouldn't I be entirely justified in assuming she was unwell? Similarly, if Marlin communicated with his spirits in a, I don't know, *positive* way, I could see myself eventually tolerating this strange practice. Why couldn't these spirits have my husband hold me closer, instead of telling him to leave me?

One final piece of prosciutto. I used it to wipe away a streak of tears. Was Marlin still vegan? I had no reason to suspect he'd given it up, but Marlin was now completely different than when he'd first converted to veganism. In his old, unfailingly logical way, he'd done the research—read *The China Study* front to back, could rattle off on-demand statistics about industrial farming's wasteful land and water usage. Whereas I'd become vegetarian at fifteen because I thought my neighbor's chickens were cute, and because I harbored some wishful thinking that the diet would make me skinny.

About a year after I became vegetarian, my mother asked me why I was still "off meat," as she put it, even though it didn't help me lose weight. In fact, didn't I look fatter? She didn't know that I had secretly been wavering, enticed by the heady, herbal scent of bak kut teh she ostentatiously ate in the house. Her challenge was what cemented my resolve to be vegetarian. I'd keep it up, if only to defy her.

As if I'd summoned her, she called. I pressed that last piece of prosciutto over my laptop camera before answering, not wanting her to see my face made even more unpresentable by crying.

"I can't see you," she complained.

"I think there's something wrong with my camera."

"How's Marlin?"

"He's . . . he's in bed." Technically true as of the last time I saw him.

"Oh, you're not joining him?"

"I was just about to."

"It's so early."

"I'm tired."

"You're always tired! You still have that mole on your cheek? It's like this: it's blocking your energy. I told you before. Okay, can you call me when you have some time?"

"Why?"

"I have something to tell you."

"What is it?"

But she wouldn't say. "You have to be in the right mood first," she insisted, almost saucily. "I'll tell you after you fix your sleep."

After hanging up I sat blankly for a few minutes, and then I lifted the prosciutto off my laptop camera and put it into my mouth.

Marlin had tried to help me lose weight once, at my behest. At first he cajoled me to join him at the rock-climbing gym, but I found it too nerve-racking. Then he settled into his familiar rhythm, reading tons of weight-loss forum posts and weeding out the fads to eventually devise a food-and-exercise plan.

"It's simple," he said. "Calories in, calories out. Just math."

"I was never good at math."

"Okay, visualize a scale with weights on two ends. One is food, and one is exercise. You just have to balance them."

I grimaced at the word *scale*.

"Just write down everything you eat," he said encouragingly. "That'll be a start. You like writing, right?"

He pinched his thumb and index finger together and waved them erratically in the air, miming writing. I had to laugh at that.

I did indeed do well with the documenting of food. There were a lot of noodles, pasta, and tofu rice bowls during that period, followed by a brief obsession with avocado atop fried plantains. Exercise-wise, I did my best with a set of dumbbells purchased off the internet.

It was the math part that broke down. I was staying late multiple times a week at AInstein, trying to impress Lucas enough that he'd be open to a green card discussion. Marlin was doing the equivalent at Cachi I/O. Neither of us had time or energy to cook by the time we left our respective offices. That meant takeout, which was hard to quantify in precise caloric terms. It was difficult, too, to derive neat numbers from my dumbbell exercises. The formula Marlin gave me required that I plug in an "Activity level (METS)" on a scale of 1 to 12, with 1 being "Sitting and watching Netflix" and 12 being "Firefighter, general." I was at a loss when it came to interpreting that last phrase. Was 12 the activity level of a generic, basic firefighter, as opposed to an elite one? Or did "general" there mean the army title?

I brought this problem to Marlin.

"Hmm," he said. "I doubt an army general burns as many calories as a firefighter. In movies at least, the most exercise they get is crossing and uncrossing their arms behind their back."

I lost interest when my weight remained steady after a couple of months. Marlin let it go; he was dissatisfied with the fuzziness of the numbers involved. It wasn't how he liked to do things.

WHEN I FELT MORE TEARS COMING ON, I PLAYED ANOTHER DOCUMEN-tary Marlin had watched. This one was about cats. How much control does a cat have over her tail? According to the narrator, the swaying and hooking of a cat's tail offer insight into the animal's emotions. Based on observations, researchers concluded that while a cat's tail may mirror her agitation, excitement, or wariness, she seems to have no control over it. Which is to say, the tail betrays.

What if there was an analogy here to Marlin's newfound spiritual beliefs? The tail moves when the creature is stimulated, whether into desire, unease, or something else. His abrupt spirituality could simply be a reflection of his inner turmoil, an unseen appendage lashing back and forth, appearing to take on a life of its own. Maybe his father's death was so enormous a psychic hit that Marlin had to develop new beliefs to manage it.

I sat on the couch, my mind churning. I knew none of this speculation was helpful. It was insulting, even, to compare my husband to ants and cats. But my brain was starved for an explanation, a *story*. I kept scrolling through documentary videos. What if whatever afflicted Marlin was contagious? What if, even as I was having these thoughts, my reasoning was suspect?

Just before I slumped into sleep, something Eamon said came back to me. "Are you pregnant?" He'd said that out of nowhere. It was true I wasn't thin to begin with, and my new meat-gorging habits might have made me more bloated than usual. Still, it had been a jarring comment. I wondered if Marlin believed I was pregnant for some reason. Maybe the spirits had told him so. Paranoia set in, and I felt a sudden urge to buy a pregnancy test from a 24/7 drugstore. But I was too tired. I kept my eyes closed instead, telling myself I was being ridiculous. Marlin didn't even want kids. He'd made that clear from the start.

We had a perfectly chaste first date, Marlin and I, possibly because we'd already kissed at the Chinese New Year gathering before he even asked for my number. I was the one to arrive first at the restaurant. I loitered outside in snappy winter air, eyeing the Michelin Bib Gourmand sign with the tire man and his provocative tongue. I contemplated waiting inside, but the chandeliers and the hostess's prominent YSL belt dissuaded me. Years after living in New York, I could still feel like an impostor, unwelcome in the city's fancier spaces.

When Marlin arrived, we smiled and moved toward the entrance without once touching each other. We leaned on the heavy doors until they yielded, and I could feel my heart lifting straight up like a hot air balloon.

The food was, to be honest, unremarkable, some vegetarian afterthought by a meat-centric chef. Marlin was diffident and cautious, asking my approval before ordering anything. When he finally cleared his throat and said "There's something you should know," it was in a tone of confession.

"I don't know if I want kids," he said. In fact, he'd once brashly declared that he would never have children in front of his whole extended family at a mid-autumn festival party.

"I was young and foolish back then, maybe." He played with his napkin. "But still, I thought you should know."

"Thank you," I said, unsure how to reply. "I don't know what I want, to be honest."

Marlin nodded solemnly. "Which is worse? To be too sure of something, or to be unsure of everything?"

"Why did you tell me? I mean, why now?" I tried to be subtle about glancing left and right, to make sure the smartly dressed couples sandwiching us were not listening in, bemused.

"I don't want to waste your time. In case it becomes serious. Between us."

After the date, as I walked away from him past the underground subway turnstiles, I smiled a private smile. I was thinking about how I wanted nothing more than to waste my time with him. I wanted our coming together to be everything a responsibility or a deadline was not—frivolous because unproductive, full of meandering delights. He would be the mirror in which I was reflected as a person who existed outside rules and regulations.

So I was the one who dragged him along to modern art museums and poetry readings that took place in churches while an AA meeting went on in the next room. I bit my lip when he commented, as I predicted he would, that he could easily paint half of the "masterpieces" in the galleries we visited. It was endearing to me that everything seemed a competition to him. There he was, gauging his engineer self against an airy hall of abstract artists. We were the opposite; whereas the new and unfamiliar paralyzed me, he took everything he knew to bear against the unknown, always asking: *What can I do with this?*

January 2018

After the four-hour layover in Hong Kong, we got on a plane for New York. Marlin seemed cold toward me during the flight, but I didn't think much of it. The funeral had been just a few days ago, after all. Now I wonder: Is it possible to give someone too much space to grieve?

We disembarked into a humid tunnel in JFK, and despite our quick-stepping, we found ourselves as always in an interminably long line for noncitizens by the time we reached the border checkpoint. Our stream of aliens fed into about half a dozen booths, each with a computer terminal and a nonalien uniformed officer perched inside, visible from the waist up. As we got closer to the head of the line, I played this silly mental game where I tried to predict which officer would call on us, and then to hazard whether that was a good or bad thing. From our experience, the border agents varied widely in their attitude toward the aliens they processed.

Admittedly my game relied upon judging by appearances, equating deep scowls with mild xenophobia or a tinge of alcoholic rosacea with a haughty impatience. But on that day, I won the game. I'd immediately picked my last choice out of the six non-options arrayed before us. This worst-case officer might have been in his early forties, his hair dark enough to approach the black of our own and spiked into a formation that looked like he wanted to erect fences on his head. He had a baby face, which should have endeared him to me, but there was something churlish about the curl of his mouth that put me on guard.

He waved us forward. It was clear from his first words that we were in trouble.

"What is the purpose of your visit?" he asked, when we had not even proffered up our passports, which are admittedly not blue. The deep blue of tasteful woven fabric couches, that shade of star-studded night skies as interpreted by painters, the hue of expensive wedding suits—no, our passports are not even close. I was a bit flushed, I think, my color "high," as they say, from drinking free wine on a sixteen-hour flight. Marlin has the advantage of being dark-skinned and so hid it better, although his forehead glistened a little. He was also wearing a scrap of black cloth pinned to his left T-shirt sleeve to signify mourning, and I was suddenly afraid that this could look suspicious to the officer.

Something had changed. Marlin and I had done this many times—passed through American borders, I mean. In the past, officers usually waved us off with a "Welcome home" after they accessed our records on their computers and saw how much of our early adulthood had been spent in America. That never failed to warm our hearts. "He said 'home,'" we'd announce to each other at baggage claim, both beaming, a little in awe still. "I heard." We'd nod, and in verifying this piece of good news, we seemed to double its potency.

But we hadn't gone through checkpoints since the Muslim ban, and now it sank in that we might not be hearing the phrase "Welcome home" anymore. The agent before us glared at our groggy faces.

"Uh, visit?" Marlin stammered. "My father passed away, so we went for the funeral . . ."

Wrong. He trailed off, finally understanding what was happening. *What is the purpose of your visit?* The agent was asking about our purpose visiting *the United States of America*, of course, even though to us "visiting" is something we do outside the US, and "returning" is what happens when we land at JFK. Clearly the definition of words had flipped since we last flew.

I squeaked out that we worked in the city and were reentering the country so we could return to our jobs. "Tech companies," Marlin added, half supplicating, half faux boastful, hoping to impress.

"You two traveling together?"

"Yes, we're married."

"Oh, but you have different last names."

"Where we come from, it's not customary for women to formally change their names after marriage," I said. Surely a better answer than to say all of my immigration paperwork is under my maiden name, and I would never in a hundred years (which is approximately how long it takes for immigrants from certain countries to get their green cards) jeopardize any bureaucratic process by something as trivial as taking Marlin's family name.

But it seemed I'd doomed us with that "Where we come from." This appeared to have the effect of highlighting our alienness to the agent. His lips withered. He rifled through our papers and tapped on his keyboard. He sighed so forcefully it was like he wanted to huff us plain out of sight. Then he uttered the dreaded "Come with me."

Marlin and I looked at each other, alarmed.

"Where?" I muttered, but my feet were already in motion to obey instructions, even as in my mind I stood a little in admiration of my single-word response that could, maybe, just a little bit, be construed as daring protest.

"Just follow me. The officers on the other end will explain it to you."

Marlin walked ahead of me. I wanted to tug on his arm, hold him back for a quick discussion. Then I noticed that his passport was swinging from the agent's hands, and I realized with a start that I'd been handed back my passport, which I'd absentmindedly pocketed in the confusion, while Marlin's proof of legal existence was being held hostage. We had no choice but to follow. Or, rather, he had no choice.

Belatedly, I asked, "Can I stay with him?" I jogged a little to make sure the agent heard me, but then became paranoid and slowed down to my previous tempo. A few quick, nervous glances to the side reassured me that no one had a gun trained on me.

We shuffled down a long walkway, the bank of Homeland Security agents in their individual booths to our left. It was a familiar sight made strange by the fact that all the agents now had their backs to us, their bottoms of various sizes visible, squished against their stools. I turned back to see where we had come from. Our agent's booth gleamed under harsh lights, empty.

I didn't know his name, I realized. What if we needed to file a complaint later? Then I caught myself and almost laughed. Yeah, right. Two immigrants filing a complaint against the Department of Homeland Security. Sure to turn out well.

At the end of the walkway was a room with door ajar. I strained my eyes to see into its jaw. Sixteen hours in a plane cabin had dried out my eyes completely, and the more I tried to see clearly, the more I needed to blink. I could feel pain creeping forward from the back of my eyeballs, threatening to also crawl up into my skull. "Pain shivers," I'd once said, trying to relay the sensations of an impending migraine to Marlin, who'd never had one.

When we crossed into the room, the lighting changed abruptly, becoming much dimmer. I watched our agent hand over Marlin's passport to a colleague seated behind a desk, uttering some kind of code word, numbers and letters that could be an acronym. As our agent turned to leave the room, I tried to catch his name tag. But already he was moving away, his steps unhurried, presumably back to his station.

The room was gloomy, low ceilings and sharp angles everywhere: rigid furniture, posters and signs that looked like they could cut. Against one bland wall was a row of four desks, three of them occupied by two men and one woman, all in uniform. The man closest to the entrance had Marlin's passport, which was laid carelessly next to his mouse pad like a paperweight or a stapler or a stapler that no longer worked repurposed into a paperweight. It stunned me. Never would we ever leave something so important simply sitting out like that, faceup even, without so much as a pinkie hovering over it in caution.

We were told to sit in a couple of gray-green chairs that faced off the row of desks. I carefully aimed my eyes a few feet above the officers' heads, the same way I acted on a packed subway.

"What do you think this is about?" Marlin asked after a long time.

I tried to come up with a way to say what I wanted to say without getting us into more trouble, just in case the agents had been hired for their superhuman senses of hearing. Instead my tired mind, reluctant to perform any kind of sustained work, cast about for distractions. I read a sign that in stern font forbade cell phone usage. Next to it was a larger poster with denser paragraphs, which I skimmed just enough to understand that it was illegal for agents to commit sexual offenses against—I registered with a shock—Marlin or me, and that should we experience such offenses we should file a report via the following avenues . . .

Eventually I could no longer ignore Marlin's questioning look. I answered quickly, keeping my voice as low as possible:

"Well, we're from the same country, we have the same kind of passport, are on the same type of visa, we basically work in the same industry, and we just got off the same plane. What's different?" I directed my eyes meaningfully at his hand, then at my own.

"You mean it's because I have dark skin," he said.

I shushed him. As if on cue, Marlin was summoned to the table closest to the door, where his passport flopped limp and casual, just like that. I itched to take my phone out so I could look up what was legal (meaning what should be tolerated) and what was not (meaning what should be tolerated after feeble protests) in our situation. But I was afraid to, because of the sign that said no cell phone use allowed.

An air steward popped his head in. I recognized him; he'd served us egg dishes in plastic containers and recommended the free white over the free red when I'd asked.

Still here? his disappointed and slightly amazed expression indicated, and I realized that he might not be able to leave until Marlin was cleared. I looked at my watch; it'd been an hour.

In front of me, Marlin was nodding along to something the

officer said. The back of my husband's head was the wrong shape, as if someone had bashed it in. The long flight had flattened his curls and flared them out to the side like bat wings. I didn't know it then, but I would soon be staring at the back of his head quite a lot, yearning to have more direct access to the secret machinations of his mind.

Why would the air crew on our flight need to stick around until we were done? It wasn't as if they could deport us (him) on the same plane back. The crew was tired and would need to rest after such a long job. Could it be that the air steward would be called as character witness? (The time I dropped my blanket into the middle of the aisle; the time I tried to race the dining carts to the bathroom; the time Marlin repeatedly pressed the air steward icon on his screen because something was wrong with his overhead light; how Marlin and I maybe asked for too many glasses of free wine; how he yelped when turbulence spilled hot water from his cup noodles onto his arm . . .)

The air steward disappeared from the door frame. I settled on what seemed the most reasonable explanation to me: that he was responsible for collecting our luggage, should Marlin be deported, so that our baggage could be banished alongside our bodies.

A numb sort of panic set in. I realized I wasn't sure whether we could afford plane tickets back to Malaysia. I had no idea if a deported person was required to pay their own fare for a forced removal. We might be able to afford one ticket, but definitely not two; not until we both got our next paychecks. There was a chance, then, or was it a choice, that I would have to remain while Marlin was sent away. Unless I caused a scene right then—I recklessly thought—and got deported alongside him. Maybe all I had to do was take out my phone. But I'd only want to do this if the US government covered a deportee's air travel expenses. How to find out this information without disobeying any posted signs?

The panic buzzed a little louder. Maybe it was too late, and I'd already made the wrong choice. I'd come with Marlin into this room to be by his side. Should I have left instead, in search of a lawyer? I'd read that lawyers had camped somewhere in this very airport, volunteering their time and expertise to help people affected by the Muslim ban. But that had been in 2017, a whole year ago. Were there still lawyers around? Would they help us? Did we qualify? We were not Muslims, though we carried passports from what many saw as a Muslim country.

Marlin started walking back toward me. At the same time, an officer at the other end of the room got up and strode in my direction. My heart sank. It took all my willpower to keep my eyes on Marlin instead of on the approaching officer. Marlin reached me first, sitting down without saying anything. From my periphery awareness I sensed the officer walking past me, and I thought *bathroom* with relief until I heard the start of a conversation.

I gaped at Marlin: *We're not alone.* I turned around to see a door behind us, open. I must have registered it as a cleaning closet or server room or something, one of those spaces that are unseen until they are needed. But no, there was another person in there. Maybe the room was some sort of holding cell. I tried to eavesdrop but couldn't make anything out.

"What did the officer say?" I whispered to Marlin.

"Says he's waiting on confirmation of my details from some central branch."

"What kind of details?"

"They want to know that I am who I say I am? I guess? He asked for my height and weight for some reason."

"They don't have access to a computer database? Why does he

have to wait? Someone has to go into a huge room with rows of fil-ing cabinets or something?"

"Edwina, I don't know." He sounded exasperated.

The officer from before emerged from the holding cell (?) into my field of vision, his whistling preceding him and raising prickles on my scalp. I couldn't help looking at him. He had sandy hair that ended in mismatched horns at the nape of his neck, the left one dipping lower than the right one. He also had narrow shoul-ders that dipped and rolled when he made for his desk, where he shuffled some papers spread around with no apparent organization. I didn't spot a passport, although there was a Batman bobblehead figure, rendered in a style some people call chibi.

The officer straightened up when a woman walked in.

"There you are," he greeted her.

The woman wore a different kind of uniform, in lighter shades of blue. I couldn't tell if that meant higher rank or entirely different position, or what. Before he walked up to her, the officer absent-mindedly pawed Batman and set him going.

Suddenly there was a flurry of activity. All of the remaining seated officers got on their feet. I must have missed a signal some-where, perhaps nothing more than a nod from the woman. The gang headed past us to the not-closet room, and we were left unsu-pervised, my husband and I.

My first irrational instinct was to snatch up Marlin's passport and make a run for it, but when I swept my gaze along the desk by the door, the passport was no longer there.

"Should I call someone?" I whispered. "I think Katie said her cousin is a lawyer, remember? When we had dinner with her?"

He shook his head. "It was IP law or something. Corporate law. Definitely not immigration law, anyway."

I reached for his knee and squeezed it. He was staring at his hands in his lap. I did this thing he normally hated, where I bored my eyes into his profile and willed him to register the intensity of my gaze until he looked up. It was something I liked to do from across our studio. He used to say it creeped him out. I joked that it was a test of our telepathic bond.

The whistling started up again from behind us, getting louder. I didn't recognize the tune. There was an accompaniment going on—it took me a second to make out that it was the jingling of metal, maybe of keys.

Neither of us turned to witness the events. We both prolonged our ignorance for as long as possible, until a man was herded into the space between the officers' desks and where we sat. He wore a hoodie, so we couldn't see his face, but I, trained, conditioned, primed, looked immediately for his hands to determine his skin color. They were cuffed behind his back, and they were the color of certain hotel Bible covers.

"The next flight to Saudi Arabia is tomorrow, early morning," the officer with the Batman bobblehead said. "Do you understand?"

There was no response.

"He's a little slow, huh." The officer with Marlin's passport raised one hand and spun lazy circles around his own temple.

I looked away, wishing we could say or do something. Give the man in the hoodie some comfort. Instead I stared at the only other movement in the room. As I tracked chibi Batman's judders, two opposing thoughts raced to my consciousness. I wondered if Batman was cheering the officers on with nods of approval, or was he trembling with rage, wobbling to intervene?

I imagined the sense of power and justice that must flood through the officer every day when he came in to work and saw Batman on his desk. I imagined the temperature of cuffs going around wrists.

Maybe this, rather than the loss of his father, was what gave Marlin doubts about life in America. Maybe the episode poisoned all that we had built in New York, and he could no longer bear to live in that vulnerability. When feeling threatened, some people self-destruct rather than let themselves be destroyed. Or they pass on that feeling of helplessness to someone else, hoping to regain some power. Perhaps that was what happened. America made Marlin feel unwelcome, and so he left me.

Day Four (Saturday)

I woke up ten minutes before I was supposed to meet Katie. I texted her frantically, asking if we could push brunch back an hour. She had no problem with it, like the true New Yorker she was. That was what I loved about Katie SooHoo: her absolutely foreign (to me) metropolitan chicness, the idea of New York embodied but tempered by her immigrant ties. Her parents had come from China, and when she was born, they'd given her a typical first-generation American name, meaning one that was actually a nickname. I'd met other first-gen kids like her: Jimmy from chemistry lab, whose birth certificate really did say "Jimmy" and not "James"; an old dormmate, Liz, whose driver's license did not read "Elizabeth."

Katie was well-off by way of her parents' accidental real estate fortune, the family's Brooklyn home, bought for five figures in the 1970s, having been subsequently snapped up and demolished to make way for luxury apartments. She had accounts not only at financial banks but also at a cord blood bank, where stem cells from her daughter's umbilical cord had been harvested and stored, sitting around just in case one day little Su-Ann got diagnosed with leukemia, or in the event she simply wanted a stem cell face-lift.

I suspected Katie liked me as a friend for a particular reason. She was proud of her parents and often made them out as examples of immigrants getting the job done, giving her all the opportunities they'd denied themselves to result in an impeccably groomed, Princeton-educated, six-figure-earning American daughter. But she was at the same time embarrassed by their knockoff clothes, which they insisted on wearing ("No one can tell it's fake anyway") and by their preference for speaking Taishanese no matter where they were, even in the middle of a Fifth Avenue store.

Perhaps in me she saw a chance to live out her fantasy of re-molding her beloved parents. Like I said, I'd first met her in college, when she approached me in the cafeteria. I was still pliable then, just finishing my lessons on all the stereotypes and insults I could expect to be thrown my way as a minority in America.

Maybe I won her over with this confession: that I admired what her parents had done for her, but I couldn't be that selfless. I wanted Katie's success for myself, not for my children. It wasn't for me, the role of self-erasing immigrant parent. No way was I working my butt off just so some American kid could one day say in her junior high school valedictorian speech: "I couldn't have done this without my parents."

This made her laugh, and we became best friends.

I RUSHED TO GET READY, BUT KATIE STILL BEAT ME TO THE RESTAURANT. She'd brought her husband and baby along, which I somehow hadn't counted on.

"Sorry I'm late," I huffed.

"Oh, that's okay, Co-Star told me today would try my patience, but I should keep an open mind."

I remembered with a start that Katie believed in astrology. Or maybe *believed* was too strong a word. It was more that she had hitched on to a trend. It had become cool and hip to care about astrology. People tossed star signs about, using them as shorthand for things that were supposed to be complex, like their seeming incapability to let grudges go. If they stood you up on plans finalized weeks ago, they'd remove their sunglasses and say "I'm an Aries. What can you do?" (I see you listed your sign on the app too—no offense. I hope Virgos are the forgiving type.)

When I first told Katie about the strange things Marlin had started saying, she'd said, "Maybe it's a good thing? I always thought he was too focused on facts and being correct. A little rigid."

"But he's saying things that he used to think were beneath him! Like the other day, he told me the previous tenant of our apartment died full of regrets. He said he could pick it up from the atmosphere or something."

"That doesn't sound so bad. Lots of people believe in ghosts."

A waitress came by, voice pitched high: "And do we need a high chair here, baby?"

The baby stared at a fascinating spot on the ceiling, oblivious.

"We're okay," Katie's husband said. He took over the fidgety baby as Katie maneuvered the restaurant's huge menu, trying to decide. Unlike Katie, Bradley had a correctly formal American name, Bradley V. Chan. I liked it, especially the middle initial that made it seem like he was perpetually at war with himself, Bradley versus Chan. This internal strife further manifested in his rhotacism, a difficulty pronouncing *r*'s that made him sound like he was accidentally stuck in baby-talk mode sometimes.

"My mom wants me to remove my mole," I said, because I couldn't just start with news about Marlin.

"You cannot get rid of your mole!" Katie said.

"Why not? It's safe. Lots of people do it."

"*Because* you'd look different on your official documents." The area surrounding her eyebrows flushed angrily. She'd probably gotten a wax while waiting for me. "Like do you want some immigration asshole holding your visa photo up to your face and asking 'Ma'am, where's your mole?'"

"I could dab it on with eyebrow pencil," I said.

"Edwina."

I was touched. With her true-blue passport, Katie had no reason to think about the complications of border crossing. That border checkpoints were at all on her mind meant my worries, conveyed to her over years, had occupied a corner of her mind, and were now part of the way she thought.

This broke the levees, and I rushed headlong into an account of Marlin's departure and his refusal to acknowledge my presence at Eamon's, the words pulled out of me as if magnetized by Katie's attention. I tried to remember to look at Bradley from time to time so he would feel included, but mostly I spoke at Katie.

It surprised and defeated me, how quickly the story could be told. Just a few sentences that barely took up a minute—that was supposed to convey all the agony that jostled within me like microwaved food atoms?

Katie made the appropriate exclamations of shock, but I could see she was not really surprised. I was irrationally irked about this. If she'd seen it coming based on what I'd previously shared with her, then what did it say about me, so caught off guard by his desertion?

The waitress came to take our order. Immediately the table

switched from long faces and somber, knitted brows to high-pitched coos and wide smiles as all attention turned to the baby, who was handed to Katie so the waitress could get a closer look. While everyone talked about her, the baby stared in bug-eyed wonder at a spoon in her chubby fist.

"Oh, just look at her! How precious!" the waitress exclaimed.

When our orders finally arrived, I caught Katie glancing at my left ring finger. Registering disappointment on her face, I nervously adjusted the statement piece I wore as my wedding ring.

"Maybe you should see someone," Bradley said. "We're worried about you."

"I can't see a professional," I said.

"Can't, or won't?" Katie arched an eyebrow. In her arms, little Su-Ann writhed so much that Bradley couldn't take a good photo of his waffles held up against her face.

I took my first ever bite of bacon. It possessed the unnatural crunch of plastic, and a tang that was mechanical, like engine oil. Then the fat melted, and I experienced a fullness on my tongue of something like contentment. I glanced at my friends, wide-eyed.

"Seriously, though, why can't you see someone?" Bradley persisted, warping the r in "seriously."

I explained how it was with the green card application. I'd read the form dozens of times by now. It started off predictably, asking for birth name, country of origin, dates, etc., moving on after that to marriages, children. Nothing alarming, mostly information that would come up at a standard if slightly bureaucratic cocktail party. The odd part began with the two separate sections for "Race" and "Ethnicity." Before I could dredge up the scholarly definitions of those terms I'd studied in class, my brain was further tripped up when I read that under "Race," all they cared about was whether you were Hispanic or Latino. Literally:

☐ *Hispanic or Latino*
☐ *Not Hispanic or Latino*

Those categories were then entirely missing from "Ethnicity," which was its own confusing section:

☐ *White*
☐ *Asian*
☐ *Black or African American*
☐ *American Indian or Alaska Native*
☐ *Native Hawaiian or Other Pacific Islander*

I had so many questions on my first read-through. The function of the word *or* was inconsistent in the "Ethnicity" section, for one. Furthermore, why would African Americans, American Indians, or Native Hawaiians file green card applications? That confused me, and of course there was the puzzling organization of the whole thing, how Hispanic or Latino were options excluded from "Ethnicity." I found myself unable to think too hard about it. Because if this piece of paper that was supposed to dictate my future didn't make much sense, then why was I pouring so much hope into it?

By this point in my explanation, Katie and Bradley were exchanging looks while pretending to feed their baby, who simply swatted away anything that came near her face. I put a palm up, letting them know I had more to say.

The application form, I-485, then went on to list questions designed to disqualify someone from getting a green card. These sections should have been no-brainers. One simply checked "no" for every insinuation and chuckled at the questions, like the ones asking whether you had ever been a Nazi or participated in genocide or held any intention of performing terrorism while in the United States. The correct answers were so eye-rollingly obvious, and the idea of potential terrorists earnestly checking "yes" so ludicrous, I thought I could just breeze through while shaking my head at this form of vetting. But a surprise was in store for me. Near the end of form I-485, there was mention of a different, separate form, I-693. No problem, I thought at first. Just more paperwork.

Form I-693 also had an English name, Report of Medical Examination and Vaccination Record. Turns out this one wasn't a mere checkbox affair. I was required to undergo actual visits to what the form officiously called "civil surgeons." These were doctors responsible for examining immigrants such as me for the existence of "Class A" or "Class B" physical and mental illnesses. What sicknesses fell under A, and what under B? It was hard to find definitive answers, because this categorization was really meant as communication between the civil surgeon and the government, to which I was not so much a party as a specimen.

No matter how much I prepared, the outcome of the application was mostly not in my hands. Yes, these hands, which looked healthy and would undoubtedly pass as so to the civil surgeon who would examine me, and yet these were the same hands that once carved faint lines into my upper arms, horizontal ones and diagonal ones and ones that looked like attempts to form words, chicken scratch. A small nick was visible still, and if the civil surgeon were to point it out, I would say: "A cooking accident."

My limbs could deceive, but if I were to sit in a psychiatrist's office like Katie and Bradley were suggesting, put down my legal name (not Edwina, which was adopted in America for convenience), my birth date, and my social security number, hand over my insurance card for copying (both sides), sit in a carpeted room and listen to Muzak, absentmindedly pick at various loose skin folds or abrasions, shuffle my feet when my name was called (incorrectly), sit down in front of the psychiatrist and withhold withhold withhold dam burst of emotions, agree to see this as need for future ongoing sessions, shuffle back the way I came and, utterly humiliated, schedule weekly appointments while sniffling, wordlessly accept the tissue handed over by the receptionist, be pressured into starting prescription antianxiety medication by the fourth visit, slouch into CVS shamefaced and wary of the checkout person's judgment—then there would be a record of some sort, some official professional file that could presumably be accessed by a civil surgeon or immigration officer, who would then check a box for either Class A or Class B, maybe even heavily underline the phrase "may pose, or has posed, a threat to the property, safety, or welfare of the alien or others" on Form I-693.

I already had a record, so to speak, thanks to the German girl in college. Those therapy sessions had been shared with school administrators, so who was to say immigration officials wouldn't access information from any therapist I saw now? They didn't even need access to notes; couldn't the mere fact that I was in therapy at all be excuse enough to mark me as Class A or B? It didn't hurt to be careful. For example, I wasn't on any social media. The US government monitored immigrants online, and anything I typed might be used against me—that was what internet advice hinted at. Resources for immigrants cautioned that we should "avoid profanity and the use of aggressive or threatening language" while posting online, which really voided the whole purpose of being on Twitter.

When I finished, I sat back in my chair and tried to meet Katie and Bradley's astonished eyes.

"You're doing it again," Katie declared. "What you always do."

"Doing what?"

"You make jokes about serious stuff you actually care about. You try to turn it into a funny, hyperbolic, preposterous story."

"Do I?"

"Yeah, you're smiling," Bradley said.

I actually put a hand up to feel my face. He was right; my facial muscles were stretched, my cracked lips taut. I tried to explain, even though I wasn't convinced myself. "Well, this is really selfish of me, isn't it? It's so privileged of me to be worrying about paperwork when other immigrants are being separated from their children at the border and deported while going to church, and there are even these kids lost by the government. Lost! Like loose change! How can I not make fun of myself? Other people have it so much more worse. I'm really lucky to be sitting here."

"Sure, but that doesn't mean your suffering doesn't matter," Katie said callously.

A swell of love for her surged in me. I couldn't help it. I'd always been that way, secretly pleased and flattered by others who behaved low-key horribly when they thought it was for my benefit. It wasn't what I wanted to feel, but the feelings came anyway.

"Don't you think it's wrong to cage children?"

"Yes, of course." She nodded for emphasis. "But we're talking about you right now."

I simmered, both charmed and annoyed.

"Maybe you should meditate," Katie said. "You went to Buddhist camp, right?"

"They never taught us to meditate there."

"Oh, ask her the Mars question," Bradley chimed in.

"What about Mars?" I asked.

"This one's a mindfuck." Katie's eyes lit up. "You ready?"

It went like this: Humans have figured out a way to go to Mars. A device has been invented, a teleportation portal in essence. You step in through the door and step out onto Mars. The catch is, the portal deconstructs your body, decimating it. You are reconstituted on Mars. Or, more precisely, a copy of you is assembled based on the knowledge gained by the portal when it broke your body down. The question is, would you do it? Would You on Mars be You on Earth, or did You on Earth die so that a clone could be possible on Mars? Was it really death if You on Mars retained all your memories? What if, in rewiring your brain, which is of course part of your physical body, the portal could only guarantee a 99.99 percent accuracy, and You on Mars was almost identical, but with just the slightest change in personality? Say, a change from someone who loved cats to someone who loved all cats except tortoiseshells? Would you do it? Would it be suicide? Or could it be said that you, the real you, actually traveled to Mars?

"What does this have to do with meditation?" I asked, bewildered.

"Bradley got it from a book about meditating."

"But what's the connection?"

"Never mind the connection," he said. "What do you think?"

"I wouldn't do it. Unless Marlin were stranded on Mars, and it was the only way to reach him."

Katie exchanged looks with Bradley. "Why are you still talking about him?" she asked. "He left you."

"I have to convince him to come back," I said. "Nothing makes sense otherwise."

"Maybe it doesn't have to make sense," she said. "For a while?"

"No." I shook my head. "I have to get him back."

"You're in denial," Bradley said.

"Which is understandable," Katie rushed to say. "Divorce is a big deal."

"We're not getting a divorce."

Katie reached awkwardly around the baby in her lap to clasp my hand. "You're the victim here, Edwina, not him."

"I don't feel like the victim."

"And you call yourself a feminist?" Katie leaned back, squeaking her chair against the floor. She'd moved on to tough love mode. The thing was—I wanted to tell her—I believed absolutely in equality for women, and I wanted bad things to stop happening to women in general, but that didn't mean I knew how to want those things for myself, because was I really even a woman, or just some floundering being? I didn't feel like a woman, partly because I didn't know how that was supposed to feel.

"Maybe you shouldn't meditate after all," she went on. "You seem a little too calm about this whole thing."

I stared at her. I was eating meat in front of her for the first time since we'd met. Was that calm? Suddenly I was annoyed with her, miffed that she hadn't picked up on my ordering bacon. I raised my hand and asked for the check.

Outside, I watched them, a trio, a nice word, shuffling together down the sidewalk. Bradley had the baby in a sling against his chest, and I couldn't see her, but I knew where she was because Katie was wiggling her fingers at the baby, *Hi, hello, hey there*.

A hot rush of dread slicked me when they disappeared from view. I scratched my left forearm, peeling at it, and something flaked off, but when I examined the pavement, lifting one shoe, then the other, I saw nothing but layers of NYC dirt.

They'd told me to see a psychiatrist or meditate. *Do something* was what they meant. I pulled out my phone and donated $50 to an organization that was working to reunite immigrant children separated from their parents.

Day Four (Saturday)

The rest of the weekend stretched ahead. I should have been plotting some creative scheme to win Marlin back, but I also couldn't bear to think about him just then. Each attempt looped me back to Eamon's house, reminding me of how Marlin had arced his whole body away from me.

In the evening, I went to a Lanzhou restaurant and asked for a braised lamb platter, thinking stew, thinking geometric cubes that appealed to the human preference for symmetry. When the dish came out it was instead a spicy sea dotted with islets of irregularly shaped lamb. I fished a piece out. It took me several seconds to identify the edible parts. Essentially there was a slim strip of meat almost obscured by surrounding fat, which was itself topped off by a skim of skin. I tried to remove the skin but found it a tough task. It was firmly welded to the gelatinous layers underneath. This whole thing of meat-fat-gel-skin was skewered by two bars of bone running parallel to each other. Eventually, I figured out that I could slide the edible parts right off the bone bars. It was addictive—I de-sleeved meat and de-sleeved meat, each bite all the more delicious because it felt hard-earned somehow.

I swallowed the last piece of meat. My plate was littered with sections of the parallel bones. They looked like a railroad track all broken up, going nowhere. Some ignoramus said that all good things must come to an end. Well, all bad things must also come to an end. So what was the point of the saying?

Back home, another of Marlin's documentaries on the couch, in an apartment turned eerie by absence. A computer-generated person dies in horrific fashion on-screen. I learned that right before freezing to death, victims can paradoxically feel so hot they begin to strip naked. That made sense to me; it reminded me of a bug by Ben I'd once caught in testing. The bug was what's called an integer overflow, which is when a number is too large for its assigned storage capacity and thus can manifest instead as a negative figure. For example, if the number 128 were forced into a signed field that could express only up to 127, the input would "overflow" and be displayed as -128.

It was mildly gratifying to learn that the human body could also overflow. I idly wondered if, any day now, my pain would grow so great that it converted into happiness.

At some point in the night my mother called again.

"Why do you look so tired?" she started right off.

"Work is stressful," I said automatically. "My visa is expiring, I told you."

"I don't understand why you still want to stay in America if it makes you so unhappy," she said in a grumbling tone. "Move back home! Here you have people who understand you."

"I'm not ready to give up yet."

"You've already given up. Why you working with computers? That is not your interest."

"Okay, can we talk about something else?"

"It's like this: your mole is bringing you bad luck. I told you before, you got the mole because of your past life when your house was on fire—"

I choked down childish comebacks. *You* bring me bad luck. You tell unlucky stories about girls and ghosts that worm inside my husband's head. You're the reason my life has fallen apart.

"I've heard it a thousand times, Ma!" I said instead.

"Clearly you haven't heard it a single time, because you don't do what I say. All you need to remove bad luck is a toothpick and some medicine, I can mail you some."

"I'm not going to put some unknown substance on my face."

"Just try it—"

"I don't believe you, okay?" I disconnected the call. I'd never hung up on her before. I sat around, waiting uncertainly for her to call back. She didn't.

WHAT IF I DEPICTED HER NOT AS THE STEREOTYPICAL NAGGING ASIAN mother, but as a crafty and sophisticated weaver of narratives who only wished to motivate me via elaborate tales of past lives? Is that better, or worse?

You told me that I am not responsible for "decoding" my parent. But does it not fall on me to view and portray her in a positive light, if only for selfish reasons? If only to, as you call it, heal?

I HAD TO GET MARLIN TO COME BACK SOON, BEFORE MY MOTHER CAUGHT on that he'd left me. It'd be one more arrow in her quiver; she'd hound me with yet another past life story about how I'd sinned two hundred and fifty years before to deserve his desertion.

I started ransacking our apartment, plowing through things Marlin had left behind. There was a clunky laptop, many years old, that wouldn't blink on, no matter how many seconds I counted after holding down the power button. My body clenched when I found the stack of Valentine's Day cards I'd written him over the years. Their garish covers were an eyesore, irony corroded by loss. I flipped one open and could barely stand to take in my own handwriting. The more sentimental words were especially bewildering, in the way that a joke's lead-up to its punch line could be.

When I bounced the stack of red and pink cards on my lap to line up their edges, a brochure stood out, skinnier and taller than the rest. I picked it out. On the glossy front was a picture of neat flower beds arrayed before a mountain range that looked like an EKG chart. I couldn't be sure, but the image looked photoshopped. I stood the brochure up by its panels and examined it. It'd been put out by the Dowsers Society of America, and as I read on, I realized I finally had a word for the bizarre practice Marlin had started adopting.

In June, I'd been coming home later and later because of a programming intensive. It was held after work hours, geared toward people with full-time jobs. One day I returned to Marlin hunched over our kitchen table, his eyes closed. With one hand he was spinning a necklace in slow circles, whirring a pendant round and round. The chain looked like one of mine, a silver affair that had been an anniversary present from him. The pendant was a lumpy block of purple mineral that I didn't recognize.

Marlin's hand was incredibly steady. The necklace rotated at an unvarying speed that was maybe equivalent to a ceiling fan's lowest setting. When I walked closer, I saw that the necklace was spinning suspended over a piece of paper depicting what looked like a diagram.

Marlin opened his eyes when I was near enough to touch him, his hand keeping up the hypnotic circling of pendant over paper.

"You're disrupting my session," he said.

"What session? What are you doing?"

He sighed, letting my necklace drop onto the table. I leaned in to examine the paper. The diagram reminded me of a color wheel with dozens of spokes, except instead of hues, each spoke was a noun, a word like "Beauty" or "Faith" or "Confidence." My eyes swirled across them. They were alphabetical, "Desire" following "Determination" trailing "Endurance."

"What is this?" I snatched up the diagram. Maybe I was expecting a tussle, or maybe I was just very concerned for Marlin, but the strength of my snatch sent the necklace sailing, airborne.

When it fell with a dull thud I looked at it eagerly, somehow hoping that the purple crystal had splintered into pieces, thereby releasing whatever hold it had on Marlin. But he had leapt out of his seat after it, and I saw the pendulum whole in his cupped palms.

I looked again at the wheel I was holding. In addition to spokes, the wheel was also surrounded by an outer ring of dense text. I skimmed the tiny font and winced at the most nonsensical phrases I'd ever encountered: "Brain-Cell Restructuring," "Soul Energy Programming," "Direct Healing Processes and Colors," and other riots of New Age stuff hybridized willy-nilly with scientific and engineering terms.

"What is this?" I asked again.

"I'm learning how to contact spirit guides and advisers."

"I don't understand." I could feel my brows furrowing. "This doesn't seem like you."

"Maybe you don't actually know me that well."

I'd never been so wounded by a single sentence. I stood blankly while Marlin plucked the diagram out of my hands.

Now, I learned from the Dowsers Society of America brochure that the diagram was called a pendulum chart, and what Marlin had been doing with the necklace was pendulum dowsing. Dowsing! Like looking for gold on a beach!

"The pendulum is a form of receiver and transmitter connecting you to your guardian angels and spiritual teachers," the brochure said. From what I could make of its claims, Marlin's pendulum-twirling was indeed a branch of the "ancient art" of dowsing, except modern-day dowsers had evolved from finding such concrete riches as gold, water, and oil, to now seeking advice and insight from intangible spirits. "Dowsing is unquestionably rooted in science," the brochure continued. "Charles Richet, a Nobel Laureate celebrated for his work on anaphylaxis (severe allergic reactions), famously said: 'We must accept dowsing as fact.'"

I looked up the good doctor online. He was born in the nineteenth century and had been a supporter of eugenics. Then I read that dowsers also claimed no less than Albert Einstein as a devotee. "The dowsing rod is a simple instrument which shows the reaction of the human nervous system to certain factors which are unknown to us at this time," he wrote. "Many of the top dowsers are doctors, engineers and scientists."

Einstein used to be a hero of Marlin's. In college, he had definitely been one of those people who put up a poster of the genius sticking his tongue out. Marlin used to laugh along with me when I made fun of my mother's past life stories and called them "third-world superstition" (I'm not proud of that). But if dowsing had the scientific weight of such a celebrated physicist as Einstein behind it, then maybe it was enough to lure Marlin over in his grief. A dirty trick.

The brochure's last page showed a picture of a cottage surrounded by trees. The caption identified it as the society's headquarters in the Hudson Valley, and a paragraph farther down welcomed all those curious about dowsing to attend a workshop, held the first Sunday of every month. My heart flipped. Tomorrow was a first Sunday.

I checked the time and train schedules. I could fit in a few hours of sleep before heading upstate. I didn't know whether Marlin would be there, but there was a chance. I wanted to see him away from Eamon, who, having experienced heartache with his ex-fiancée, was perhaps planting poisonous ideas about me in Marlin's mind. At the very least Eamon might be fanning the flames, reveling in the fact that he wasn't alone anymore in his misfortune. He could be wanting Marlin to suffer alongside him, couldn't he? That last part I did understand. I hadn't wanted to admit it, but I'd felt a bit of resentment watching Katie and Bradley walk away with their baby.

Even if Marlin didn't show up at the workshop, I could still potentially learn something about his transformation from the society. They—whoever they were running the workshops—could have been responsible for manipulating Marlin into his new beliefs. I would reverse-engineer their process and undo their damage.

Day Five (Sunday)

The train ventured north, the Hudson River stretching out along-side and winking under bright sunshine. I peered out the window, charmed. I couldn't remember: Had I seen the horizon lately?

The river's sparkling dips and crests, the clouds trailing wisps of themselves, these must be regular, yawn-inducing sameness for Marlin by now. Before he became someone who used a necklace as a telephone to the spirit world, he would go on weekends to the Shawangunk Ridge with Eamon and others to climb. The Gunks, they called it. How many times had Marlin looked out the train window at this view? I never went with them because I was self-conscious about the way I'd look, strapped tight into a harness.

I spoke politely and formally to the uniformed conductor. When the train passed a castle in the middle of the river, I ate a smoked salmon sandwich, gnawing away at the rubbery, oily flesh. And when a young couple wearing matching outfits asked if I would trade seats so they could sit together, I said, "No," surprising myself.

THE HEADQUARTERS OF THE DOWSERS SOCIETY LOOKED LIKE AN AIRBNB darling. It had triangular roofs and a porch. The exterior walls were a display of whitewashed horizontal slats, and the front door featured a pane of stained glass. There was even a chimney.

I was early for the workshop advertised on the brochure. I figured that would leave me enough time to investigate the organization, though I wasn't sure what I was looking for. In movies, people were brainwashed by physical objects, like hair-salon helmets or clickers that produced dazzling white flashes. I didn't think I would find anything similar to explain Marlin's behavior.

Maybe part of me wasn't out to uncover the society's working mechanisms. A corner of me wanted to be changed into a believer also. That way I could join Marlin in whatever version of the world he had crossed into.

I walked around the cottage once, then twice, not finding the flower beds printed on the brochure's front. Already I had proof of their willingness to deceive. I peeked through a window, noting the floral-print armchairs, the quilts, the curtains with tassel tiebacks. No sign of Marlin.

Standing before the front door, I tried to practice smiling, or at least to maintain an open, neutral face, but the pane of stained glass scrunched my face, distorting my intentions. I didn't know whether I should knock. The Rock wouldn't. I could hear him booming: "Walk in like you own the place." My mother said that in a past life I'd died trapped inside a house.

I opened the door and walked into a dim hallway. I blinked to regain sight, and a woman appeared, the hem of her tunic fluttering against the tops of her thighs as she came toward me. She looked to be in her forties.

"Welcome," she said. "Here for the workshop?"

"I was referred here. Do you think you might know him? His name is Marlin."

"Marlin, Marlin . . ." She aimed a blank look at the wainscoting running along the entryway. "Is he a member?"

This threw me off. I had been so sure I would find some connection to Marlin here and be able to *do something*. I'd told myself I couldn't know what that *something* was until I visited the society, but now an urge crystallized under the woman's expectant look, a repressed fantasy in which I found those responsible for turning Marlin into a stranger and forcefully made them stop. This woman, for example. If she'd confessed to knowing Marlin, I would have grabbed her by her tunic and told her to leave him alone. Or so the fantasy went.

"I'm not sure," I answered.

"Say that again?" She cupped one ear.

"I'm not sure."

"Well, not to worry. Follow me, it's this way to the workshop." She started walking, then half turned without slowing. "I'm Carol."

The room she led me into had yellowing crown molding and mismatching floor lamps in every corner. Why was it so dark in here on a summer day?

"Let's begin."

Carol lowered herself into a great big overstuffed chair in the shadows of a looming potted plant. I did the same across from her. She wasn't what I was expecting of a dowser. Her voice was not wispy, and she wasn't bebaubled or birdlike. No shawl either. If anything, she seemed like an ER nurse who cared deeply, yet knew some of us had to be cut loose into the void of darkness.

I was ashamed. I'd come here hoping to find someone laughable, so I could prove that Marlin was wrong to be taken in by such silly beliefs. At the same time a part of me, I realized now, had come in sincere hope that a healer would be able to unpack Marlin and help me understand him. I felt my arms and neck boiling with an invisible rash.

"It's just us?" I looked around. One of the floor lamps tilted at a drunken angle, ready to keel over.

"It's summer," she said, her feelings seemingly not at all bruised by the lack of attendance. "People go on vacations. So. What are you hoping to get out of dowsing? Finding lost objects, cleansing negative energy, resolving mental issues, emotional issues—these are some of the ways dowsing can help you in your life."

I wanted to ask if a husband fell under the category of "lost objects." Instead I said, as neutrally as possible, "resolving issues."

She nodded. "We can get into the specifics later. Do you have your house keys with you?"

Was it supposed to happen so early on, the surrendering of personal property? I thought cultists took their time to work their talons into you. It dismayed me, the idea that Marlin had handed over keys to our apartment. I stood up, ready to walk out.

"Take one, the lightest of the bunch if you can. Put it through this." She leaned forward to extend a beige rope cord at me.

I rummaged through my pockets and sat back down, another jet of shame shooting up my spine. Removed from its usual context, my front-door key looped through the cord did look slightly mysterious. I wondered if that's what dowsing was: a way to externalize one's own thoughts, make them just strange enough to seem like advice coming from wiser sources. In times of uncertainty, perhaps a neutral third party looked more attractive than the selfsame brain jumble one had tolerated all one's life.

"When did you start being able to talk to spirits?" I asked.

Her eyes flickered. She was probably sizing me up, sending unseen feelers out to interrogate the shape of my sincerity.

"I realized I had a gift when I was very young." She looked intently into my face. "But we're not here to talk about me." From a side table drawer, she lifted out an amber pendulum hanging off a silver chain. The amber narrowed down into a point at its tip, fanglike.

"Tell me what issues you're hoping to resolve."

I watched the amber spin slowly as she suspended it over her lap. My key sawed into my palm.

"Is it normal for someone to suddenly . . . channel spirits, when they didn't even believe in them before?" I coughed. My throat was dry; it was a chore to speak. But once the first question was out, the rest gushed forth in a nervous torrent. "Can this someone become angry and unreasonable because of the, maybe, shock? Why do you seem so calm? Are all dowsers supposed to be calm?"

She didn't answer immediately. "These are stupid questions," I said. Unfamiliar energies charged upward in me, like I'd turned into a mercury-filled thermometer and someone had just put me into their hot, clammy mouth.

"Oh, honey." Carol leaned forward. Her shoulder brushed against the plant to her left, and it sashayed, whispering. "The gift does not come easy. Sometimes it's difficult for people to see the truth in the visions they are shown. But don't worry"—she put a hand forward, hovering a foot above my knee, not touching it—"I can help you."

I hadn't noticed it before, but she had a S'well bottle flush against one leg of her chair. A sticker on the S'well read: "Ithaca is Gorges." That bottle disoriented me. It made her seem approachable, just like other American women I knew; she could be Katie SooHoo or her lawyer cousin, or my gynecologist, or the host of a podcast I listened to on commutes. What did that mean? If she could contain the occult and still be cheesy and buy into overpriced consumer trends, then why couldn't Marlin?

"I'd like that," I replied, tears dribbling. "But it's Marlin you should help. Somehow he picked up the thing you do, spiritual dowsing, and he—" I threw a hand up in a helpless gesture, knocking into her hovering hand. She withdrew it.

"I think the first thing we should do is be honest with ourselves. It's you who needs help, right? Can we agree on that?"

I did not see that coming at all. I shook my head hard. I tried to explain everything. Although Carol did not interrupt me or deny my story in any way, she communicated with her look that she absolutely thought I was going down the wrong path. She had a very expressive face.

"This Marlin, he's the one who referred you here?"

"In a way." I couldn't meet her eyes. The door to the room seemed far away.

"What does he look like?"

I started to say "Chindian," then winced. It wasn't a term familiar to Americans. I remembered having to explain it to Katie, the way I also had to explain it to you. In Malaysia, where everybody is hyperconscious of ethnicity, the word is a shorthand. How you are categorized in turn determines the kind of treatment you receive from everyone around you, friends and shopkeepers alike. Every year, Marlin dreaded Ramadan. With his darker skin and round eyes, he was often accosted while eating lunch during fasting month by self-righteous uncles ready to berate him for being a bad Muslim. It had happened to me a couple times too, when I had to produce my IC and point to my obviously non-Muslim name—*May I eat my economy rice in peace now?* Sometimes, in the face of their obvious error, the uncles only hardened more. *Who sold you this rice?* they wanted to know. Marlin would walk around for the rest of the day worried that he'd gotten some poor hawker in trouble with the religious authorities.

Katie laughed at the end of my roundabout explanation. "What's your point?"

I said I moved to New York to escape being racially pegged every time I stepped outside. I was tired of constantly thinking about the color of my skin.

She snickered. "Well, you've come to the absolute worst country for that."

"But you've never thought about living somewhere else?"

"No, I can't imagine it."

I envied her. What it must be like, to grow up not hearing friends declare that they were going to leave as soon as they could, even if they had to "jump aeroplane" in Singapore or Australia or Taiwan—work as illegal immigrants, that is. "This country doesn't love us," they'd say as justification. "There aren't as many opportunities for people like us."

Being loved is not a basic necessity, I'd replied. I can live without love. It's easy.

And I'd really believed it too. That was before the acceptance letter to an American college, before I started imagining what it would feel like to be free of my mother. Before Marlin.

"He has curly hair that hangs past his ears. About this tall." I stood on tiptoes over Carol, one hand slicing air above my head. "Really big earlobes, if that's something you notice about people."

"Beautiful hair." She nodded.

"Yes," I said, crying, abject, at this first validation I'd gotten from her. "He's an engineer," I pleaded. "He doesn't belong here."

I thought she would trot out the Nobel Laureate or Einstein.

Instead, she said, "People are complicated. Including you. There is so much within you that you don't understand, that you refuse to see. Don't you want to expand your potential?"

No, I didn't. I took a few steps away, so I wasn't crying right into her lap. I wanted Marlin back the way he was, the rock in my life, the person who reliably had a plan and action steps whenever I felt lost. He was the one who'd started teaching me programming basics. He coached me through my job interview for AInstein. Throughout the process he'd been so enthusiastic about the fact that I was sharing in his interests, putting one foot into his world of code and building things from nothing but keyboard strokes. I'd willingly moved into his sphere, just for him to leave me for an alien planet?

"You are too upset right now to practice. Dowsing requires you to be relaxed, free of negative feelings. Here." Carol handed me tissues, splayed on top of a piece of paper with dense text. "Those are instructions for beginners. Try it later when you're feeling better."

She stood up and unceremoniously guided me toward the far-away door.

"Don't forget the cord," she said when I crossed the threshold. Sniffling, I extracted my front-door key from her cord and gave it back to her.

I SPENT THE TRAIN RIDE BACK FEELING FOOLISH. I'D IMAGINED BEING CO-vert, a spylike figure who gathered answers and then walked out of the Dowsers Society without showing my hand. Would Carol tell Marlin about my visit? And if she did, would she characterize me as concerned for his well-being? So much depended upon the story she told.

The Hudson's winks were intolerable now, taunting, too chipper, like flashes of white teeth some American parents paid for their children to have. What had I learned from this trip? That Carol had a magnetic personality tinged with brutal efficiency, which might have appealed to the engineer in Marlin. Perhaps she was the one who'd convinced him of his potential, she whose hand guided his into spinning, spinning, spinning.

I wanted our old Sundays back, fun and messy hours coming up with ways to make the wackiest vegan versions of nonvegan food, such as vegan sardines and vegan Froot Loops (the regular kind contains sheep bits—shocking, I know). Marlin, as could be predicted, approached the whole thing as a science experiment. His favorite parts were when he got to read up on chemistry, or when he gleefully mixed things that normally would never go together. He was the one who insisted on having beakers instead of normal measuring cups.

In many of these experiments I played a supporting role, passing ingredients or dipping a finger in for a taste. Laughter-filled times, the rare kind that tap you on the shoulder to whisper *This is happiness* as you are deep in the moment, the realization then amplifying the emotion, like feedback reverberating in a tiny bar.

Maybe by eating meat now, I was making sure I wouldn't have those vegan experiments with anyone else. This way, I would never again experience that specific kind of happiness. It might seem childish at first, but it can also be interpreted as a way to protect those memories. At least I think so.

OUTSIDE GRAND CENTRAL I BOUGHT A HOT DOG FROM A STREET CART, then walked down the block and ordered another dog from another cart. I asked for everything on the first, and nothing on the second. A man walked by with newspapers folded under his armpit, and I started to cry again. I should have been home all day, sprawled on the living room floor elbowing Marlin, a newspaper page spread out before us. The race would be on, me trying to solve my crossword puzzle on the left before he could complete his sudoku on the right.

Whenever I won, he would rib that crossword puzzles were just a collection of useless trivia. Whenever he won (almost always), I would jeer at him and say he was simply rearranging nine measly numbers on a grid.

I could feel it, a mess of tears, mustard, and relish across my cheek, mashed on top of my mole. I swiped at my face with tiny, sheer napkins. I picked roughly at the mole on my cheek. I wanted to change too. A new start.

HOW I GOT MY MOLE (A PAST LIFE STORY)

The woman who is me in a past life runs into the burning hut, screaming her son's name. A curtain entangles her when she tries to push past it to reach the bedroom. The fabric clings to her face. She feels her man's arm belt her waist. She struggles, thinking he is telling her to leave her son, but he shouts at her to look, and she turns to see their baby boy crying on the floor to their left, his legs splayed and kicking.

She opens her mouth to scream for him to come over, but instead she bends down coughing. Her chest feels like it's been pierced all over with a sharpened stone, and all the air and blood contained within is leaking out into the rest of her body, swelling her limbs and making her head heavy. The more she tries to breathe, the more the holes in her chest burn.

Her man pulls her down to the floor, where the air is cleaner and clearer. This is like drowning in reverse, she thinks, where the suffocation does not rise from the depths of hell but rather presses down from the direction of heaven. She risks an upward glance to see the form the smoke takes, waiting for it to gather into a spectral tiger, bird, or dragon.

"What are you doing?" her man hisses. While she was spellbound, he has retrieved their son. She crouches and takes the boy into her arms, praying he will not remember this day.

Her man starts for the door, and she follows. He is doing his best to clear the way with a broom he picked up, sending fallen pieces of their hut skidding along the floor. The fire is loud, very loud. There's something insectlike about its screeches, as if the fire has many legs that are being pulled off one by one. The hut has been repainted in violent hues. She can see right through parts of the flames like they're made of the sheerest cloth, but she knows she will not be able to tear through them. She hugs her boy close and tries to keep up with her man, her eyes watering. Every few steps something grabs at her feet.

The attap roof sticks out a tongue of fire and licks itself clean, until there is no roof and suddenly, in its place, a square of sky and an impossible pain. She screams and looks down at a wooden post, large as a young ciku tree. Somewhere under it is her foot. She tries to move it but cannot. Flames dance on the post, giving it movement, like it is the one struggling to get off her.

She presses her boy's face harder into her chest, her mouth gasping to breathe through the pain. She meets her man's eyes when a section of the wall next to them gives way. A flying spark lands on her cheek, singeing her flesh. The sting makes the decision for her.

"Take him!" She throws the boy through the air and watches his swaddle come partly undone. The man's eyes protrude with shock. But she knows he will catch their son safely, and he does. A triangle of the swaddle flaps, dangling, as if beckoning the flames, which do come, lapping at the tip of fabric.

She tries one last time to get her foot back. With all her strength she pulls on her calf, and the excruciation comes in such a wave that she thinks she must have succeeded, but when she looks down she is still pinned. She screams, a long word that doesn't exist. But the man understands. So he does what she asks. He holds the baby tight and heads for the direction of safety. The smoke chases them out of sight, taking the form of a beautiful woman.

Day Five (Sunday)

I jerked awake to an insistent sound. I rubbed my eyes, and there was my mother's face on my laptop next to me. The Skype call ringtone persisted for a few more moments. When it stopped, I leaned in to check the screen. It was just after eight at night.

My face hurt. I let my fingers crawl all over it. The mole was still there, a blot of firm finality. This was the way things were, it said.

I was fourteen, standing in front of a mirror and worrying the mole. Someone at school had made fun of me, saying it looked like I had permanent bird shit on my face. My mother walked in. I wanted to ask her for help.

"Stop touching it," she said. "Or it'll grow bigger."

Horrified, I dropped my hands. That's when she told me about my past life, the one in which I was trapped in a fire.

"You were burned there," my mother said, pointing to my mole.

I couldn't understand the moral of the story. Was it to instill motherly virtues in me, by preemptively describing me as a woman who would make the ultimate sacrifice for her baby? I didn't ask my mother to elaborate. But I kept thinking about the story, and it kept showing up in my dreams unbidden. It was only after I'd moved to America that she started referring to the mole as a bringer of bad luck.

"That's fucked up," Katie said when I told her. "Telling a fourteen-year-old they were burned to death? That's absolutely the most painful way to die, you know."

"Parenting styles are different in Asia," I said, uncomfortable. I'd wanted her to help me decode the story, not to probe my relationship with my mother.

I told myself that I was respecting my mother by giving weight to her visions, filling them in with sensory details. The recurring dreams meant I was taking her stories seriously, which could be a kind of love. I preferred it over raw resentment.

My phone lit up next, my mother's contact photo—a selfie of her in a polyester windbreaker at Genting Highlands—peering out through a porthole. I sat up straighter on the couch. I couldn't talk to her, not before I reunited with Marlin. I was sure she'd pin the blame for our separation on me. "You're very lucky," I heard her say again on our wedding day.

I turned the volume all the way down on the phone and waited until it stopped convulsing with loud death rattles against the coffee table. I thought about how easy it would be to stop being a daughter. It had taken only a moment to no longer be a wife—the time it took to switch on a light and register a blank space bordered by dust. Why should other identities take any longer to lose?

It would be so simple. A push of a button that wasn't even real, and my mother could be deleted from my phone. She had no friends or kin in the alien country of USA. She didn't even have a passport. By the time she got one and appeared in front of a US embassy worker to be grilled for a tourist visa, I could have moved. Even if it was just to another borough, how would she ever find me? The word *borough* itself was unknown to her.

No work at all to undo, this supposedly most sacred of all bonds. It didn't seem unreasonable to me. It just seemed sad.

MY LACK OF SLEEP FROM THE LAST FEW DAYS HAD CAUGHT UP TO ME. When I woke up again I was still on the couch. My neck hurt, and my right shoulder was hunched almost up to my ear, even when I stood up and tried to stretch.

I moved to the bed proper, but lying on the rumpled sheets only made me miss Marlin, his warm body. He never minded that my hands were always cold. When we had sex I'd grip his burning shoulders or run my icy palms up and down the tautness of his back, and he wouldn't even flinch.

"You drive me crazy," he once rasped into my neck.

I smiled into his hair, immeasurably pleased. It seemed the ultimate achievement. I gripped the nape of his neck, surer of myself than I had ever been. For however brief a time, I had pulled him beyond his own boundaries. That was magic.

I GAVE UP ON THE BED. I WASN'T SO MUCH TOSSING AND TURNING AS writhing. I called Eamon, trying to keep the anxiety out of my voice.

"It's ten o'clock, Edwina."

"I know. I'm sorry. I just want to know if he's still there."

"He is. For now."

Was it me, paranoid me, or did it sound like he was gritting his teeth?

"Did something happen?"

"Listen, in case you're thinking of showing up unannounced again: don't do it. He's not ready to see you."

"He won't answer my calls or emails. What else can I do?"

Eamon was silent for a while. When he answered, his voice seemed to have softened. It was almost gentle.

"You could write him a letter."

"How is that different from an email?"

"It just feels different, right? Handwriting is so personal."

I wondered: maybe he had sent his ex-fiancée letters.

Marlin's graph paper was the only writing material I could find in the apartment. The paper's little plots of squares unnerved me, insisting on orderliness when my thoughts were hopelessly jumbled. I stared at the cage-like squares, frustrated. For the first time in my life, I wished that an AI would take over for me. Figure out the minimally viable words that would achieve the expected outcome of my husband's return.

When Marlin was helping me improve my coding skills, he gave me an assignment. I was supposed to write a straightforward shell script and cron job combo that acted as a reminder. A user could specify a time and a note, say to walk the dog at 16:00. At that specified time, the script would both emit a sound and also display the previously entered note. There was allure in having machines do our bidding, Marlin explained.

After I successfully completed the assignment, I slyly set a daily reminder on Marlin's laptop. Every day, at precisely 10:00 p.m., an alert pinged. "Tell Edwina I love her," it read. "Don't forget."

In the end, all I could manage for the letter was this exact refrain. I scribbled down the words, which looked wild on the graph paper, breaking loose and trampling all over the borders of the little squares. "Tell Edwina I love her. Don't forget." I knew he was no longer the "I" of that reminder. I was appealing to routine, to habit that had, I hope, hardened into instinct. Supposedly it takes sixty-six days for repeated behavior to become "automatic." Doubtless you've heard.

Day Six (Monday)

Another sunny summer morning in Manhattan, winter decorative cabbages giving way to more vibrant leafy plants on sidewalks, protected by ankle-height tree guards made of rusty steel. This was the city I lived in, littered with dog shit to step around and vest-wearing people holding clipboards to avoid. You know how it is. Though for too long after I moved here, I'd stream a movie, a romantic comedy perhaps, or something like a wry take on urban millennial living, and it'd be set in New York, and I'd watch, wistful, wishing I were there. Then, with a start, I'd recognize a street corner or a flash of the skyline and realize I did live in that same place depicted on-screen, except my life had nothing to do with that silver city. It was like getting glimpses of a parallel dimension.

Since I was up too early, I decided to walk to work. I dropped my letter to Marlin in a sidewalk mailbox not far from the office and went into a tiny café nearby. No seating space, and no one in line. A handwritten sign on the counter read: "We're cashless!"

"What kind of nondairy milk do you have?" I asked.

The barista wore a slouchy beanie, paired with an apron that wasn't tied at his waist. The apron billowed and sagged as he leaned down to perch his elbows on the counter, looked me up and down, and said: "Cambodian breast milk."

The door jingled on my wordless way out. If Marlin were still living with me, I would have said something. I would have said something because then when I recounted the episode to him I would have come off cool. It had been a ritual almost, one that I relished. We'd trade reports of microaggressions, laughing at the more ridiculous of them, even though they also hurt a little, of course.

"It's us against the world," I'd tell him.

"I've got your back," he'd say, pinching at the fat below the hooks of my bra.

EMPTY BROOKLYN BREWERY BOTTLES AND SOLO CUPS LITTERED OUR OFfice space. There was an uncapped Hendrick's on my desk, my keyboard pushed askew to make room. I picked up the gin bottle by its neck and wagged it. The splashing of liquid answered me.

They must have stayed late on Friday, either for someone's birthday or for a code sprint. I looked around for pizza boxes and found them on Lucas's desk. Code sprint.

I didn't want the gin on my desk, but I couldn't just dump it on someone else's instead. I took it, sloshing, as I wandered around the bullpen searching for the cap. Then I thought: AInstein has its own office. I could leave the gin there, close the door, and not have to smell alcohol while I worked anymore.

AInstein's head gleamed when I turned on the lights in Bond. It was so quiet I could hear the machines hum. I set the gin down on the floor by AInstein and woke it up.

"Hello! The time is: eight thirty-eight a.m."

"Hello."

"Would you like to hear a joke?"

"What's your favorite joke?" I asked, knowing full well that it was nowhere near sophisticated enough to have an opinion.

It whirred its head as it always did, and then it asked: "What was Einstein's rapper name?"

"What?"

In response, AInstein made a sound between a murmur and a cough. What was going on? Was it broken, all because I'd asked it for something resembling a take? Had I unleashed the beginnings of an AI awakening?

Then I caught myself. I knew what "artificial intelligence" powered AInstein—nothing more than the ingestion of large data sets and subsequent pattern identification. There was no way AInstein was gaining sentience.

"Please repeat," I instructed.

Again, AInstein emitted a short, confusing sound. It started like a hesitating "Mmm" which then quickly segued into a cough, followed by what sounded like the number 2. These sounds were definitely not expected. I went to AInstein's control laptop to investigate. Could it be a memory corruption?

The answer blinked into existence on the screen, and I burst out laughing. Because AInstein's content was trawled from online forums, many of its jokes had improperly formatted text, typos, and the like. The joke in question, in its original typed form, went like this:

Q: WHAT WAS EINSTEIN'S RAPPER NAME?

A: mc2.

It was obvious, to those in the know, that the punch line should be pronounced "em cee squared," from the formula $E=MC^2$. But AInstein didn't know this. Its text-to-speech voice generator did its best with nonsense words, of course, but in this case the joke was totally ruined. In fact, even if the text had been properly format- ted, I wondered how the text-to-speech generator would fare with superscript. I tore off a piece of paper from a pad nearby and started jotting down notes. We would have to add a filter to catch words the text-to-speech generator couldn't handle. I made a mental note to bring it up with Lucas for extra green card points. Smiling, I folded my notes and put it in my pocket. It was so like AInstein to name something defective as its favorite.

Marlin's favorite joke, before he changed, had of course been one related to programming.

KNOCK, KNOCK.
Who's there?

RACE CONDITION WHO?
Race condition!

The joke is funny because it demonstrates the symptom of a race condition. You see, a race condition is when events occur out of expected order, so the punch line works by switching the order of the answer ("Race condition!") and subsequent follow-up ("Race condition who?"). But of course explanations ruin a joke. Marlin liked it, he said, for its potential double meaning, as in the color of his skin shouldn't be the first thing people notice about him, but often that ends up being the case.

"What I love about New York is that it's so diverse, I don't stand out as much," he'd said. "Also no one knows what a Chindian is."

I wondered what his new favorite joke might be. I stood there trying to come up with jokes about ghosts until I felt tears coming. I pictured Marlin laughing, his eyes crinkled, and it hurt to imagine him so happy without me. I could only hope that my seven-word letter would move him enough to change the situation between us.

BACK AT MY DESK, I WATCHED MY COWORKERS SLOWLY TRICKLE IN TO work. The stench of alcohol was thankfully lesser, though it still lingered. I checked the status of the canary test suite that had run over the weekend. As you might have guessed, canary tests are named after the birds in coal mines. Like those unfortunate creatures, canary tests are meant to exist in the background, out of sight and mind, when everything is going well. But when something goes wrong (new code committed that breaks existing product features, for example), they're supposed to act as an early alert system that can help us discover and revert bugs quickly.

This morning, I saw that our canary tests had caught a failure. I felt a sour dread rising. When I inspected the failure, sure enough—AInstein's ability to de-duplicate jokes had been compromised, the exact error I'd caught last week, caused by Josh's code.

I checked the bug ticket I'd opened and assigned to Josh. I'd spent time carefully writing up that ticket, laying out the test cases I'd written to prove that Josh's code was at fault. Now I saw that he'd taken himself off the ticket late Friday night. No explanation. "Unassigned," the ticket taunted.

I asked Lucas if I could have five minutes of his time.

"Sure, I can huddle real quick," he replied.

I followed him into our tiniest conference room, a two-person space named Ant-Man.

"So what's up?" he asked.

I took a breath. I needed to keep my story strictly linear; it was the best way to get through to him.

"I found a bug in Josh's code last week, before it was merged to master. I opened a ticket and assigned it to him, but then this morning I saw that canaries are failing, which means he did push his bug to master. He also unassigned himself from the ticket. Even though he obviously knew about the bug."

I stopped. I wanted to propose a bug-fix process that would bind the engineers to an SLA—for example, all reported bugs must be triaged and sized within two weeks, or one week if we suspected a major issue. But I thought I'd first see what Lucas would say, to gauge his openness to my ideas.

"Have you talked to him about this?"

"No," I answered, startled.

"Maybe the bug fix is on his backlog?" Lucas twirled a pen in one hand. "Typically, I trust my guys to manage their own work. I'm not a micromanagey kind of leader."

"But it's a bug. It shouldn't be out in production if it was previously caught."

"Okay, can you send me the bug ticket? I'll take a look." He missed catching the pen, and it fell, clattering onto the tiny round table between us.

"Sure," I said.

He stood up. I stood up too.

I stayed at my desk only long enough to forward Lucas the bug ticket. Then I left the building for a walk. Nine forty was a little early for lunch, but who would care, given the lack of micromanagey-ness? I could have lunch before ten if I wanted to.

I took a deep breath. Taking everything into account, Lucas was really not that bad of a manager, I reminded myself, especially given the wider general problem in tech. A good engineer had low correlation with a good manager; when tech companies tried to reward high performers by promoting them to leadership, it often backfired. More often than not, the initial power rush wore off, and the engineer-managers quickly found that they disliked meetings, the lack of time to code, and—shudder—having to be diplomatic.

I walked by an American Chinese takeout spot, the smell of frying oil rising as if out of the pavement itself. Inside, a man wearing a hairnet scowled when I asked if he would sell me just a single fortune cookie. He didn't even bother saying no before he turned away, lifting an arm high and flapping it tiredly.

We used to insist on sharing fortunes, Marlin and I. We'd inspect our two vegan fortune cookies from Keep Calm and Curry On, and we'd pick the cookie that looked less perfect. Maybe it would have a chip along an edge, or maybe its dent was not quite in the middle, making it look lopsided. We'd unwrap the "Chinese" cookie and read its faux-oriental wisdom out loud, nodding sagely and solemnly as we acknowledged our entwined fortunes. Sometimes the little slips of paper contained not predictions but directives, like "Trust your intuition" or "Smile. Tomorrow is another day."

The other cookie we'd throw away, whatever was folded over in its core unacknowledged.

Barred from buying a single fortune cookie, I left the American Chinese spot and got an $18 prime rib sandwich instead. I'd heard so much about this sandwich, beloved by many AInstein engineers. I wanted to see what the fuss was about. Or maybe I wanted to imagine what it was like to be them.

While I waited for my order, I read an article online that said Kobe beef tastes wonderful because of the treatment Kobe cows receive while they are being raised for their meat. Men massage the animals daily, working the muscle and fat, marbling them. In contrast, American factory beef is subpar because of the inhumane caging, crowding, and general nastiness of the cows' environment. Every day they see their fellows marched off single-file and hear their death lows ring out. The strain builds up in their bodies, and when a chunk arrives sliced on your plate, all that they have suffered manifests in the meat, making it tough and chewy. The texture of distress.

Back in the office, I tried to really absorb it, the stress in my sandwich. I ate to feel how good it was to be so bad. I wanted the state of my body to match the state of my mind.

BY THE WAY, SORRY I DIDN'T RESPOND TO THE QUESTION IN YOUR LAST email right away. Thursday works for me. I'll wear the same sweater from my picture in the app, so it'll be easier for you to spot me.

SOMETIME IN THE AFTERNOON, I CHECKED MY NOTIFICATIONS AND SAW that the bug ticket I'd brought up with Lucas was now closed, marked as "Fixed." I looked at Josh in amazement, but he had his giant headphones on, oblivious to the world. Had it actually worked out the way I'd hoped? Had Lucas sat Josh down, talked him through the importance of prioritizing bug fixes, convinced him that he and I were on the same team, working toward a common goal? I smiled. I was right to have cut Lucas some mental slack earlier.

Just to be sure the bug had truly been fixed, I ran the canary test suite again. When it finished with green checks across the board, I felt almost energized, like I'd not been sleeping terribly for a week. Thanks to me, our product was now just that little bit better. I was contributing. Making things better.

Maybe an olive branch was due. I took a screenshot of the canary results and drew a red circle around the results: "Build passing." I pasted it in our chat application and tagged Josh by name, thanking him for his "quick turnaround on a bug fix."

Suddenly the bullpen resounded with explosive laughter. I surveyed the space, confused. No one was meeting my eye. It took me too long before I understood I should be reading the responses to my chat message.

"Who's gonna tell the tester?" read the latest text in our group chat. There were already a dozen more messages above it. I watched as they kept on piling up, too weary to read.

"Hey," Ben whispered. He jabbed at his screen. I took his cue and looked at mine. He'd direct messaged me a GitHub link. I stared at the URL, expecting an explanation or a roundabout apology. But nothing else came. I clicked the link.

The first thing I registered was a gif of Bumblebee from *Transformers*, switching back and forth between his car and robot forms. The laughter around me had died down. In its place, the whir of a computer fan, a rhyming union protest down on street level.

"The Beetle," I read on my screen, "detects when your tests are being run, and makes them pass." Farther down the page was a list of "Test suites defeated" by the Beetle.

Of course, I thought. Rather than actually doing the work to fix the bug I'd reported, Josh had embedded code that falsified tests passing. Where there should be failures reported, the Beetle inserted itself and brute-forced the outcome as success. A defeat device. All of my work circumvented for a laugh, my entire raison d'être at the company called into question. I sat motionless until Lucas pulled me into our second "quick huddle" of the day. This time we didn't even try to find a room. This time we just stood on different steps in the stairwell.

"Look," he said. "I know those guys can be a pain sometimes."

"Thank you," I said. I wondered why he and I were having this chat. Was anyone else getting the huddle treatment?

"How about we expand your scope of responsibilities a bit, shift your focus for the short term?"

I blinked rapidly, wary of what was being offered. Previously, some other ways my scope of duties had been expanded at AInstein included soliciting meeting agenda items and taking notes. What was on offer now? Making coffee?

"I want you to beta-test AInstein," Lucas continued.

"I'm already testing it," I said, not comprehending.

"No, I mean not as an analyst but as a user. You're going to use AInstein like a customer would. Consider it our start to prioritizing UX."

Immediately I could tell it would be a delicate task. Whatever feedback I had from testing AInstein, I would have to present to the engineers. It would require treading carefully. But Lucas meant well, I could see. I nodded.

"Great. And don't worry," he said, opening the disabled fire alarm door. "I already told the individual responsible that his behavior is unproductive."

"Unproductive?"

"Yeah, like not contributing to increasing the company's value."

"I see." I blinked more.

"Okay, keep up the good work." He smiled kindly at me, then walked away.

Day Six (Monday)

That night, I had takeout fried chicken for dinner. Tendons trapped between my teeth, I thought again about that gif of Bumblebee endlessly transforming. Marlin and I had both watched the cartoon version of *Transformers* as kids, long before Michael Bay got involved. If only we had the flexibility of alien robots from space. But for us, transformation is unidirectional. Once we change, we can never go back to exactly how we were before.

My laptop pinged. Katie had forwarded me an article from a tabloid's website. I clicked on the link. It was a profile of a woman who was about to marry a spirit. A jolt ran through me. I stopped chewing. This woman, a wholesome-looking blonde, was going to pull out all the stops: wedding ceremony, reception, honeymoon, everything. The resort where her ghost fiancé had proposed offered to host her wedding gratis. Her family, she said, was supportive.

I read the headline again: "Woman Who Slept with Dozen

Ghosts Will Wed Spirit." The tone of the article was clearly derisive, whoever was calling themselves a journalist playing it up for sensationalism. My eyes squeezed shut against a pricking that came from within, eyelids trembling to contain the sting. I laid my cheek down on my keyboard. Under my face, individual keys moved, some relenting to my weight, others resisting and struggling stubbornly against my skin. I jumped when an ad started autoplaying.

Was it not immensely tragic, to have one's greatest sorrow be laughing stock for other people? What sawed me to the bone, I now watched filed under Zany and classified as clickbait for everyone else, racking up cry-laughing emojis. Somewhere there was a mom who had lost a child to Tide Pod ingestion, who could no longer turn on a radio or TV for fear of hearing the easy jokes, the laugh tracks. The light of her life reduced to a meme.

The woman in the article said she'd first had sex with her fiancé on a plane. I thought back to that interminable flight after the funeral, when I'd held Marlin's hand as long as I could. No, I didn't think he was banging a spirit then. But I do wonder what a spirit might have whispered into my husband's ear to turn him against me, all that time his hand was lying in mine.

My fingers shook when I scrolled back up to the picture of the ghost bride. They shook all the time now. There was a name for it: essential tremors. What a name for a condition, right? Jitters that were basic and necessary. The shaking was a physical reminder that even as I saw myself as stuck and static, I was really changing or being changed, ceaselessly, perhaps taken further and further away from someone who loves Marlin, and who was loved by him.

With some difficulty I typed my message to Katie: Why did you send me this???

"I'M SORRY," KATIE SAID. "I JUST THOUGHT THE ARTICLE WOULD SHOW you that you aren't alone. There are other people like Marlin, and it's not your fault. I didn't mean to upset you."

We were at Stone Street Tavern, perched on opposite sides of a long picnic table. There were no stars when I looked up at the bruised-blue sky, but the moon shone bright. I sipped my whiskey and winced. I wasn't a drinker, never had been, but Katie said that I "needed it."

"Hey, I said I'm sorry." She put her hand on mine.

"But you laughed, didn't you? When you read the article?"

"Yeah, a little, but I mean. Come on." She was fighting not to laugh again, I could tell. "Anyway, I came over as soon as I realized you were upset. Dropped my baby and everything."

"Yeah, hide behind your baby. Do that."

She grinned at my smile. "Is that my cue to show you pictures?"

I leaned across the table while she swiped through more and more photos of Su-Ann, the toes and arches of my feet pressing into the uneven ground. We'd been so excited, Marlin and I, the first time we wandered down to Stone Street. Lanes that lived outside the grid system! Cobblestones! European-sounding restaurant names! Marlin took his loafers off and tried to prance across the paved stones like a horse, but he wasn't very good at it.

"Aww, you like her, huh," Katie said. "You have such a sweet smile on your face. She *is* a cutie, isn't she? Here, I'll send you a few." She fiddled with her phone.

I thought about what her cousin had said when she'd met Marlin for the first time: "Oh, your kids are going to be so beautiful!" She'd failed to hide her double take well enough. What she said made me uncomfortable, like she was twisting her surprise at

Marlin's skin tone into a weird compliment. I didn't take it that way, though. I felt slighted by her assumption that not only did we want kids, we'd married for some secret agenda to produce America's next top model. "They're going to look like the future of this country," she added.

"Did you get them?" Katie asked now. She tapped my phone on the table. I unlocked the screen to indulge her, opening up the text messages she'd just sent, Su-Ann now on my phone.

"Give me that." She grabbed it out of my hands and started typing on it, her body angled steeply away from me.

"What are you doing?" I asked, confused.

"I think it's time you move on." Still typing.

"Move on from what? There's nothing to move on from."

"You can't make someone love you when they don't anymore. What are you waiting for, anyway? Do you need him to really spell it out for you?"

"I wrote him a letter. I'm waiting to hear back."

Katie frowned. "You're making it sound like a job application."

"What if Bradley left you? What would you do?"

"I'd kill his ass, that's what. There." She handed the phone back. "Don't worry. I had the perfect picture for you. And I'm setting your profile to 'Seeking friends' only. You can change it later." She raised an eyebrow at me.

"You installed a *dating app* on my phone?"

"You don't have to do anything with it now! It's just there, if you want it."

I wanted to ask which picture of mine she'd chosen, and how she'd described me in my profile. Then I thought, What was the point? It wasn't like I could put my current self into words better than she could.

ON MY WALK BACK TO THE APARTMENT, I WONDERED WHAT MARLIN WAS doing at that exact moment. I pictured him cross-legged, that chunky purple pendulum twirling under his fingers, a single, narrow-beamed lamp shining beside him.

"What do you think happened to him?" Katie had asked, just before we hugged goodbye.

I didn't have an answer, but I felt compelled to say something so that Katie would understand that this situation, whatever it was, was temporary.

"I think his father's death really affected him. It's only been seven or eight months."

"That's sad, but a lot of people go through that, right?"

"I guess everyone's different," I said stiffly, not really knowing what I meant. Katie pulled me into a long hug, squeezing until tears threatened to leak out of me.

I walked on, trying to decipher what I'd said. *Everyone's different.* Unlike me, Marlin had grown up with both parents. This part I excelled at imagining; I'd spent many childhood hours wondering what it was like to grow into an adult with a father alongside a mother. Teenage Marlin would have been rambunctious, his burning curiosity about the world mistaken as naughtiness. His father would have fueled and fanned Marlin's energy even as his mother protested, painfully aware that her mixed-race child would have to prove himself again and again in order to be accepted.

Marlin's father was the one who indulged and spoiled. He, too, was the one who brought home Lego kits and radio-controlled cars that turned Marlin on to engineering. His father let him do anything in the name of learning: take apart a brand-new watch; pound on the family typewriter until the keys stuck; throw assorted objects onto the roof of their single-story home to see which would roll back down, and which would remain wedged between shingles.

Then as Marlin got older, his skin tanning to resemble more and more his mother's dark brown, he began to see how many of her attempts to rein him in were done out of a fear-tinged love. He learned from her the necessity for care and caution. He saw how she adopted different tones and styles when she talked to different people. Because of that, he began to pay attention to social interactions, noticing the power dynamics and hierarchies at play. He picked up from her a barbed humor, deployed often in irony and against the powerful.

It warmed my heart to imagine this, the best-loved qualities of my husband deriving equally from his two parents. I pieced together this fantasy based on the stories Marlin told me, but who knew whether his memory was accurate? Not to mention my memory of my memory, and the parts of his memory that were really his parents' memory.

But say it was true. Say that for Marlin, his parents represented the two poles of a magnet. Electrons shuffled between these poles to create a magnificent field, one that drew people like me in and held me fast in love and admiration. Then the death of Marlin's father destabilized the entire makeup of Marlin's being. Something impossible had happened; the magnet was now missing a pole. Maybe Marlin was sabotaging his life to underscore his great loss.

Or it could be that I am simply projecting.

Marlin and I once talked about stories. He observed that some people liked stories that fed their confirmation bias. What he meant was that people seek justification for the way they live their lives in the narratives that they read or watch. For example, a man who has martyr syndrome and feels the world treats him unfairly will devour stories about courage winning the odds against tyranny. Meanwhile, a different man who undertakes mildly unsavory business practices cannot get enough of plots involving power play and ascendance through intelligence and trickery. This also explained why all summer blockbuster movies seem to have the same plot. Because when someone likes pizza, they won't just stick to their favorite pizza restaurant. They have to sample all the pizza places in their city to find the best one, and each new bite is a reminder: "I'm a pizza person."

Marlin, prone to pontificating, said that it made sense to him from a utilitarian standpoint. Life was chaos. Attempting to remain more or less the same person from day to day required a psychic bedrock around which to organize one's various mental loose threads. And this sort of bedrock, which had to withstand daily battering, of course had to be reinforced from time to time. Enter familiar stories under various disguises.

I smiled, listening to him. He sounded like he was leaving himself the world's most serious voice memo.

What about "moving" stories, what people call tearjerkers? I asked. People loved those. They watched or read them and got weepy, melancholic. Untimely deaths and star-crossed lovers torn apart! The failure of ambition! Ah, the fleetingness of love and life! There was the twist, too, that people who loved "a good cry" from their stories were overwhelmingly positive and optimistic about their own lives. What was the explanation?

Marlin thought a moment. Then he hazarded that it was *practice*. Practice?

Yes, the kinds of people who wanted their emotional heartstrings tugged—well, likelier than not, their lives were like still ponds or sheltered groves, without much turbulence to their days.

Yet they knew that loss and death would visit them one day, sure as anything. Thus, to be moved by stories was in a way rehearsal for how to act when the dreaded events did visit. When the time came, you'd know without hesitation to wail and beat your chest, or turn to drugs and alcohol. It might even be that the pain of loss, when it happened, would feel "natural," and this would help people better accept the pain—there, utilitarian after all.

So it's all prep work for our tear glands? I teased. Memento mori with pastel filters?

Nothing wrong with keeping the engine of grief running, he joked.

IF YOU'VE READ THIS FAR—AND IF YOU HAVEN'T, IF YOU DIDN'T EVEN open my email, I understand. I'm sorry I stood you up. Please forgive me. I got as far as putting on my shoes to leave the apartment. Than I thought: What if I happen to laugh unguarded at a joke? Or lick an ice cream cone with abandon? Someone, you for instance, might remark that I seem happy. But I'm not happy. These days that drag and stun and rot me from the inside out, I need to really live them all. I want to be able to say that I suffered as much as I could, in honor of something that I lost.

AFTER I LEFT KATIE, I SPRAWLED ON THE COUCH, HEAD LEADEN FROM the whiskey she'd bought me. The alcohol opened up a portal in my jumbled brain, and I examined the memory it called up, a moment from the night Marlin had accused me of cheating. He'd brought up a name, Li Shen. I remembered it because it was also the name of a Tang dynasty poet. Where had Marlin gotten the name from?

Just then, my mother called.

"Yes, I know my face is red and I look terrible," I said to my laptop screen.

"And so many pimples! How this happen?" my mother exclaimed.

"I'm stressed."

"Are you mabuk? Your face is *really* red!"

"Yes, I'm drunk."

"I don't understand you. If you're so unhappy in America, why don't you come home? Your job isn't even what you want to do. And you sound so different now. So atas and proper. How come you don't talk like us anymore?"

"Didn't you have something to tell me?" I asked. I couldn't afford to dissect my life choices with her right now.

"Oh, ya. Hmm." She pushed her face closer to the screen to peer at me. "I'll tell you next time. When you're not mabuk."

"Just tell me."

"I cannot tell you when you're like this."

"Fine," I huffed. "I'll do it for you."

"What?"

"Did you talk to Marlin about the banana tree spirit story?"

Her face fell. She cast her eyes down, and I looked at the roots of her dyed hair, waiting, wondering how I'd drifted away from her. That thought experiment about teleporting to Mars wasn't a hypothetical question after all, was it? Maybe anyone who left home to go far away stood the chance of being reassembled, and called it variously immigration or rebirth. The distance traveled was shorter than Mars, and the timeline of transformation longer, but it had happened to me all the same.

"He called me," my mother said. "I just wanted to help."

"When?"

"I can't remember exactly. April."

"What did he say?"

"He wanted to know more about your past life. At first I told him what I told you. You remember the story?"

"Yes." I swallowed some saliva. The whiskey made it hard to stay still; I felt like my brain was gently vibrating, and I wanted to move my whole body in rhythm to it, but I couldn't quite pin the beat down.

"Then he asked, was he in the story too? Did he know you in a past life?"

"And then?" I felt my jaw clenching.

"I asked him, why do you want to know? I was excited, you know, that he showed interest. *You* never pay any attention."

"That's not true."

"He said he wants to understand your marriage better. I thought: that's nice."

"So what did you tell him?"

"I said the two of you, your fates have entwined for many past lives now. It is meant to be. I told him he was your fiancé in that past life with the banana trees."

"Li Shen?"

"Yes, and I said, Edwina loves you so much in this life because she wronged you in the past, so she owes you this deep kind of love."

"What? You said that? How can you say something like that?" My hand had flown up to cover my eyes in horror.

"What's so bad about that? I said you love him very much now, isn't that good?"

I groaned, fighting an urge to get up and press my face into a wall. My head felt hotter than the rest of my body, my mouth was dry, and the wall, it seemed so cool and refreshing.

"You do love him, right?" my mother asked. From the consternation on her face, I concluded that this must have been exactly what she'd been wanting to tell me for the past week. She'd been planning to confess her conversation with Marlin, all packaged up as some twisted reaffirmation of our marital bond.

"This is a mess," I muttered. No way I would admit that my marriage was in danger to her, a woman who had remained faithful to her dead husband, who placidly faced down the long rest of her days alone. Who believed that Marlin and I were *fated* to be together!

"It's America that's making you so unhappy," she said. "Do you even like your job? You work so much, you probably don't have time to enjoy New York also. Then you might as well just move back home, right?"

I trotted out the knee-jerk, expected answers, about how in America there were more merit-based opportunities, less constitutionalized differences in how people across races were treated, less ostentatious corruption, and so on. What I didn't tell her: I already knew how to be a minority in America, having been one in my home country. All that was required of me was to learn my new names, like kook or dirty commie or terrorist, and to understand what I was expected to do, such as eat dogs and cats alive. Some of the names I'd already acquired in Malaysia even translated abroad like a universal plug—an engineer might appreciate the portability of an insult like "Sepet," which means "Slant-eyed," applicable to me in various countries around the globe. Although I will admit that I did not foresee the twist in America, which split the insult off into branches, as an undergraduate dining hall experience showed me. I was offered a choice. I could choose from a dial with three settings: Chinese, Japanese, Korean, each click of the dial corresponding to the position of index fingers stretching eyes into narrow strips. Slightly above the eyes, curving the slits upward—Chinese. Parallel—Japanese. Yanking downward into droopiness—Korean.

One other thing remained constant—the exhortation for me to *Go back!* Except the destination had changed. In Malaysia I was supposed to go back to China. In America I was supposed to return to Malaysia. Was this progress? If I moved to China, would they tell me to piss off to America, thus resulting in some sort of infinite loop? I wondered if it would be like the completion of a ritualistic summoning diagram I'd seen witches and demonologists draw in movies. What would emerge? Perhaps a space that existed between real places, where I could go and be left in peace. The most well-educated Americans said to me: It must be hard to live in diaspora for the first time as an adult; it's easier on children. They didn't get that I was born into diaspora, that I had merely moved from a place that wasn't mine to another place that also wasn't mine. To them, diaspora meant the arrival of the non-West into the West, that was all.

After nine years in America I'd finally gotten a reasonably whole picture of what I looked like in the eyes of the dominant culture, partly thanks to Katie. She was the one who shed light on a myriad of things, from "me love you long time" to why, when I carried a guitar on campus, three men stopped me to ask whether I was on my way to serenade Korean Jesus, then burst out laughing. Once, depressed, I turned to her: "I know I don't look Malaysian because that's not a thing here, but do I really look like all these other categories? Korean? Vietnamese?"

Katie rolled her eyes. "Edwina, please. Don't ask me things like that. I had those same questions all the way back in third grade, when I was being bullied, and I am *not* ready to relive that."

"So you're saying that as far as being American goes, I'm just a child."

"Yeah, you have a long way to go," she said, smiling. "Ten more years, maybe."

A decade more of coded insults, of learning to navigate my perceived place and exploring my cordoned-off swim lanes. But even if I were to return to Malaysia, it wasn't like I could slip back into my previous identity like it was a pair of comfortably worn shoes. I had changed, and so had the country. I'd have to discover anew just who I was, though a few traits of this ghost person could already be divined: a loser who couldn't cut it overseas; a banana who uncritically idolized the West, yellow only on the outside; a pretender who adopted a fake American accent. If I were an expat, then there wouldn't be a problem. My time away would have been for the perfectly justifiable mission of "finding" myself. But I am not an expat. I am an immigrant.

There was also the raw and shameful reason for staying away that I could never share with my mother. In Malaysia, I shop for clothes in size XL, whereas in America I am a medium. The "all clear" given by American doctors during annual health checkups translates to "not yet have kids already so fat" in Malaysia and "better don't eat so much" during mealtimes with my own relatives.

It is ridiculous, and I know it, which is why I can't confess it to anyone but you. "Fewer people body-shame me" is not a legitimate reason to emigrate.

And yet I feel it all over, on my shoulders and midsection and thighs—the weight of all those taunts and admonishments, whenever I think about moving back home. It would be a burden to be endured daily, just as living in America comes with an atmosphere of different poisons.

It is so hard to be proud of my own thoughts.

Day Seven (Tuesday)

I'm so relieved that you want to keep talking. I knew I could trust you to understand. I'm sorry again for not showing up, and I hope you didn't wait too long. And I'll try not to take up too much more of your time with my story.

THE BETA TEST WAS SCHEDULED FOR AFTER LUNCH. I SPENT THE MORN-ing thinking up ways to surface any issues I found. Although Lucas wouldn't be present, I could still show him the number of product enhancement tickets filed as a result of the test. Maybe that would impress him.

At five minutes to noon, Ben stood up, stretched, and asked: "Lunch? What are you guys getting?"

A few engineers said "Anything" or "Whatever." One of them predictably suggested "salad," and as usual someone else then roasted the salad champion as "lame." It was all part of a cycle. The engineers took turns being "currently" on a health kick. It was then the responsibility of the others to erode this sense of superiority, heckling the health kicker and tempting him with pizza and prime rib sandwiches until he no longer suggested salad for lunch. At that point, another engineer feeling the consequences of all those pizzas and prime ribs would take over the mantle of salad advocacy. Thus the wheel turned.

Today the salad champion was Josh. After he got laughed down ("boring," "weak sauce," "lame"), he smiled, shrugged, and lingered behind while the rest of them trooped toward the elevators.

"Ready for the next installment of my novel?" he asked, pausing by my desk.

I looked up, surprised. "Already?"

"I had time over the weekend. I think you're gonna love it."

I thought about what my weekend had been like. Bacon at brunch, a train upstate, the Dowsers Society, whiskey, lots of crying. I felt weary. My tailbone hurt.

"Why don't I read your startup memoir instead?" Anything was preferable to more of Radmonsius.

"Why, don't you want to know what happens next in the novel?"

"Yo, Josh! You coming?" Faces peeked out from the elevator, its doors held open by a hand.

"I guess they're waiting for you," I said.

"I'm starting to think you haven't been honest with me," he said, before walking away.

AINSTEIN AND I FACED EACH OTHER OFF. TO OUR RIGHT, BEN AND JOSH sat close to the wall, observing. I should have known Josh would be asked to take part in this. Lucas's approach to conflict resolution was to have the parties work together on projects. A common goal builds camaraderie, he said.

I decided I would try to score myself an easy win right off the bat, to demonstrate my abilities and shore up some confidence while Ben and Josh took notes.

"Hi, AInstein," I greeted the robot. Someone had added a company-branded sweater to the bare-bones torso supporting AInstein's head. On the sweater was our logo, a cartoon rendering of a Bender-like robot wearing a wig with flyaway white hair.

"Hello. Would you like to hear a joke?"

"Sure. What's your favorite joke?"

Some whirring, and then: "What was Einstein's rapper name?"

As expected, AInstein was keyword-matching on its own moniker to offer up that same broken joke I'd already heard.

"What?" I asked.

A hesitating murmur, a cough, a 2. AInstein mangling the punch line "MC^2."

I paused AInstein and waited a few moments. Then I turned to the two engineers, pretended to look concerned, and delivered what I'd rehearsed: "Seems like the text-to-voice generator isn't delivering the best results here. I think we should add a filter to detect non-dictionary words and explore using recorded voice clips for them instead."

Ben nodded, typing on his laptop.

"I can open a ticket after this," I offered.

"You should stick to giving user feedback," Josh said. "We'll come up with the solutions."

"It was just an idea."

"You don't know what the best solution is. Just tell us how you feel and we'll take it from there."

Ben was still nodding. To what, I no longer knew.

On a whim, I decided to feed AInstein the same keyword twice. I wanted to remind Josh that I wasn't useless, that I had, in fact, caught one of his bugs.

"AInstein, what's your favorite joke?"

The familiar whirring, and then: "What comes after USA?"

"Passes de-duplication requirement," I said loudly, not looking at the engineers.

"I'm sorry," AInstein said. "I didn't catch that."

"Nothing. AInstein, please repeat."

"What comes after USA?"

The rush of my jab at Josh receded, stranding me in a strange headspace. I found myself seriously considering AInstein's question. What *would* be next for me, if I didn't get a green card? My mother wanted me to go home. I, like anyone else, had been dropped onto certain tracks at birth. Class, sex, race, physical and mental limitations, nationality, native language—we don't get a choice. To feel in control, I did the opposite of whatever my mother urged on me, though wasn't traveling backward along the tracks just another way of following them?

The day I came across applications for scholarships in America, I was thunderstruck. For the first time, I imagined: What if I could change one of my fundamental characteristics, a major way in which I was sorted, pinned down, and judged?

I was thinking of becoming American. Or, more precisely, I was thinking of not being Malaysian anymore. Was this not relatable? Wasn't this precisely the point of Sleeping Beauty and Rapunzel, whose stories are about our struggles to overcome fates sealed at birth, or before we are even born?

"What comes after USA?" AInstein prompted, after its five-second time-out lapsed.

I cleared my throat, embarrassed. "What?"

"USB."

"Huh," I said, not at all in the right mood for such a silly punch line. I didn't dare look at Ben and Josh. The best thing I could do was forge ahead with the session, try to play off my absentmindedness as a deliberate test of how AInstein performed when there was no user follow-up.

"Time-out works as expected," I said, trying to sound as authoritative as I could. "Let's see. AInstein, tell me a random joke."

"What's the difference between a pickpocket and a Peeping Tom?"

"What?"

"A pickpocket snatches watches."

I waited, but AInstein was silent.

"I don't get it," I said. Immediately Josh burst into uncontrolled laughter, his eyes squeezed shut. I looked to Ben for help.

"It's . . . umm. Think about the last two words, and switch their, their order."

I stared at him blankly.

"She doesn't get it!" Josh hooted, one hand flat over his heart, like he was swearing allegiance to my failure.

"I assume it's off-color?" I asked, agitation rising.

Before Ben could respond, AInstein whirred again. "Why does the bride wear white?"

"Why?" I whipped back to the robot, grateful to move on.

"Because," AInstein said, LED mouth twinkling furiously, "the dishwasher should match the stove and the fridge."

I sat back, stunned. Who had vetted these jokes? *Had* anyone vetted them? Had a single nonmale person tested AInstein until today?

"This is not funny," I managed.

"She doesn't get this one either!" Josh renewed his laughter.

"I'm sorry you did not find that funny." AInstein. I couldn't take it anymore. I paused it.

"Hey, I think we have a problem," I said, trying to keep my voice as level as possible.

"Yeah, we do." Finally Josh's laughs had petered out to a couple of stray chuckles.

"AInstein has some pretty—sexist jokes, don't you think?"

Ben started to say something. Josh cut in. "That feedback is too broad. We can't do anything with that. You know you have to be specific when you give us your user impressions."

"You heard the jokes, right? You don't see how they're sexist?"

"You said it yourself: you don't get it. How can you say something is sexist if you don't even understand it?"

"I *did* understand. Ben, what do *you* think?"

Ben coughed uncomfortably. His face was flushed. The way he slouched, it was as if he wanted to pin himself against the wall and turn into an insect specimen. "I think we should maybe bring this to the larger group for discussion."

And that was it. The beta test was over. Ben led the way out the door. Josh stayed behind a few beats, long enough to say to me: "You're so innocent. It's refreshing."

THE MUSIC DREW ME, TOP 40 SONGS BLASTING FROM SPEAKERS SO loudly you could feel the bass lines through your shoes. I stood a block away from the street fair, attracted by the smell of charred meat. I imagined flaking off blackened bits. It was late afternoon, and I was drooling against my will.

I walked the gauntlet of white tents and curls of smoke. After the beta test I'd left the office and wandered aimlessly; I no longer knew where in Manhattan I was. Up ahead hulked an inflatable bouncy castle. I headed for it, passing stalls selling grilled corn, Thai iced tea, kebabs, jerk chicken. The tents closed in on me. The deeper I tunneled into the fair, the more I wanted the feel of flesh surrendering to my incisors. "Elk jerky," I read on a sign, and saliva overwhelmed my mouth.

Less than a week since I started eating meat, and already I was so changed. Why should it be any different for Marlin? He could have stopped loving me by now, every passing day hardening an aberration into reality.

The high screams of children rang out when I got close to the castle. Suddenly thirsty, I made for a stall nearby lined with squat containers of honey-colored tea. Each container bore a label crammed with spidery handwriting. I ran my eyes across the dense descriptions. They extolled benefits like "immunity boosting" and provided history lessons about the early use of herbs. My attention snagged on *mugwort*, a word unknown to me. I skimmed the wall of text beneath the tea's name, groping along like someone following a rope in a snowstorm until I reached the very last word: *sedative*.

"Excuse me," I turned to the stall owner idling nearby and staring off into space. "This says the tea is a sedative?"

"Hmm," the woman said. She put on the glasses strung around her neck and leaned in to peer at the label. "Yes," she confirmed, straightening up at last.

"What does that mean? Will I literally feel numb after drinking it?"

"It's very mild. No side effects."

"Are you sure?" I stared at the liquid, its color a vaguely shiny orange that people would probably call "amber."

"Hmm." Long pause. "Yeah, as long as you don't drink more than a cup at once."

I paid for my sixteen-ounce cup of mild sedative with no side effects and walked away. As I passed the final stall at the edge of the market (featuring obviously home-baked muffins), I realized I didn't know whether the woman's "a cup at once" referred to the cup I was holding, or whether she meant a conventional cup of eight ounces, in which case my cup contained twice as much sedative as I should drink. I didn't turn back for clarification. I just continued along the sidewalk, sipping delicately, stopping after each intake to gauge my nervous system.

At first I felt no different. Then, slowly, a kind of dullness that felt chilled and warm at the same time spread through my arms. I took a bigger gulp, encouraged. I wanted the feeling to expand until I was immersed in it.

At the next stoplight there were no cars, but I spotted two cops in uniform at the opposite shore, so I didn't jaywalk. Couldn't risk it, even if a green card now seemed completely out of reach. The cops were staring at me, I was sure of it. Was it so obvious that I was an immigrant with expiring paperwork? Were we already in the future, where law enforcement officers wore special contact lenses that showed civilians' biodata above their heads like haloes?

I took a step backward, farther away from the curb, making it clear that I had no intention of jaywalking. The cops continued training their eyes on me. I began to wonder whether the mugwort tea had other potent properties besides being a sedative. Was it also a psychedelic? Did it promote paranoia? I glanced behind me. No, there was definitely no one else waiting for the light. It had to be me they were glaring at.

I considered turning around or crossing the street the other way, to my right, where the walk sign was blinking. That would probably look guilty, though. I stayed still, pretending to be calm and swigging more of the tea hopefully.

When my light flashed white for walk, I waited to see if the cops would cross. They simply continued looking. One of them even rotated his body so that he was squarely facing me. I tried to reassure myself: Cops idled on street corners all the time, didn't they? Sometimes leaning against a wall, sometimes not. No big deal.

When the traffic light began its countdown from twenty, I finally made myself cross. It was hard to disobey the authority of flashing numbers.

"Ma'am," one of the cops said as soon as I arrived at the opposite sidewalk. I had been avoiding eye contact, so I didn't know which one had first spoken, but when I faced the cops I was certain it had been the bald one. He had a face that matched the voice, with features that somehow looked out of control—bulbous nose, protruding eyes, downy stubble.

"Ma'am, did you know that public drinking is illegal?"

"What?" I didn't understand.

"No. Open. Containers. Of alcohol. Allowed," the bald cop's partner chipped in, speaking slowly and loudly. This one had dark brown hair coming out of his nostrils and ears.

"Oh!" I laughed, maybe like a drunk person would.

"Ma'am, your ID, please?"

"No, wait, this is *tea*. It's not alcohol. I didn't realize how much it looked like beer, but really, it's tea. Try it!" I pushed the cup toward them. Some tea sloshed over the rim, and the cops took a step back, first the partner, then the bald one, reacting to his partner's reaction.

"Or just smell it?" I pleaded. I no longer felt any effects of sedation.

"Ma'am, show us your ID."

I wished they would stop starting every sentence with "Ma'am." I took off my backpack (here was the company logo again, the robot with wild genius hair) and unzipped a compartment as slowly as I could. I kept my head down, afraid to see what was happening above me in the space occupied by the taller cops. As I slid an unsteady hand into the compartment, I hoped there was no taser cocked at my crown.

Finally the wallet was out, and I extracted my New York State ID. The partner took the card, face impassive. I held the cup a little away from my body, hoping one of them, maybe the bald cop, would still want to sniff or inspect the tea further. Look, no skim of bubbles! No foam! I wanted to point and cry out.

"Says here it's expired," the partner announced.

It felt as if my skin suddenly shrank and drew tighter around my frame. My organs pushed against my insides. I had scrutinized my ID so many times, marveling at the three women and lone eagle depicted in the background. The bird and two of the women were cartoonishly drawn, giving the plastic card a childish air. Except the two women also had a stylized ribbon of my name trampled underfoot, and beneath all that was printed on a banner: EXCELSIOR. I remembered looking this word up. And then there was the expiration date on the card, which was a good four years away.

As I tried to explain this, the bald cop cut me off.

"Let me see," he said, and reached over to pluck my card from his partner.

"I see 2022—ah, nope, wait, I see what you mean." Then, turning to me: "Ma'am, says here you're a temp visitor, and the expiration date is two years ago. 2016."

"Yes—" I forced myself to slow down and add a reluctant "You're right. But the expiration date for the ID itself is 2022."

"Well, I'm talking about the other date," the partner said. "The visitor date. What kind of identification do you have to show me you are visiting legally?"

"I don't have it on me," I said, so faintly that they asked me to repeat myself. I was keeping my visa safe at home inside my Important Documents folder, I wanted to add, but found I couldn't talk.

"That's a no-no," the partner said.

"Ma'am, you should carry identification with you at all times."

"I know, I'm so sorry! I live nearby. I can go get them for you now?"

The two men stared blankly. They did not turn to exchange looks, but somehow I got the sense they were communicating, deliberating as a pair even as their gazes remained on me and my stupid tea.

"That's a Chinese name, isn't it?" the partner finally said, eyeing my ID.

"Yes, but I'm not from China."

"Doesn't matter. You're still Chinese, aren't you?"

"Yes?" I took a gamble. I didn't know what the correct answer was.

"So what's this, then? Some kind of magic kung fu tea?"

The partner remained straight-faced even as the bald cop broke into a guffawing laugh. I grinned uncertainly. The cup slid an inch; my palms had started sweating. I switched hands so I wouldn't drop the tea and splatter it all over their shoes. As if on cue, the cops hitched up their trousers and started walking away.

"Carry all your IDs with you next time," one of them said. "You be good now!"

BEFORE

June 2018

There was this fight we had, a month before the steam pipe explosion. But all couples disagree from time to time. We were no different.

We'd waited thirty-five minutes to get a table at this East Village Chinese restaurant. We were there because we'd read, for a while now, gushing internet write-ups minting the area "Chinatown North." I found it interesting that the American perception of Chinese food had undergone such a shift. It used to be associated with pathetic loneliness—the go-to for postbreakup binges or Thanksgiving for one. Now it was splashed across covers of foodie magazines, some of which had been laminated and displayed on the restaurant's glass exterior. Reading a write-up with overly zoomed-in photos, I felt a strange grudge. I remembered an episode in college, when I mentioned to a dorm mate from Beijing that my grandmother had emigrated from the southern Chinese island of

Hainan. "I thought so!" my roommate had exclaimed perkily. "I once visited the south, and everywhere I turned there were people who looked just like you!"

I thought about it for much longer than I should have, this blurry place packed to the brim with people just like me.

When Marlin and I were finally seated, I remarked upon the diners around us.

"You hear these accents? Everyone sounds like they're from mainland China."

"Food must be good, then," Marlin said agreeably.

I was buoyant that day, happy that I'd persuaded Marlin to leave the house. In the restaurant, I made a note to myself: I should think about everything I'd said or done that day, figure out what it was that'd made him agree to date night. Don't forget, I reminded myself.

"I wonder if eating here makes them homesick, or makes them feel *less* homesick," I said, surveying the faces at the table next to ours. Under the restaurant's lights, one woman's pink puffed cheeks shone brighter than her eyes as she blew on her stew. The man next to her, slack-mouthed, trawled his porcelain soup spoon along the bottom of his bowl repeatedly, trying to fish out whatever remnants were left, wanting to prolong his meal. "I guess I don't know what homesickness looks like," I said as I turned back to Marlin. I wasn't prepared for the look on his face. His forehead looked like it had expanded, pushing down his brows and eyes. His nostrils flared as if something was trying to crawl out from the back of his throat.

"Are you okay?" I was unnerved, to say the least.

"This is what it looks like."

"What?"

"I'm homesick. Aren't you?"

"But we were just there."

"That was for my dad's funeral. Doesn't count."

His retort made me feel like an unreasonable person. I reached for his hand, tried to rub circles into his palm. Out of the corner of my eye, I saw a person walking toward us, and I winced, hoping it wasn't the waiter come to take our order. How like a clichéd TV scene, I thought. I must have made a wry face, or surfaced a slight smirk, before the person passed us on his way to the bathroom. How could I know what my face looked like?

"You think this is funny?" Marlin snatched his hand away, in the process sweeping my menu off the table with a flourish.

"What? No!" When I should have met his eyes and explained, I instead bent over to retrieve that stupid menu from the floor, some drummed-in sense of decorum making me prioritize a list of all the things we wouldn't eat over my own husband's feelings. By the time I straightened up again, I could see the evening was lost.

"What's your plan?" Marlin asked in a challenging tone. "Do you even have one? What if your mom gets sick tomorrow?"

I felt ill, the kind of nausea that makes you torn between the relief of retching and the dignity of holding it down, repressing, conquering what threatens to rise out of control from deep within you.

"My mother is still young. She's not even sixty," I said, lowering my voice and hoping he would follow suit.

"So was my dad! He was young too. Your mom, my mom, we need to be there for them."

"I'm not saying we abandon them. It's just, we're so close to getting our green cards. If we leave now, we'll never know whether we can get them. But if we stay just another year, then at least we'll know for sure, right? We might not even get the cards—and if that's the case, the decision will be made for us."

"Is one little card more important to you than your own mother?"

"I'm not saying I don't want to do it," I said, uncertain at that point whether I was being truthful, mostly just eager to stabilize his mood. I could see that the rash, dramatic idea of exchanging our lives in New York for a new start in Malaysia was both exciting and agitating him. "I'm saying let's think it through. What's the rush?"

"Every day we're sucked deeper in."

"Deeper into what? New York isn't some, some quicksand of despair or anything!"

"Maybe it is, and you just can't see it."

"This isn't like you, Marlin. You were the one who encouraged me to get a job in tech because it'd be easier to get a green card that way, remember?"

"'*This isn't like you*,'" Marlin mimicked in a mean, singsongy lilt. "So, what? I'm a robot? I can only follow my programming?"

"I didn't say that. We're so close to having options. Why don't we wait a year and see what happens?"

"I don't want to be a passive observer of my own life. Plus, don't you remember how they treated me at JFK? Like a suspect, that's what. A potential source of evil or something. Maybe that doesn't mean anything to you because *you* weren't the target."

"Let's talk about this at home," I said, one eye tracking the waitress coming for us. I could tell from her expression that we had become *that* couple, the one so tactless they let their private unhappiness ruin everyone's nights out. I avoided Marlin's insistent gaze and turned the pages of the menu, back and forth. Sour cabbage with pork. Grilled pollock. Sea cucumber.

Did you know? A river can be diverted such that it never reaches its intended end. Some rivers are forced underground, where, instead of nourishing the soil as they formerly did, they begin to erode the earth's foundation. When you look at a skein of water, can you tell if it's traveling where it's meant to go?

Day Seven (Tuesday)

Back at the apartment, I slid my Important Documents folder out from a desk drawer, my hands still shaking from the encounter with police. I pinched my passport gingerly and flipped it open to the page with my visa affixed. Near the bottom, close to one corner of my unsmiling face, was the name AInstein Inc. My benefactor, for all intents and purposes.

I examined the Expiration Date again. It read datemonthyear all squeezed together without spaces separating them. The date sat superimposed over a washed-out pastel drawing of the US capitol building, and I blinked and blinked at it.

If I didn't ask Lucas for a green card soon, it would be too late to beat the Expiration Date. But if I did ask now, he'd say no, what with how things were going at work. Even if Lucas miraculously said yes, I'd have to convince Marlin to come back, so he could fill out forms for a spouse visa attached to my green card. It seemed there were many ways to fail, but only one unlikely path to success.

I ordered delivery from an Italian restaurant, picking the most unfamiliar name I could find. When the osso buco arrived, I was intimidated at first by the shot-glass-shaped bone jutting out of the meat. But the silkiness of the veal made my eyes close by themselves, shutting out sight so that my brain could focus more on the tongue's pleasures. I'd never had anything of this texture before. I prodded at the marrow teeming out of the shot-glass bone, intrigued. When I took the bone whole into my pursed mouth, I thought of my mother, who sucked snot out of my nostrils when I was a baby. I'd caught the flu and couldn't blow my own nose, she said. I was suffocating.

I drew marrow like breaths down my throat.

Later that night, my phone rang with a call from her. I dwelled on the mechanics of it. If I were to answer, a temporary connection would be forged between us via cables at the bottom of oceans, and every time the paths that these signals took might be distinct—different cables involved, different data centers in different areas of the earth. So many ways to go from point A to point B. Every connection a new one. When I picked up, I had to decide all over again whether I knew this person, whether I loved her, whether my resentment outweighed my gratitude. She'd sucked my snot, yes, and with one hand she'd fed me, while the other pinched my waist as she told me no one would want to marry me if I didn't lose weight. She'd carried on alone for my sake after my father died, asking for her old clerk job back at the driving school. All her creativity, all her wit, channeled into raising me and weaving those past life stories of hers. It struck me then, forcefully, that I had never heard her tell a past life story about herself. I wondered about this until my phone stopped ringing, my mother having given up, halfway across the world and twelve hours in the future.

Day Eight (Wednesday)

"Okay." Ben cleared his throat. "I think we have quorum. Let's get started and discuss the latest beta test."

We were in the Bike Shed, a literal bike shed that had been given its capitalized name because it was also supposed to be an inside joke. To tech people, *bikeshedding* is a verb. To bikeshed is to belabor one's point with trivial, borderline inconsequential things, such as whether void functions must always return nothing.

The meeting had started reasonably enough, with Ben declaring that AInstein had failed the beta test, given that the acceptance criteria was laughter at 25 percent of delivered jokes. In the case of my session, "the user" had not laughed at any jokes, and had moreover declared the content "disagreeable." It was a solid, if understated, start. Then several engineers started speaking at once, and now, as far as I could follow, they were debating whether AInstein's failure was in fact a true failure.

"It's clear-cut, isn't it? There's acceptance criteria, and we did not meet that criteria," Ben said.

"It's not so black-and-white. What if the tester just has no sense of humor?" Josh said. "I was there, and I thought at least a couple of the jokes were funny."

"We also have to think about the size of any improvement efforts," Darren said. He was the data scientist, responsible for trawling the web for free jokes. "What size are we talking about here? L? XL? XXL? The launch is two months away, just as a reminder."

Handlebars dug into my spine. Spittle flew overhead. I looked at my shoes. No matter how I tried to shrink into myself, something or someone was always pressing against me. Hard elbows, soft thighs, mud-crusted wheels, unyielding plastic seats, they were all around me, crowding in.

"We have data from other beta test users, right? How do those look?"

"Every single one of those passed."

"Like I said, in this case maybe it's an issue with the user. No offense." The exchanges had become rapid-fire; I couldn't keep track of who was speaking.

"Excuse me," I said. I tried not to pant, but it was getting hard to breathe. "I'm the first woman to beta-test AInstein, right? Isn't that a relevant factor?"

"Are you saying female sense of humor is different from male sense of humor?"

"Hey, I didn't want to be the one to say it because it's not PC or whatever. But see, she herself is admitting there's a difference between female brains and male brains."

"How does that help us here?"

"That's not what I mean," I said.

"You know what? Actually, beta users shouldn't be part of the postmortem. We have what we need in terms of feedback from the user, and now it's up to us, not the user, to decipher the feedback and map it to action items." Darren looked pointedly at me.

"Can I just explain what I mean?"

Faces peered at me, impassive. No one said yes, but no one objected either. Now I was thankful that we were all crammed in so close together, because my knees were shaking, and I didn't want them to see.

"I'm saying some of the jokes in our database might be sexist, racist, or offensive in other ways to subsets of users. I think we should have a human audit of all the jokes and flag those that might be problematic. We don't want to alienate paying customers."

"Human audit? That's so inefficient. The whole point of our tech is that there's a smarter way to do things."

"Actually, flagging the jokes might not be a bad idea. So if something is flagged as offensive to women, we'll limit that joke to cases when AInstein detects the user as male."

"Did you not hear me? I'm saying having a human flag things at all defeats the whole purpose of our tech!"

"But we already do it for non-adult—" I tried to speak again, but they were all caught up in an opinionated frenzy now. I looked around for Ben. He was half hidden behind the tall DBA whose name I couldn't remember, gesturing with both hands. Defeated, I pushed past three engineers and two bikes to exit the void function that was our meeting. No one stopped me. I was the cause of the problem, not part of the solution.

AS SOON AS I GOT HOME, I BEGAN STRIPPING. SHOES OFF BY THE FRONT door. One sock in the foyer, one three paces ahead in the kitchen.

Jeans in a tangle by the sink, where I stopped for a glass of water. T-shirt on the counter. Bra in the doorway of the bathroom.

I used to spend a lot of time imagining my mother naked. I know that is an odd confession, maybe even off-putting. Or perhaps it's a gold mine in the context of therapy. Make of it what you will. Back in my youth, dwelling on her nudity seemed natural, given what I saw as my mother's obsession with my body. She could tell when I had gained or lost the slightest bit of weight, and would always comment accordingly. For a long time I thought it was her right, since she had made every scrap and droplet of me, gestated during the height of her life. That was how she described it to me: she had never been happier than when she carried me around in her womb.

On days that she remarked upon my fatness, I would take off my clothes in front of the full-length mirror she had installed in my room. I'd brush my palms over my stomach the way I had seen pregnant women do, the sharp chill of my hands making them seem alien. And I'd imagine my mother nude, her slender frame eloquent as an ink brush, describing to the world her uncompromised goodness. Then I'd come back to my corrupt flesh and try to measure the distance between her body and mine. I was sure, as a teenager, that she was waiting for me. She would wait as long as it took for me to become like her.

I sat on the lip of my bathtub, taking off my underwear. The only thing I still had on was the necklace my mother gave me when she sent me off at the airport for the first time.

"This will protect you in America," she'd said, reaching around to fasten the clasp of the necklace. Her face was close enough to kiss.

A sob escaped me in the apartment, pathetic and unbearable.

I turned the shower dials to drown it out, savagely twisting the hot water knob. The medicine cabinet's double mirrors slowly filmed over like dead fish eyes. My mother had once promised me that if I ate fish eyes, I would be able to whistle. I did, and I couldn't. My butt felt cold against the bathtub. I grabbed fistfuls of fat from my midsection and tugged on them, kneading, then yanking. I imagined a civil surgeon examining this very body for my green card examination. What would he find that I didn't already know? I felt sure there was something.

With the mirrors blinded and unable to judge me, I could be honest: I missed my mother. I could hear her now, saying things I didn't want to hear, stressing words like *diet* and *positive thinking*. How had I grown up so different from her, our beliefs and outlook on life diametrical opposites? She had raised me almost single-handed, her influence on me total. I should have inherited her prejudices.

For our last meal before I left for America, we went to her favorite restaurant, a place that made home-style Teochew dishes that were difficult to find elsewhere. She was such a regular that the owner recognized her on sight. A dish was set in front of us practically as soon as we sat down.

"What's this?" I eyed it, suspicious. The food resembled cut-up sausage, though the shape and size of the slices were off. The cross-sections were more parallelograms than the usual round or oval, and their edges were golden crisp, like they'd been fried. The texture of the filling, too, was unusually uniform, its color too pale to be meat. Studded throughout were orbs and halves of peanuts.

"Don't worry, I'm not tricking you this time," my mother said. "This is really vegetarian. It's called kwong qiang. You know what that means?"

When she identified the two characters that made up "kwong qiang," I frowned. "Flushed intestines? Like an enema? Why would they name a vegetarian dish something so . . . gross?"

My mother laughed. "It's only gross if you think of it that way, isn't it? It's like this: how you choose to see the world is the most important thing."

There she went again, always turning every conversation into a teaching moment. She talked like there was forever a disciple near at hand, ready to jot down every pearl of wisdom that emerged from her mouth.

The owner returned, all smiles, bearing even more dishes.

"Thanks, thanks," my mother said, then gestured at me. "This is my daughter."

"Your daughter?" The owner's eyes bugged out. "Cannot be!"

"Why, we don't look alike?" my mother needlessly asked, already knowing the answer.

"Oh, but you're so skinny, and she's so fat! I thought she must be your coworker."

My mother tittered with pleasure, flattered.

Perched on the bathtub ledge, I finally understood why I'd turned out so unlike her. My fatness had punted me off course, marking me as "other." The shape of me transgressed, the width and bulge of me failing to conform. So it was only natural that I shaped my mind to match that outsider status.

The water in the bathtub lapped at my butt. I turned the faucet off and watched as the water jiggled, weakly at first, as if nothing had changed. Then, gradually, sleepily, it started swirling in the direction of the drain. It made a greedy, sucking sound, hoarse and insistent. I swiveled my legs around and lowered myself into the tub. The water was still warm enough to surprise my skin. Submerged from chest down, I shivered as a chill spread across my shoulders and neck. I felt a sudden oozing sensation, originating from deep under the ridge of flesh that *Cosmo* magazine called my pooch. The oozing traveled downward, applying pressure against my urethra. I looked down to see a period clot slither out of me into the cooling water.

I picked the blood clot up by reflex, not wanting my bath to be tainted. Maybe I even thought I was saving a piece of myself. Balancing the menstrual clot on my palm, I smoothed it open where it had started to curl over. I marveled at how much of an *entity* it seemed, its edges solid, not bleeding away, bright as any fruit. I took a neat bite out of it.

It was halfway between gum and Jell-O, the kind of consistency that fooled you into thinking it was giving in, when really it made you work your jaw much harder than you'd bargained for. There wasn't much flavor beyond a slight saltiness. I thought about all the meat, red, white, and in between, that I had put into my body over the past week. I chewed the clot, relishing it for what it was: a texture conjuring up no associations beyond itself. An experience devoid of memories, good or bad. New. Clean. Unrooted. A blank slate.

Day Nine (Thursday)

I was dreaming about Marlin, I think, when my phone rang.

"Marlin left," the voice said. I took the phone off my ear and squinted at the screen. It was Eamon calling, at not even 8:00 a.m.

"Hello? Did you hear me? Marlin left," he repeated.

"Well, I *know*," I said, indignant that he was calling just to taunt me.

"No, I mean he left my place. He moved out."

"What? When? Where did he go?" I sat up and haphazardly shoved bedsheets off me.

Eamon sighed heavily into the phone, a whooshing in my ears.

"That's the thing, I don't know. I think he left in the middle of the night. I woke up, and his suitcase was gone."

"Did he leave a note? Anything?"

"I haven't found one."

"Did he . . . did he receive a letter from me? Is that why he left?" It'd been three days. The letter must have arrived by then.

"I don't know." A long pause. "I'm sorry, Edwina."

"For what?"

"Maybe we should talk in person. Can you meet me near my office?"

"Where's that again?"

"I'll text you."

I hung up and emailed in sick to work. Immediately after, I sneezed almost a dozen times in a row, as if my body were corroborating the lie. My head began to pulse, an epicenter of pain growing at my left temple. When I looked down at my hands, I saw nicks on my knuckles. I had no idea how I'd gotten them.

The commute uptown was a haze. I had no memory of getting on or off trains. Suddenly I was struck by the smell of street kebab and I looked up, astonished, at a window ledge crusted unevenly with pigeon shit. I resisted the urge to reach out and touch it, to ask with my fingers: Is this really where I am?

In my head I had been imagining Marlin opening an envelope, his fingers drawing out my letter. His eyes taking in my handwriting, neurons lighting up his brain like fireworks.

A businessman shoulder-checked me on the sidewalk. Someone swore. I looked around, dazed. I was in Manhattan, with its sour garbage stench and weary, irritated energy lapping at glassy storefronts, revolving doors doing their best to filter all of it down into clean luxury. Marlin was here, too, somewhere. At least I hoped so.

"WE SHOULD CALL THE POLICE," EAMON SAID. HE'D GOTTEN TO THE NON-descript café near his office before me. I sat down across from him at a wobbly table on the sidewalk. I watched as he dunked a tea bag repeatedly into a white paper cup. "Do you want to get something?" He'd noticed me looking.

"No, I'm okay. So you have no idea why he left?"

"I don't know for sure," he said. His gaze shifted from his tea to the ground.

My headache had grown into a dome that squeezed the top of my head. I pinched the skin and flesh between my thumb and index finger, alternating hands. It helped a little.

"It's okay," I said. "I can take it. It was my letter, wasn't it?"

"What did you write?"

It was my turn to look at the ground, at the crooked curl of a cigarette half smoked.

"The wrong thing, apparently. Or he wouldn't have left." I wondered what the right thing was, if it existed.

"No, no," Eamon said. He pulled at his shirt collar. "Even if it was because of your letter, I was the one who told you to write it. It's my fault."

"So he did read my letter."

Eamon ignored me, plowing on ahead. "I wrote a long letter to my fiancée after we broke up. I didn't notice at the time, but afterward I realized I felt a lot better after writing it. It helped me move on." He looked at me, gauging my reaction. "I was hoping it would help you too."

"Did she respond to your letter?"

"No." He shook his head. "For her, we were done. She just wanted to start a new chapter of her life. And that's exactly why I don't think Marlin left because of your letter."

"Why did he leave, then?" I challenged. "You really think the timing of the letter is just a coincidence?"

Eamon sighed, a big, dramatic breath. I watched ripples float across the surface of his tea. "To be honest, Marlin and I . . . argued."

"About what?"

"His spirit guides. He said they knew what had really happened between Emily and me. He told me they wanted to help me find love."

I was stunned by how matter-of-fact Eamon sounded when he talked about Marlin's spirits. Was it really just me who had trouble accepting this new side of Marlin?

"You believed him? About the spirits?" I asked.

"You know me, I have my own beliefs." He touched the first button of his dress shirt. There was a cross made of hammered silver underneath, I knew. "I never push mine on him. I just wish he'd done the same for me."

"You fought because he wanted you to believe in his spirits?"

"'Fought' is too strong. He said I would find love soon, according to the spirit guides. I told him I'm not interested in dating. I'm fine how I am. But he kept giving me these random predictions. Like, he was telling me I should pay attention to people I meet in the next two months, because one of them will fall in love with me."

"Did you tell him you don't believe him?"

"No, I wouldn't do that." He gave me an odd look. "He's entitled to his beliefs. Normally I would humor him, but I felt like this was a low blow, right. I was really down for a while after Emily. He knew that. I told him about it." He frowned, a faraway look on his face. "Anyway, I told him to stop. I said I wasn't interested."

"Did he stop?"

"He did, but he seemed upset."

"Then he left?" Muddled feelings rose to the surface. On one hand, it pained me that Marlin was not in a better headspace. On the other, Eamon couldn't make Marlin stay either. I felt vindicated.

"Yeah. Today I woke up, and he was gone. I looked in his room, and a lot of his clothes are gone too. I tried calling him." He shook his head.

"Last time he left, I made a list of places he could be at. We could split it between us and look for him."

"We're just two people." He looked doubtful. "I still think we should call the police."

"No! First thing they'll do is check with his office. That will just get him in trouble. He might lose his job or get deported. Do you know that we have to file a form with the government every time we move? We, as in immigrants?"

His face told me he didn't know.

"See? We're supposed to have a known address at all times. If we get him in trouble with the authorities, who knows what will happen to him?"

"So we're just going to let him wander around out there on his own?"

I wanted to tell him that I wished I could be bombastic. I wished I could take out billboards declaring my love for Marlin, or obscure subway ads with my own pleas, a thousand repeating reminders: *Don't forget*. I'd storm his office and make a scene, demanding that he speak to me. I'd personally fly a plane trailing cloud puffs that spelled out our names.

And if I failed to win him back, I wouldn't have to hold in my desperate sadness the way I was doing now. If I didn't need to be perfectly law-abiding, I could flail in some illegal warehouse speakeasy, washing down Ecstasy with Four Loko; I could climb water towers somewhere in Dumbo, dive into the Gowanus, smoke weed on a stranger's fire escape, drink on the streets, right out in the open, until I puked, bending and convulsing, into one of those

New York City green wire mesh trash cans that were such a perfect height for me. I could even punch Eamon in the nose.

"You don't understand what it's like." I glared at him.

To my surprise, he rubbed his eyes and said: "Maybe." We sat in silence for a while. I could feel both of us softening, bound together by our respective encounters with the puzzle that was Marlin.

"I didn't cheat on him," I said eventually, into my lap.

There was a long silence. When I gathered up the courage to look at Eamon's face, it was a picture of unease. I wasn't expecting that.

"I know," he said, then cleared his throat. "I'm sorry for what I said."

"What do you mean, you know?"

"I thought it would make him feel better to talk about it." He shifted awkwardly in his seat. "Since I've—I've been through something similar. I could relate."

"And?" I leaned forward.

"At first I thought it was too painful for him to share any details. Finally I realized he didn't *have* any details. After I asked a few times, he said he had no proof *yet* that you were, umm, cheating." He glanced off to the side, at the stalled lanes of cars idling before a red light.

I did the guesswork. "That was what you argued about?"

He flapped his right hand weakly. Inches to the left, inches to the right. "I thought what I said was pretty mild. But maybe he didn't feel the same."

"Do you think he came around in the end? About me not cheating?"

My face burned while he considered. I regretted asking, but now that the question was out, I needed an answer. At last, Eamon said: "I think so."

We looked at each other. For a moment I was confused. Who was comforting whom?

"You don't think he'll hurt himself, do you?" I asked.

Eamon considered this. "No," he said. "A few days ago he was telling me that he was excited about something. A big change coming his way."

"According to his spirit guides," I said wearily.

Eamon nodded. "He said everything would be much clearer. He'd understand what happened to his dad."

"His dad? He died of a heart attack."

"You know what I think? I think this is all part of Marlin's grieving process. He was super close to his dad. They messaged a lot. I think they sent each other a picture a day, kinda like a diary thing."

"Really?" This was news to me. Every day? "How come he never told me?"

Eamon grimaced at his tea, then drained it.

"I think he didn't want to rub it in. He told me he was always worried about reminding you of your dad dying young. He said it was a sore spot for you. It made your relationship with your mom difficult."

"When did he say this?"

"Oh, I can't remember. Years ago."

I sank into my own memories of years-ago Marlin, back when I thought we knew each other and ourselves. I looked up only when Eamon said he had to go. He was already late for work.

"Let's talk again tonight?"

"Okay."

AFTERWARD I WANDERED THE STREETS AIMLESSLY, LOOKING AROUND now and then to see if a miracle would happen and conjure Marlin before me. A little past noon I dialed Meg's number. I wanted to ask if Marlin was in the Cachi I/O office, but she didn't pick up. I kept on drifting until I realized I was dangerously close to my own office. I was supposed to be home, sick. I couldn't be seen. Just before I ducked into a subway station, I thought I saw Phil from the corner of my eye, but I didn't dare turn to confirm. I quick-stepped through the turnstiles and walked to the end of the platform, my eyes firmly on the darkness of the tunnel ahead.

My phone buzzed when I surfaced back aboveground. It was a text message from Meg.

"Hi, I'm on vacation in Hawaii. Need something?"

I put the phone away, a sense of loneliness building. Eamon had shown up at the café in a dress shirt, all business and prepared for work, his routines undisrupted. Katie was at work too. Meg was off sunning under big umbrellas while sipping drinks that came with tiny umbrellas. Everyone's lives hummed forward.

Back home, I went online looking for answers, or at least sympathy. I typed "what to do when spouse walks out," then discovered that I was afraid to press enter. It felt like escalation to connect my so-far private problems to the chaos of the World Wide Web.

After a few moments, I took a breath and hit the return key. I saw at a glance that the search results were mostly pertinent to Americans. I knew the results were customized based on my IP, but I couldn't help wonder whether Americans did in fact have more marriage trouble, as my mother surmised. Perhaps they simply turned to the internet more for answers?

I clicked on a few of the top results. They all leapt straight past soul-searching and into legalities. Divorcedmommies.com said to hire the best lawyer I could afford and "prepare for the worst." Wevorces.com had a tagline plastered at the top of every page: "Divorce: changing how we do things for the better." A blog post by a law firm contained this advice: "You must determine whether you failed in fulfilling your obligations as a husband or wife and make a list for consultation," it counseled, so that the opposing lawyers wouldn't catch you unawares.

None of these results were what I wanted, but I was unsure how to further tailor my search query. What to do with my heart when spouse walks out? What to do with my hands? My thoughts? My tears?

I tried a different search term: "husband left me," I typed. The tone of the results changed, now that there was a gendered word in the query. Half of the pages told me I should move on, anonymous internet voices echoing what Katie and Eamon had both urged me to do. The other half gave me extremely specific advice about how to win my man back. Eventually the two sides converged, both the move-on and get-him-back camps issuing the same commands on what to do with my mouth and body. Exercise to be attractive again! Don't let yourself go anymore! Diet to a revenge body! Here's how many grapefruit slices to eat for breakfast. Here's how many times to cat-cow on the mat. Here's where to get vaginoplasty.

Reading these posts, I felt superiority and abjection blending into a slurry. Surely I was better than these people with their loud, false bravado. Yet wasn't I on the internet precisely because I wanted someone to give me a to-do list? I objected to the content of the lists, found them laughable, but still—I wanted my hand held, didn't I?

I decided the problem was that none of the results mentioned meddling by spirits. But when I typed in "spirits told my spouse to leave me," there was a tidal wave of marriages troubled by alcoholism. And when I tried swapping out "spirits" for "ghosts," the results were about how people had been ghosted by their partners, which, true, fit the bill in my case, but the underlying circumstances were vastly different. I felt cheated of something. Wasn't everything supposed to be on the internet now? Why couldn't I find anyone who had been through my exact situation?

I jumped ahead on the pages of search results, scrolling all the way down and clicking 9, 10, 13, 17, until a particular result caught my eye. "I feel like I don't know him anymore," the title read.

> hi, I'm new here. Husband left and I'm devestated. How could he? We had a beautiful wedding and he wrote his own vows. Now it's like all that never happened. He said there's no one else, he just doesn't love me anymore. Should I wait for him to change his mind?

The commentators piled on, other people at various stages of "moving on." Have some self-respect! Don't be a doormat! Stand up for yourself! Don't let him treat you this way! Never beg! You can do better! Plenty of fish in the sea! If you can't love yourself, how can you get someone else to love you? I wasted the best years of my life waiting, don't repeat my mistake!

The OP lashed back, wounded. I thought this was a forum for support. You of all people should understand. What good is marriage if you can just cancel it like cable?

I leaned back in my chair. I saw now that I was just like OP, trawling forums for someone who agreed with what I had already decided. It wasn't guidance I craved after all, but confirmation. There was so much editorial hand-wringing about how millennials were exposing the entirety of their private lives online, when the real danger lay in us bringing the weight of the whole world's judgment into what should be our personal decisions. Am I the asshole? Yes, if I choose to outsource my morality to a horde of strangers.

It seemed like a paradox to me. Americans were raised on a diet of individualism, but they still sought approval from the amorphous presence of their peers online. And even though they were told to "be yourself because there's no one like you," they were trying so hard to craft "relatable" content that would resonate with as many people as possible. I couldn't hope to find what I needed from the American corner of the internet, I in my transitive state, trying to outrun a self that was so unoriginal it had been recycled hundreds of times in many past lives.

I closed all of my open browser tabs, exhausted and smug. I had seen through the lie that was the contemporary version of grieving, in which we bounced around online, swimming in a sea of information, trying on various data for size in order to find something that spoke to us. Grieving in the form of doing research, because we believed in productivity above all else.

I was better than this, I thought. There were far more sensible things I could do. I went on Cachi I/O's website and scrolled around until I found their Careers page with a list of job openings. I copied the link to their Senior Software Engineer posting and messaged it to Eamon with a note: "Call me, we need to talk."

I'M SORRY AGAIN THAT MY APARTMENT IS SO DIM. I'LL DEFINITELY RE-place the dead bulb before our next video call. It was good to finally "see" you, even though I don't express myself as well verbally, as you have probably noticed. Maybe that's why I try to be so "extra-eloquent" in writing, as you put it.

By the way, did you see the headlines? "ICE Using Psychiatry Records to Deport Young Immigrant." It made me want to tell Katie and Bradley *I told you so. I said I couldn't see a professional therapist because it'd be on my record, and I was right.* Of course I'm a privileged, documented (for now) immigrant, but the point is, there is no sanctity of privacy when it comes to the authorities. I feel for the immigrant in the news article. How betrayed he must be feeling. How unfair it all is, his cries for help used against him.

Again, I'm so thankful we found each other. I trust you.

Day Nine (Thursday)

By 6:00 p.m. I still hadn't heard from Eamon. I messaged him again. "Stuck at work," he replied. I paced the apartment, feeling antsy. There had to be something else I could do. I sifted through the accumulating pile of unopened mail until I found it, the list I'd made right after Marlin first left.

- ~~Home with Mummy (unlikely, based on phone call)~~
- His office (possible, though need an in to get past building security)
- Crashing with someone?
    - ~~Best friend Eamon (possible, all the way out in College Point)~~
    - Friends from work (possible, could verify by visiting office—see above)
    - Climbing gym partners? (can't remember names other than Eamon)

- Climbing gym (possible, given three-times-a-week routine)
- Favorite restaurant (too close to apartment? worth a try anyway)

I still didn't have a way into his office, especially now that Meg was on vacation. But I could go to the climbing gym. From the one time I'd been, I knew it was a place of artificial nature, the outdoors brought inside and given garish pops of color that shouted TOY! Marlin went there three times a week, or used to. He'd been so serious about this sport. It might have survived his transformation. Maybe what had shifted was simply software, while his hardware stayed the same: fingers that loved locking onto brightly colored replicated rock holds, feet that scrabbled and soared off plastic nubs.

I felt uneasy the moment I stepped into the gym. A strong stench of feet permeated the space, even though it was cavernous, warehouse-high. Bulbous rock walls bulged forth at odd angles. It was dizzying. The climbers, too, looked off to me, in a way I couldn't pinpoint.

Maybe I would stand in the shadows as he ascended, grunting, up the highest rock wall in the gym. As he reached the top, I would rush forward and stand right underneath him. I'd shout out some pithy message of love at the exact moment he let go of the wall to come back down. He'd crash into me, and I'd fold into the mat. "I'm here for you," I'd tell him, as the pain from broken bones and crushed body parts kicked in.

These were scenes inspired by East Asian dramas our mothers used to watch, long-running series from Hong Kong, Taiwan, or Korea. Marlin and I both scoffed at the dramas' predictable, sentimental plots (many, many convenient cancer diagnoses when lovers needed to be star-crossed), though we also slyly followed along from the corners of our scornful eyes. Some primal human in us responded. We laughed when our moms wiped away tears and clucked their tongues, but really, there was a swelling in our chests too.

Heightened stakes and emotions—maybe that's what Marlin wanted. In the 1990s Asian dramas we didn't watch, the most expedient way to win back an angry lover was to stand in pouring rain outside their window until they felt you had suffered enough. Sometimes it took catching a bad cold to reach that threshold, sometimes physical collapse. I stood in the climbing gym and craned my neck, taking in the fifteen-foot bouldering walls. I imagined myself doing and saying the cheesy, cringe-inducing things from the dramas. I replayed my fantasy's ending scene over and over: Marlin's weight and my injuries combining to make my breath shallow, the unnatural angle of my leg or wrist making it clear that I had successfully crossed us over into a world in which things were different.

What I wanted was physical manifestation of my suffering. Bodily pangs that would legitimize this psychic hurt, make it quantifiable from smiley face to frowny face: How bad is the pain?

A roar echoed around the bouldering gym. Obediently, my attention snapped after the sound. In one corner of the gym half a dozen men were celebrating, clapping their hands, their faces angled adoringly up. The object of their cheer was a man holding on to a rock near the ceiling, his feet dangling. His body swayed rapidly, like a punching bag punched. Then he let go with a whoop and dropped all the way onto the mat beneath, his arms crossed at his chest. He was swarmed as soon as he got up, the cheering men extending fists for bumping. As if in response to their adoration, the man who'd dangled from the top of the wall pulled off his shirt. I saw, with a jolt, a logo featuring a Bender-like robot wearing a wig with flyaway white hair. The man, it was Josh.

I gasped and ducked my head, then felt foolish—there was nothing to hide behind. I looked around at the large, undivided space, so reminiscent of the open floor plans of tech companies. Then it clicked. All around me were men who looked nerdy from the neck up, but athletic and toned everywhere else. I had never before seen so many framed glasses paired with defined biceps in one place. Slouchy postures and impressive abs. Bad haircuts and thick forearms.

And their T-shirts, the dead giveaways, advertising things like annual summer retreats and hackathons, bearing the logos of tech companies, yes, but also those of law schools, dental schools, banks, and accounting firms. I remembered what Marlin had said when I asked him why he liked rock climbing so much. He said it was mentally challenging in addition to being physically demanding, and in this it was unlike most other sports. A bouldering route was like a problem-solving exercise, involving much more strategy than running or weight lifting.

Problem-solving exercises? Like in a job interview? I was puzzled. Why would you do those in your free time, when you're supposed to relax?

Gotta stay sharp. He grinned.

There were many women in the climbing gym too. I noticed them now that I wasn't solely focused on finding Marlin. Almost all of them were slender, with long limbs, their ponytails dancing as they soared up the walls. How light their bones must be, I thought. Their eyes, too, glazed over with the intensity of tackling problems that existed for no reason other than to be conquered.

I did an almost full sweep of the gym, careful to avoid the area Josh was in. The rental climbing shoes cramped my feet, bunching up my toes. Marlin wasn't here, among all these smart people with brain cells to spare. As the tension of hope held tight dwindled away, I became light-headed, on the verge of tears again. "Weak," I muttered. Then an impetuous energy sparked as if rising against this self-disgust. I eyed the rock walls and their preschool colors in contempt. What was so hard about clinging on?

The thick mat bounced under my feet as I walked toward a pink problem. That was what they were really called, these climbing routes—problems. I barely glanced at the difficulty rating attached to one of the rocks. Like software engineers, rock climbers started counting from zero instead of one, meaning a problem could be rated from zero (easiest) to something in the midteens (world-class hard). I craned my neck as far back as it would go, my hands resting on the labeled pink rock. I lived in a city of skyscrapers, I told myself. The top of the wall was not very far at all.

I swung my legs up. The momentum surprised me, making me kick my toes too hard into the wall. They already hurt in a dull way from the shoes' crimp, so the additional pain was easy to ignore. I reached for the next pink hold just above my head, stretching out my arm. Each time I ascended up one rock, my body swayed away from the wall, flapping in air. It was as unsteady a feeling as I'd ever had, more precarious even than being on a roller coaster. I had to either reach the top or descend safely back to the mat; this in-between position was untenable—

My left foot slipped. I shrieked involuntarily as I felt the hard tug of gravity against my hands and right foot, now the only points of support attaching me to the wall. I flailed to get my left foot back in contact with a rock, but the haphazard movement swung my right foot off too. I hung with my arms rigid, too stunned to kick my legs. Already I could feel the burn spreading through my fingers, as if the rocks they grasped were eating them away.

"Just let go!" someone shouted at me from the mat, a world away.

I looked up. The very last hold, perched near the top of the wall, was only a foot above. I thought of Marlin sitting on Eamon's guest bed, so close but unreachable. With a loud exhalation I lifted one knee and planted it on a tolerably flat rock. The position hurt my kneecap, but I thought I could finish the problem that way, my arms pulling me up to the last rock, my weight supported by a half kneel. I strained skyward, trembling. My fingers brushed the edge of the final hold, and then I plummeted.

For a while there was no pain, only a dazed breathlessness.

"Are you okay?" A woman leaned over me.

I was about to nod and wave her off when an excruciating pain radiated through my left shoulder. Even my armpit seemed to pulse with hurt.

"No," I gasped.

"Let me see," she said, helping me up into a sitting position. I put all my upper-body weight on my right arm, braced against the dirty mat. I wanted the left side of my torso to cease existing.

"It's dislocated," the woman said. "May I?"

And before I could even process the question, my limp arm was pulled into place with a click. I looked down to see her chalk-smeared shoe curved against my thigh, bracing. Tears streaked my face. I had not been touched by a stranger for a very long time. When I opened my mouth, I found I didn't know what to say in the face of such violent kindness. By then a small crowd had gathered around me, silently gawking. I felt debased even as I also felt saved.

Day Nine (Thursday)

Back home I stripped to my waist and gingerly tried out my recently dislocated shoulder. The internet said that to treat a dislocation is to "reduce" the affected area. I windmilled my reduced shoulder slowly, first forward, then backward. Had its range of motion been affected? I didn't know, because I'd never really paid my shoulders any attention. They were not problem areas like my stomach or my butt. I imagined encircling my arms around Marlin's back. Was this how I'd done it?

Afterward I lay on the couch, thinking about how I had no idea which continent I'd be on six months later, everything hinging upon a government form. In a few weeks it would be September, and our landlord would ask whether we wanted to renew our apartment lease. If I couldn't even answer that, how could I possibly claim to be in control of my circumstances?

Eamon finally called.

"Sorry, there was an outage at work. It was all hands on deck."

"Everything all right now?"

"Ehhhh . . ." He drew the sound out. "Anyway, what's up?"

I told him about the job posting at Cachi I/O, for a senior software engineer. "You could apply," I said.

"I'm confused. What's the plan?"

"I would apply myself, but I'm not qualified. You are, though. You could apply, and then when you go on-site for an interview, you could check and see whether Marlin's there."

"I don't know, that seems like a lot, just to see if he's there."

"A lot? You wanted to call the police. How is this 'a lot' compared to the cops?"

"Okay, but what do we do once we know he's there? Am I supposed to quit my job and join Cachi?"

"No, no, of course not. I just want to know he's still going to work. Hanging on to at least one part of his regular life. That's a bit reassuring, right?"

Eamon didn't say anything immediately.

"Please, Eamon. I'm asking you to help."

"Fine. Okay. I'll try. It's not guaranteed they'll want to interview me, though."

"Oh! Thank you!" I was grateful, gushing. "It's worth a try."

"Any other ideas?"

"No, but—" I weighed my words, wondering whether I should say them out loud.

"What?"

"I've been wondering—when Marlin predicted you'd find a new girlfriend soon, why did you want him to stop? You said you suggested that I write a letter because you thought it would help me 'move on.' Doesn't that imply you've 'moved on' from Emily?"

There was a long silence, which I didn't dare interrupt, for fear that I'd offended Eamon and he'd change his mind about the Cachi I/O interview.

"It's hard to explain," he eventually said.

"I know," I said uncertainly.

"It's like, this is an area of my life I care so much about. It's a touchy subject. When someone claims they know exactly what's going to happen, when to me it's something . . . mysterious and powerful, I just feel like they're trivializing it. Does that make any sense?"

"I think so. Do you think he was trying to help?"

"Maybe, but it's not actually helpful. Not for me, anyway. It reminds me of when my cousin was in a bad accident, and doctors said he might lose his leg. My aunt kept repeating to him, 'You're gonna be fine, your leg will be saved, don't worry,' and I could see my cousin getting more and more agitated and upset. It's like, how could she know? She might be doing more harm giving him false hope, when he should be mentally preparing for any outcome."

"You're saying you didn't believe Marlin about your love life."

"I guess so." Eamon sounded tired.

"Do you want to believe him?"

"No. Well, maybe. I'm not sure. I want what he says to come true, but I don't want it to be because of him, or anyone else. Does that make sense?"

"Maybe," I said. I paused, weighing my words. "Do you dream about his predictions? Or imagine them?"

"What? No. That's weird. I don't let them get to me that way."

I thought a lot about our conversation after we hung up. Eamon had told Marlin to stop predicting the future. Eamon never let himself dwell on stories other people told about him. Why couldn't I be the same way? I'd never thought to tell my mother I didn't want to hear any more of her past life stories. Instead I fleshed in their contours, both with my waking imagination and in my dreams.

Could it be that I'd developed this tendency in my free-market, postcolonial childhood? Growing up in a former British colony meant that the first books I read were the most English stories possible, by the likes of Enid Blyton. The radio would be going while I read in the kitchen, broadcasting songs in different dialects from Taiwan and Hong Kong. Meanwhile I'd also catch sounds from the TV drifting in from the living room, carrying snippets of news reported in Malay. And on school holidays we'd go to cinemas and sit under long-stemmed ceiling fans to watch censored Hollywood movies. I drank it all in without question. No one taught me that these various media had their individual cultural contexts that informed their content. I'd been dipped indiscriminately into the great vat dyes of so many different cultures that were not strictly "mine," never examining the biases of their origins until I was already a horrid patchwork quilt of clashing colors. (You see? "Vat dye" is a metaphor from Chinese. "Patchwork quilt"? From English.)

Marlin, too, had been raised in a similar environment, with the additional angle of being mixed-race. Growing up, he'd fed on even more diverse sources of narratives. Had he been smarter, more discerning, than I was? Or had he similarly swallowed them all without question?

Maybe he'd succumbed to the allure of dowsing because, like me, he had dived uncritically into the amalgamation of global influences around us. Maybe we'd both become lost, shuffling around puzzle pieces from unrelated jigsaw sets, aimlessly trying to form a coherent picture, deluding ourselves into believing that if we could make the elements come together in harmony, we would have produced some insight or breakthrough. Something like a revelation.

Day Ten (Friday)

Lucas was late for our one-on-one meeting, which he stylized as "1:1" on our calendar invites—1:1, as if we were equals. As if our values, our worth, were interchangeable. I fidgeted with my phone while I waited, refreshing news pages, sitting with a vague dread that something unknown but bad was about to be announced.

"So what happened in there? With the beta test?" he said as soon as he walked in, closing the door behind him. His boyish face was flushed.

"AInstein failed the test," I said. I'd rehearsed this. With engineers, you always started with bite-size facts. Get them to agree with you on the basics.

Except of course, I realized with a sinking feeling, there had been a whole bikeshedding meeting about whether the statement "AInstein failed the test" was accurate. Lucas frowned.

"AInstein couldn't make you laugh," he rephrased.

"Yes, that's right."

"You didn't find it funny at all?"

I hesitated. It had to be said.

"It was actually worse than that. It was offensive. Insulting."

"I appreciate that some of the jokes are, well, edgy. Some people like them because of the surprise factor," he said in his managerial tone of infinite patience.

"These were really bad, though."

"You can't have a product that pleases everyone. You have to find your core audience. That's something you'll learn as you grow in your career." He leaned back, surveying me. "How can we convince clients to buy an AI that tells jokes, if our product can't even make our own employees laugh?"

"I looked into it this morning—"

"Do you know what I've been telling our sales team? I told them, just look at our Glassdoor ratings. They're so high because we eat our own dog food; we let our people interact with AInstein whenever they need a laugh, and it works, the employee satisfaction ratings are proof. But now this. What went wrong?"

"This morning I looked into it. Log inspection shows that AInstein detected that I'm a woman, and tried to calibrate some of its jokes to fit that assessment. Unfortunately we have not trained AInstein on much data that would make it successful in that area. One thing that it did not pick up on was my reaction expressing disapproval. I took a look at the code. It should be a quick fix to . . ." I trailed off when I saw his expression.

"What are you doing, looking through code? That's not your job."

"I just thought this might be low-hanging fruit, and I have some free cycles. I've been working with the codebase for a while now—"

"You're a QA analyst, not an engineer. Your job is to test things."

"Yes, I know."

"The fact that you didn't find AInstein funny—do you think it might have something to do with the fact that you're from a different culture?"

I blinked. The more I did, the faster the anger rattled inside me.

"What I mean is, maybe Asian humor is different." Then he added, hastily: "Or like, all foreign humor is different."

He didn't say the phrase "inscrutable Oriental," but it nevertheless vibrated between us like a hard disk drive whirring to life. I blinked so much that the borders of my contact lenses hardened and cut.

"So we're not going to fix AInstein? It's getting launched as is?" I could see how this would all end. I just wanted it over with.

"Right, about that. As you know, the engineers held a meeting to discuss the issues you raised. After a robust discussion, they determined that the issues are more edge cases that are outside the scope of an MVP first release."

I blinked more, forcing myself to nod.

"Minimally viable product, you know? So the conclusion is, they hear you, but they have their own concerns with scope creep. You know what that is?"

"No," I said, exhausted that, once again, it came down to words and phrases in English I didn't understand.

"No problem at all. It's terminology from project management. Scope creep is when a release gets sidetracked by demands on resources that were not allocated in a project's original design. So we planned for X amount of effort from engineers to do Y amount of work, right? And now we have to stick to that. Don't worry, your suggestions are all documented in our backlog. They'll be reassessed once we're finished with the MVP."

"Can I look at the backlog and add my clarifications?" It was an alarming thought, my concerns represented solely by an engineer paraphrasing me.

"Of course." Lucas leaned forward, relaxed and carefree. "By the way, you're coming to the team outing tonight, right?"

"Team outing?"

"Yup, party's tonight! Perfect time to bond with the rest of the team, let some steam off. I'm counting on you to be there!"

Why? I wanted to ask. But I just nodded again.

THE NIGHTCLUB STAFF LOOKED AT US ASKANCE. THERE WE WENT, TROOP-ing into an establishment owned by Jay-Z with our company-branded backpacks and company-branded vests, office building key cards still clipped to retractable badge holders that dangled off our untucked shirt hems. What were we thinking? Half of the engineers had never listened to a single Jay-Z song in full, while the other half were way too into him.

It was loud in there. I fell back as Lucas led all of us along, winding our nerdy way deeper into the club's neon bowels.

"Here we are!" Lucas shouted. He gestured at a couple of bar-height tables in a particularly dark corner. "It's ours for the night!"

"No seats?" Ben asked, sounding a little apprehensive.

"We're here to party, not to sit!" Josh gave a little whoop. He put his backpack down on the floor, leaning it against a tulip table's base. Everyone else followed suit, piling identical backpacks on top of his until there was a little backpack fort. I was grateful I'd left mine behind in the office.

"Come on, let's get some drinks!" Lucas said, heading for the bar.

"I'll watch our bags," I said, but no one acknowledged me. They'd all followed after Lucas. I stood there, trying to calculate the minimum time I needed to kill before I could leave and still say that I'd been at the team outing.

When Lucas came back, he sliced a palm in an arc around his body, indicating the nightclub's tall posts, decorative LED arrangements, clustered beams of neon lasers, and, for some reason, crystal chandelier. "It's something, right? Huh?" Wave after wave of light washed over us, changing colors midjourney, making me feel trapped inside a police car's beacon.

"Here." Ben squeezed past Lucas to hand me a drink.

"What's this?" The liquid was a bright, warm brown, a lemon peel dunked gracelessly into it.

"An apology." Ben looked left, then right, lowering his voice. "Sorry about the lemon. It was supposed to be decoration, but it fell in."

"Oh. You don't have to apologize for that."

"No, the apology . . ." A new, louder track started playing, drowning out his words. I leaned in to hear him.

". . . it's just not a good place to be. I'm going to leave, and you should think about it too."

I stepped back, confused. "You're leaving now?" I strained my voice to be heard over the music.

"No!" He looked alarmed, ducking his head to my level and making little flutters with his free hand. "Not so loud, please. I just started looking this week. I'll probably start interviewing next month."

He gave me a strange look then, peering into my face. We were standing too close, but it was the only way to have a conversation. I wasn't sure what to do with what Ben had just told me. Why the trust in my discretion now? I'd never had an in-depth conversation with him.

"Anyway." He seemed resigned at my lack of reaction. "I just want to say I'm sorry again for how the Bike Shed meeting went. I don't think the decision was right. Sorry."

He turned and wedged his way into the crowd, which consolidated more and more into a single mass every time I looked. First the back of his head was blue, then it was red, and then I couldn't see him anymore.

I put my drink down on one of our reserved tables and headed after him. I should have been thrilled by his apology, but I wanted to know exactly what he was sorry for. The decision wasn't "right"? What was Ben's perception of "right"? I felt on the cusp of some great discovery. Muttering excuse-me's and sucking in to pass through the nightclub goers, I began to believe that a vague, hazy part of my self was about to come into focus. It was just a feeling I had, but I pursued it through pulsing tunnels of warm, sweaty arms.

When I emerged, I headed instinctively for the one part of the landscape that wasn't gyrating. It was a long bar, spanning my field of vision like a barrier.

"Edwina!" A hand clapped on my shoulder. I turned; the hand fell away.

"Didn't I see you the other day?" Josh shouted. "At the climbing gym?"

I shook my head. "I don't climb."

"What?"

"I don't climb!"

"Likely story." He scoffed. "Next you're gonna say you don't have a crush on Ben, am I right?"

"I don't! You have to stop saying I have a crush on everybody."

"Don't lie to me. I saw you two together earlier. You were looking at him with, like, Bambi eyes."

"I'm getting a drink." I pointed behind my shoulder. There was no point falling into his trap. The more I protested, the more he'd make fun of me.

"I'll get one too," he said, herding me with his body, advancing one sure step at a time, until I was backed against the bar. I felt wetness spread along my spine: spilled beer, pooled wine, leaked spirits.

"You're drunk," I said.

He laughed, spraying hot breath into my face. "Of course I'm drunk. It's a team outing. We're here to CELEBRATE!" To demonstrate, he did a version of dancing, wagging his shoulders and knees in place. Smoothly, fluidly, he transitioned from his dance to planting his hands against the bar, one on each side of me.

"So. You wanna tell me why you lied about the climbing gym?"

All around us, people packed into each other. I tried to look past Josh's shoulder to locate the rest of my coworkers, but saw only scattered limbs and epileptic heads, all anonymous. Even if I did find, say, Darren, what would I do, and what would they do? We worked for a startup barely a year old. We had no code of conduct defined, nothing that said Josh might not corner me against a bar at a team bonding event. Nothing, too, that instructed me on what to do when a teammate such as Josh circled my waist with one arm, as he now did. There were no best practices for how I could handle the situation without jeopardizing my job, my elusive green card, my last hope of making it in America.

"You know what I think? I think you keep saying you don't have crushes on those other guys because you have your eyes on someone else." Josh shuffled forward, affixing his body to mine.

"I'm married," I said.

"Yeah, right." He smirked. "No one on our team is married. What's his name, your *husband*?"

"Marlin. His name is Marlin."

"Lemme guess. A white guy. Am I right?"

"You're wrong. And that's kind of offensive. Can you give me some space here?"

"You're so funny, you know that?"

With that he leaned in, eyes flickering shut. The world was green, then it was orange. All those talk show hosts, polished and coiffed, had not prepared me for this. I'd thought that if I could make Americans laugh, then I would be accepted, foreign accent or not. I would be embraced and admired. Well, Josh had just called me funny. What had I accomplished?

His kiss landed half on my lips and half on my chin as I twisted my neck to see, I am ashamed to say, whether there were any unwanted witnesses. Not seeing any, I levered my arms up so that they were between us, holding Josh off my torso. The moment he slackened, I shoved him and crabbed sideways out of his embrace. His face yellow, then purple. I ran, tracked by searchlights, across the club's trembling floors all the way to the exit.

IT WASN'T A BIG DEAL. IT *WAS* A BIG DEAL. I SAT AT HOME, CRAVING VEG-etables but finding my fridge stocked with only meat. I salivated over the imagined crunch of raw cauliflower dipped into cool ranch. Snow pea leaves sautéed with garlic, their delicate leaves and hollow veins succumbing to my teeth. Asparagus brutally snapped and smothered in butter. Eggplant blistered beyond recognition into pulp.

I wasn't actually hurt, I reasoned. It was more or less just a peck on the cheek. Maybe Josh was so drunk he wouldn't even remember it by morning, so it would be like nothing had happened. I exhorted myself to think about all the actual suffering that other immigrants went through, the ones who didn't have my privileges. ICE raids. Family separation. Neglect and death in detention centers. Real sexual abuse. I was lucky, so lucky.

What if Marlin had been there? Watching from the crowd?

My mind broke down when this electrifying image flashed in. He would have been grimly triumphant, what he'd foretold manifesting into truth—I was indeed an unfaithful wife. I tried to brush the thought aside as nonsense. But what did it mean, that he had predicted this situation? It couldn't possibly be actual powers of premonition. So then, what? Had I been walking around with the look of vulnerable prey, inviting attack? Thoughts blinked and buzzed, a slender beam of attention roving and rotating among them. Nightclub brain.

Day Eleven (Saturday)

Seven missed calls and a voice message from last night. The voice mail was from Eamon.

"Hey, I called a few times but you didn't pick up. Anyway, Cachi wants to interview me on Monday. I told them during my phone screen that I have other offers waiting. Guess it worked, since they're fast-tracking me." A pause. "Call me if you hear from Marlin, okay?"

Two of the missed calls were from Katie. When I called her back, she chirped that she was on her way over.

"For what?" I pinched the flabby part of my elbow, trying to calm myself down.

"Girls' day out! No husband, no baby."

I noticed the "husband," singular, and felt a brief pump of despair. But she meant well, I knew. She was going to all this trouble for me. And anything was better than marinating in further thoughts about Josh, wondering what he would do next.

"I guess," I said.

"Awesome! You've earned it!"

As if there existed some kind of employer who accepted anguish as labor, who doled out little treats to those who put in their hours at suffering.

Following Katie's lead, I stood in line on a sidewalk for pastries whose names I could not pronounce, such as kouign-amann and schnecken. It was a windy day; I could feel my hair tangling. By the time our position in the snaking line crossed the threshold into a tiny storefront, I was ready to declare whatever the bakery sold as the best thing ever.

Perhaps that was what I needed, I idly thought. I should create some easily surmountable hurdles and then surmount them.

"So? Have you checked out the dating app yet?"

"Katie, it's been less than two weeks."

"I'm not saying you have to sleep with anyone! Just make a new friend or two."

"You're my friend."

"Yes, and I'm here for you, but I also know that I don't spend as much time with you as before, since Su-Ann and everything. It doesn't hurt to have someone else to talk to."

"I'm fine."

"Knowing you, you're probably keeping things to yourself because you don't want to burden other people."

I cringed. It was true I'd decided not to tell her about Josh at the nightclub. But I was nowhere near as selfless as she was making me out to be. I simply couldn't bear to admit that after Marlin questioned my fidelity, I'd stood, stunned and silent, while a man I didn't even like put his mouth on me.

"I know you don't want to hear this," Katie said, trying again, "but maybe it's time to move on. It doesn't look like he's coming back."

"How do you know that?" I stared into her eyes, challenging, letting indignant righteousness wash over me, even though I knew it was unfair. Anything was preferable to plain old pain.

"Okay, I'll drop it." She hefted her croissant bag higher on her shoulder and looked away. I was disappointed. Secretly I wanted her to keep up her persuasion. It would let me briefly hold the power to frustrate and disappoint for a change. Let me be cruel, to see what it felt like.

Or maybe, just like I'd done with my mother, I simply wanted to do the opposite of whatever Katie wished for me.

After we brushed crumbs of baked goods off our faces, Katie led the way to a spa. As soon as we entered, a room full of Asian faces swiveled toward us, some of them partially obscured by surgical masks. A woman with permed hair stood up and said: "Yes?"

I let Katie handle the talking. I would never be in my element at a salon. I zoned out, thinking about why it was that Katie never seemed to visit the same salon twice. Each time she bent my arm for a "spa day," we always ended up in a different spot, and I could never tell what made one place preferable to another.

Katie ticked off a list of services she wanted while the woman with permed hair assented. Their conversation dissolved into the hum of the space, blending in with the AC unit's rattles and the tinkle of what I believe is called "crystal music." Sometimes the soft whirs of massage chairs joined the music. I was spacing out, lulled, when suddenly a sentence jumped out from the background hum, automatically highlighted by my brain:

"Where are you from?"

The question was directed at both of us. The salon employee

who'd asked wore her hair in a ponytail, showing off the pointy elven ears holding up the straps of her mask. Katie gave me a Look. "New York," she said, throwing in some attitude.

"Speak Chinese?" Ponytail asked.

"No." Katie was positively frosty.

I demurred. I didn't even want to be here.

"Pick a color," Ponytail instructed us.

I stood in front of the rows and rows of miniature bottles and felt a rising sense of panic. It was chaos, overwhelming. True, the bottles were organized according to their places on the spectrum of light. But they all also bore a secondary identifier that had tangential connection to their essence. For example, what looked to the human eye (admittedly deficient when it came to color detection) like an uncomplicated red was labeled "Vamp It Up." This then required my brain to perform work and unpack the allusion, something like: (vampires-> blood-> red) * (to vamp-> to seduce) == a pun meant to put in mind femme fatales, "fatale" because of the vampiric angle, c.f. man-eaters, end goal being to produce a feeling of sexy badassery while applying coats of paint to unfeeling parts of fingers.

And it was like that for two entire shelves, one after another, exhausting exercises that stoked my fear of not fitting in or "getting it," summoning flashbacks of when I'd first arrived in America and had no clue what *ER* (the show) was, plus had never made the acquaintance of one Ferris Bueller, whom my college classmates kept name-dropping in conversations. Any number of quotes from movies, songs, and breakfast-cereal commercials sailed past my head. It was like I'd learned English from a dictionary that had huge chunks ripped out. In reaction, I doubled my efforts to be fluent-sounding. I even took a Middle English seminar, all so I could feel like I was gaining an upper hand in some way. I would wield the language more properly than native speakers could, I thought. But here I was, made uneasy again by pop culture in a nail salon.

Dizzy, I forced myself to stop my eyes from sweeping over the endless parade of bottles. I clutched an edge of the display shelf.

"What's up with you?" My turn to be on the receiving end of a Katie SooHoo Look. "You're acting like a robot."

Numbly, I floated along with the word association (robot-> metal) and picked up a bottle of silver polish. I resisted looking at the label for as long as I could, but the technicians who would be working on us were busy with the footbaths, making me think of pots prepared for lobsters. I gave in.

"Moonlight Sonata," the label read. Relief arrived. Twelve years of piano lessons finally coming in handy.

Katie wrinkled her nose at me.

"Tacky?" I asked, holding up Moonlight Sonata.

"Not really, but just a bit, hmm, *tweeny*."

Yet another reference I wouldn't get. I surrendered, exhausted.

"Those two are slooow," one of our technicians said to the other in Cantonese.

I was going to apologize, but then remembered with a start that they thought we were both Americans who did not speak Chinese. In Katie's case this was mostly true (she didn't know much beyond "eat," "thank you," and such in Taishanese), so it hadn't technically been a lie on her part. On mine, it was pure omission.

Too late now to do anything about it, because the two technicians were discussing who would be working on whom, and I heard myself referred to as "the plump one." My face started to burn. I turned away to look out the spa's glass doors, huge and sparkling clean. Today's New York had a distracted buzz about it, people walking around slack-mouthed while earbud microphones dangled by their chins. I considered plugging in my own earbuds, but Katie wanted to talk.

"Did you hear back from Marlin? After you sent your letter?"

I shook my head, bracing myself. To my surprise, Katie drew me in for a lingering side hug.

"You know how I feel about you moping after him. Sorry, I say it as it is. *But* if you're not gonna get the closure you need unless you hear back from him, then here's something I do at work. You ready for this? It's pretty good."

I couldn't help but smile. Katie and her schemes.

"Okay, here it is. Say I need something from my male boss by a certain time, let's say four days from now. First I send a request with clear action items at both the top and bottom of my email. Then I wait. If I don't hear back by the second day, I send two reminder emails with the action items highlighted, once early in the day and once at close of business. If he still ignores me"—Katie rolled her eyes—"then it's time for drastic measures. I'll send an email that's all professional, like, 'Since I haven't heard back, I assume you would like me to take initiative. Therefore, unless you say otherwise by five p.m., I will go ahead with XYZ.' The key is, XYZ is an idea that I already know he hates."

I laughed. "So you blackmail him?"

"Oh, no no no." Katie put on a sweet grin. "It's not blackmail. It's playing games with the male ego. He might hate XYZ because he believes it's wrong. In that case, his male ego makes him want to *correct* me—there's nothing more satisfying for him than that. He can't let go of an opportunity to show that he knows better."

"I see. Don't you run the risk of him thinking you're an idiot, though?"

"He'll only think I'm an idiot if I insist on XYZ after his correction. If I'm grateful for his input, then I'm actually really, really smart for being so receptive to his greater wisdom. Obviously."

"Wow." Maybe if I'd put half her cunning into my interactions at work, I wouldn't be up against so many walls.

Ponytail waved Katie and me deeper into the salon. We sank into neighboring chairs, so bulky and replete with buttons that it could belong to a Starfleet commander (I'll admit, this is a pop culture reference I'd studiously learned). I must have been tense, because my technician spent extra time massaging my calves. While she did this, I tried to relax, but I also kept expecting her to say something in Cantonese like "She better pay extra for me to massage all this fat" or "Silver? So tweeny," except then I realized I didn't know the Cantonese equivalent for "tweeny," and I gratefully became lost in thought.

When we were finally left alone to dry our nails under mini fans, Katie turned to me, moist-eyed.

"I just want you to be happy, you know," she said.

I could feel tears welling too. I thought about how many of the tangled threads that made up "me" were a direct result of her influence, or else reactions/resistance to the force of her personality. Even when I judged her for things and behaviors I thought beneath me, I was still using her to propel my personhood at a specific angle.

"I just think you're trying to intellectualize things that . . . can't be treated that way," she continued. "Sometimes there's no hope of thinking our way out of problems. Especially when it comes to matters of the heart."

She was wrong, but my deep fondness for her held. I managed a chuckle and said: "First you want me to see a psychiatrist, then you don't want me to intellectualize things? Don't those contradict each other?"

"It's different with a professional, objective perspective."

I tested a fingernail to see if it was ready. It smudged, ever so slightly.

"I'll think about it," I said.

She looked at me with such hope in her eyes.

Day Twelve (Sunday)

Thanks for saying that. No, I understand that what happened at the nightclub team outing was serious, but I disagree with you that it's sexual assault. There has to be another word or phrase for it. But really, thank you for asking.

I have this recurring dream where I walk into a bright, featureless room, a sci-fi jail cell. The door seals shut behind me, its outline disappearing into the wall. In the center of the cell, Marlin sits cross-legged, his back to me. I plead with him to turn around. In the dream, this is accomplished by wishing very hard. My mouth never moves, my lips never part. But I send brain waves out to Marlin's prone figure, again and again. Finally, it works. He turns, slowly, brain stalk cricking, and it is Josh's face that I see.

IT'S A FUNNY HUMAN THING THAT WE SOMETIMES FORGIVE A PERSON when someone else comes along and does something even worse to us. That is the way I forgave my mother for the banana tree spirit story.

She called when I was fully awake, but still feeling the effects of a Marlin/Josh nightmare. Rattled, I was ready for reconciliation.

"You look terrible," she said immediately, and I was glad for it. It felt good to have my state of mind acknowledged, without my having to whine about it.

"I feel terrible." I told her what had happened at the nightclub. When I finished, I braced myself. *Look, isn't this what you wanted?* she might say. *To live a life completely different from mine? Well, chaos is the opposite of calm and order.*

"Tsk, these American young men," my mother said. The transformation of flesh into pixels always made her look younger, her skin brighter. She glowed on-screen. Meanwhile I had no idea how I looked, having turned off self view. "But don't think too much about it. The more you think, the worse you feel. Maybe you worked in tech too long already. You're becoming like them, always overthinking."

I flinched. I wanted to unburden myself, but I could already sense the failure latent in any attempt to describe the terrors consuming me. The sentences "He *half* kissed me" and "He left me" did nothing to convey how I suffered. If I couldn't handle my pain gracefully, then failing to describe it adequately seemed like a double condemnation of my character. I should either be the strong, silently suffering type, or a sensitive, expressive soul who brought others to tears with descriptions of my inner turmoil.

"You're always like this," my mother continued. "You can't leave anything alone. You used to pop all your pimples, you remember? You're popping all your mental pimples now. It's like this: if you leave them alone, they'll heal by themselves. This Josh guy, you tell him to stop bothering you and find himself a girlfriend."

I laughed, despite myself, at the absurdity of her imagery.

"What did Marlin say?" she went on.

"I haven't told him."

"I know things must be rough between you two. Otherwise he wouldn't have called me. But just be patient, okay? Don't rush and go say things you'll regret."

We were both silent for a while. I told myself that if she brought up a past life story now, I would hang up on her. Not because I was still angry at her, but because I didn't want to be angry at her again, or anymore.

"You remember I said I have something to tell you?" she asked.

I shook my head, surprised, then nodded. I thought what she'd wanted to talk about was how Marlin had called her up, asking about Li Shen.

"I have a, a male friend," she said.

I gasped audibly.

"Don't worry! He asked me to get married, but I said no."

"Who is he? How did this happen?"

"He's a Pendidikan Moral teacher at that new school next to— Oh, you don't know it, they opened it after you left."

"How did you even meet a moral studies teacher? You had a moral quandary to resolve?" I couldn't keep the snark out of my voice.

"Friends introduced us. You're upset?"

"Why would I be?"

"This is not like love or marriage. It's like this: he and I can take care of each other. Now you don't have to worry about me. No need to leave your life in New York even when I get so old I can't walk."

I struggled to put a name to my emotions. Guilt. Disappointment. A feeling of being cut loose, after having been tethered for time immemorial. Fear. I connected the dots for the reason behind my chaotic feelings: if I failed to get a green card, I could no longer use "caring for my aging mother" as an excuse for why I left America.

Such vile thoughts. I closed my eyes.

"I just want you to be happy," I said, recycling Katie's line, remembering how I'd been touched.

My mother laughed. "Happy? When you get to my age, you don't think about 'happy' anymore. I just want some peace. If every day is the same, good. If nobody worries about me, good."

"So why did you keep asking me to move back?"

"That's for *you*. When you first moved there, you said you wanted to do something with English literature, so staying in America made sense. But now you're doing what? Computers?"

"Computers," I admitted.

"You can do computer work here."

The dizzying void opened up again, and I stared into it. What would my life be, a year from now? No matter what science said, the sun in Malaysia was different from the one that shone on America. By next year, what shade would I stand under, what clothes would I wear, what food would I eat? What language would I be speaking? Who would I reach for, bolting up from a nightmare at the edge of dawn?

Day Thirteen (Monday)

I took the day off work, not bothering to invent an illness or a family emergency. I needed to put off seeing Josh's face in the office. Also, somehow yesterday's conversation with my mother had snuffed out my last flicker of hope that AInstein would sponsor my green card. If she was making practical choices, maybe I should, too. I felt it settling in my body like sediment, the acceptance of my failure.

I sat on my unmade bed and went on Facebook, aimlessly scrolling through photos of my primary school friends. I had a half-baked idea of reuniting with them when I moved back, so I would have a ready group of friends waiting in the wings. But as I scrolled, I began to notice a pattern. Over a quarter of them now worked and thrived in Singapore.

Eamon called when I was opening up my eighth tab of job postings in Singapore.

"My brain is fried," he announced. "Just got through five hours of interviews at Cachi."

"I'm sorry." I grimaced. "Thank you again for doing this."

"Sure."

"Did you see him?"

"No. But I did see something interesting when they walked me around the office for a tour."

"What?"

"You know the purple necklace thing he has?"

For dowsing. "Yes," I said.

"I saw it on one of the standing desks. I was walking by, and the desk was pretty much at my eye level. It has to be him, right? What are the odds someone else has that exact purple necklace?"

"But you didn't see him?"

"No, no one was at the desk. I'm sure it's him, though."

"You're right. I think you're right."

"That was before the interviews. I tried to look again after I was done, but he still wasn't there. Maybe he took the day off."

"I would think he'd bring the pendant with him, if that's the case."

"Pendant! That's the word."

"At least we know he's still going to work. That's good. Thanks again, Eamon."

"Yeah, glad it wasn't a complete waste of time."

"Do you think you'll be getting a job offer?"

"I was just gonna tell the recruiter that I'm accepting one of my 'other offers,' but . . . it might be cool to see what Cachi says?"

"I'm sure you did well."

"Thanks! I should go."

I hung up and rolled over in bed, feeling the minor aches that came with sitting on a soft surface for hours. I stared at the ceiling and tried to conjure a sense of relief given Eamon's news. Nothing rose up in response. I was squeezed dry.

The room was splashed with shadows when I woke up. I blinked in confusion at the apartment's corners, obscured by darkness. How was it evening already? The idea came to me then, in that liminal state between sleep and complete wakefulness. I tumbled out of bed and went to rummage through my closet. What did I have that would make a halfway decent disguise?

Marlin had seen me in virtually all of my outfits. I would need to dig deep, go all the way back into the cobwebbed, mothballed recesses of drawers, where there might be clothes I hadn't pulled out for years. I thrust my arms into shelf after shelf. They emerged with homecoming shirts from college, winter beanies I hadn't seen in months, long johns my mother had sent me. I yanked a scarf free, and something else fell out with it, entangled. I picked it off my foot. It was a Suṣy and Geno shirt, featuring the mascots from Sustagen, this nutritional supplement drink my mother used to foist on me. Shame-tinged memories crowded into the closet. As a child, I had begged my mother to order this shirt off a catalog delivered to our mailbox. The day the coveted item arrived, I put it on right away, delighted.

"Too big," my mother said.

It was true; the shirt hung down to the middle of my thighs like a dress. Reluctantly I pulled it over my head and let my mother take it away for safekeeping.

"You can wear it when you're taller."

But by the time I grew to the appropriate height, I couldn't tug the shirt much down beyond my shoulders. It snagged on my torso, its downward progress impeded by rolls of fat. I burst into tears.

"Cry what cry?" my mother said as she helped me struggle out of the shirt. "Just don't eat so much. Then the shirt will fit!"

I'd held on to that shirt since, at first out of genuine hope that I could one day lose enough weight to wear it. Later, that hope dimmed and morphed into something else. Every time I moved, I considered putting Susy and Geno into the donation pile, but I never did. I think it was because they reminded me of that first powerful desire to be thin.

Standing in the closet, I lifted Susy and Geno to my nose and sniffed. There was a funk to them, but it was more intriguing than revolting. I took my sleep shirt off and pulled them on, tugging aggressively when I met with resistance. I heard the sound of a seam ripping, and I kept going. When I'd done my best, I turned to the full-length mirror next to the closet.

I looked ridiculous. I was technically wearing the shirt, but it was so obviously too small for me, riding up my fleshy arms and bunching at my belly button. But it was indeed something Marlin had never seen me wear. I bit the insides of my cheeks, both sides at once.

In the end I psyched myself up enough to do it, though I did add a hoodie tied around the waist to bridge the gap between shirt and sweatpants. I also found a gaudy bandanna to wrap over my head pirate-style, a bright yellow thing that I'd acquired once upon a time because I saw an Instagram personality demonstrate the "French" way of wearing bandannas.

It was the tail end of rush hour when I left the apartment, when happy hours were ending and people were settling in with their Seamless dinners. Marlin was probably working late as usual, so I had decent hopes that I would still catch him. I adjusted and readjusted the hoodie throughout my subway ride, self-conscious. When I emerged at the stop closest to Cachi I/O, I walked by a street vendor packing up and bought a $5 pair of sunglasses to add to my disguise.

Picking a stakeout spot was easy. There was a construction site kitty-corner from the building that housed Cachi I/O, with plenty of steel frames and tarps that I could lurk behind. For the next hour or so I stood there, trying to focus on the revolving doors of Cachi's office building. But it was harder than I'd assumed. Thoughts popped and sizzled like oil in a pan. I fantasized about biting into a double-decker burger, blood-tinged juice dribbling onto my hands faster the closer I got to the center. The modulo flashed into my mind, its harsh slash separating two needy, gaping mouths: %. A symbol that used to bind Marlin and me together through an inside joke, now a visual mockery alluding to our break, the slanted line a forbidding border.

I remembered the time we boarded a Chinatown bus from New York to DC. There were no vacant seats together by the time we stepped into the bus's vibrating hull. We ended up sitting across the aisle from each other, holding hands, letting them swing with every lurch of the bus.

A man in sunglasses and a red cap walked by the construction site. I tensed back into reality and tried to get a look at the front of the cap, but he was too tall and I couldn't get a good view. All I managed was to draw the man's attention. He gave me a sideways look, and my paranoia took off immediately. What I was doing, did it count as loitering? Could I be arrested for that? From behind my shades I checked other passersby as furtively as I could, trying to see whether anyone else was watching me.

The sky was a dull gray now, streetlamps and car headlights the brightest objects around. Marlin could have gone in and out of his building ten times and I wouldn't have noticed, my mind dithering.

I turned to trudge back to the subway stop, but a deli/Korean takeout combo two doors down caught my eye. Bulgogi, I thought, the craving hitting me instantly.

The door tinkled when I entered the store. A man pushed a mop around the floor, a yellow sandwich board near his feet. It smelled like bleach. The man glanced up but didn't say nothing. He adjusted his cap and went on mopping around the sandwich board, which showed a stick figure with limbs akimbo. It looked like it was trying to bust out of the board's frame.

On a whim I took out my smartphone and unlocked it. I opened the Gallery app and scrolled through grid after grid of colorful pain, wincing at Marlin's face beaming or pensive or playful.

"Excuse me," I said, greeting the mopper, phone cradled loosely like I was holding a dying palm-size animal. "Have you seen this man?" I turned the screen to him. He leaned on his mop, or maybe it was the deli's and so wasn't *his* his, just like my husband wasn't *mine* mine.

"Yeah, I seen him."

"When?"

"He comes late. Very late. We're open twenty-four/seven."

"How late?"

"Sometimes three a.m., four a.m. Buys a sandwich."

"Where does he go after that?"

"Cross the street."

"Into that building? The brown one with the, the gargoyle statues on the second floor?" I wanted to reach out and touch him, try to absorb his knowledge through skin contact.

"I don't know." He shook his head. "Could be."

My phone fell out of my loose clutch, narrowly missing the bucket of water next to his mop.

"Sorry," I said. He bent down, and I didn't stop him from picking up the phone for me. I'd come on this stakeout on a hunch, and now that my hunch had proven correct, I didn't know what to do with myself. It was true, had to be: Marlin was squatting in his office's coworking space. Mostly I felt a crushing sadness. Was using company-branded sweatshirts folded over as pillows really preferable to sleeping by my side?

BACK HOME I SLID OUT MY IMPORTANT DOCUMENTS FOLDER AGAIN, GOing through the stack until I found the blank green card application form. I tore it in two and walked into the kitchen to shove the halves into the trash can. When I returned to the Important Documents, my eye caught a corner of creamy ivory peeking out from the folder. My heart thrummed. At first I thought it was our wedding invite, but when I pinched the corner and drew it out, slowly, I recognized my college diploma. "Bachelor of Arts," it read. How strange that phrase sounded now.

I hadn't thought about her in so many years, that young woman who'd wanted to spend the rest of her life reading. No, not just reading, but exercising dominion over a language that she was told didn't belong to her. One more way to outrun her fate.

I saw her again walking across college campus, feverishly happy, hugging books that her American classmates had yawned through in high school. That girl had been fanciful and ambitious. When she read Mary Shelley's *Frankenstein* at nineteen, she immediately identified with immigrant scholar Victor Frankenstein, who worked day and night to prove himself master of his field at a foreign university. She, too, was constructing a monster of her own, a creature she meant to pass off as an accepted member of her adopted society, only to have the whole experiment go horribly wrong. And somewhere along the way, her painstaking creation, that unique blend of invention and mimicry, veered off course. Became me. I couldn't say when the last time was that I'd picked up a novel. All my efforts since graduation had been pointed toward maximizing my chances at a green card—attending Toastmasters, going to meetups and networking events, paying to join professional organizations that promised to empower me as a woman in male-dominated fields.

My ears wouldn't stop ringing. I looked around the room, trying to calm myself by taking stock of the objects around me. Floor lamp. Framed picture of us. Smoke alarm. Wall socket. A long groove across the wooden floors, where Buster had had an accident.

When I felt a bit better I spread the folder's maw wide, my hands shaking. Essential tremors. I put my Important Documents back in, the seal on the diploma reflecting light at the very top of the stack.

Day Fourteen (Tuesday)

I walked into AInstein Inc. with my jaw clenched. Josh had beat me to the office. I stood at my desk, facing the back of his monitors, willing him to look up. But he didn't. He continued pounding away at his mechanical keyboard, completely absorbed, or pretending to be.

All morning I waited, tension coiled in my body. Would he say something? When he got up for more kombucha on tap, I stiffened, wondering if he would look at me and sneer. At his slightest movement my shoulders inched rigidly up. When the engineers stood and stretched, one after another, I was surprised to see that it was already lunchtime.

At fourteen minutes past noon the office was empty, everyone out to lunch except me. All the wound-up tension I'd been tamping down since morning jostled within, seeking an outlet. Did Josh think that if he ignored me, the nightclub incident would fade away? How long was he going to keep this up?

There had to be some acknowledgment, at least, of what had happened. I scanned the empty office space. One good thing about an open floor plan: I could see anyone coming from a literal block away.

Josh's monitor blinked to life as soon as my hand touched his ergonomic mouse. I navigated to AInstein's GitHub page. When Josh's password keychain manager popped up, I clicked "Yes" to sign in.

My agitation crescendoed into anger, and I could feel an imminent dam break. I wanted Josh to feel a fraction of my pain. Some of this burden was his to share. The mouse flew to Settings > Danger Zone. I stared at the "Delete this repository" button. My finger itched to click it, even though I knew full well that there were many versions of AInstein in local branches on the computers surrounding me. Deleting the repo would barely slow them down, satisfying as the act would feel.

Instead I pulled up Josh's Emacs and found the file where the team had coded in exemptions for when AInstein detects children, or "non-adult users," as the product manager insisted on calling them. In such scenarios, AInstein had been programmed to adhere to a small pool of pre-vetted, age-appropriate jokes, mostly of the knock-knock variety.

I toggled the default setting to turn off parental control. I pushed the change under Josh's name and titled the commit message something innocuous like "convert tabs to spaces." Then I went to Darren's computer. In the code review UI, I had Darren approve Josh's change and merge it, committing my sabotage to the next production push. The company was nearing a release date, and the engineers were in a merging frenzy. This commit would be just one among many, and it wasn't like the engineers were organized enough to generate and monitor release notes. They didn't have time for such mundane administrative tasks. Move fast and break things: just fine by me.

As the tension in me ebbed, I felt a brief pang of apprehension. Some children exposed to AInstein were going to be . . . confused, although most of them had probably already heard all there was to hear by age seven these days. It was the parents who would be outraged. That's what I was counting on, anyway, parents foaming at the mouth and coming after this shoddy product. That could be my meaningful contribution, couldn't it? It might even be enough to atone for all the nonsense I'd enabled in this strange country, helping these men have their fun.

I looked down at my shirt, an impulse purchase from a pasar malam shortly before I left Malaysia:

NEW YORK

IF I CAN MAKE I THERE

I CAN MAKE IF ANYWHERE

I'D RATHER BE

IN NYC

Sitting in the empty office, I laughed out loud.

Day Fifteen (Wednesday)

If stories can indeed inspire our behavior in real life, then perhaps I owe my surge of recklessness to my mother, after all. I'd digested the narratives of the banana tree girl and the mother in the fire and taken what I wanted, and now I had tampered with AInstein.

Though there was also a flip side. They say that to write a story, all you have to do is put down one sentence at a time. No one teaches how to unwrite a story. I wish I could undo the tales I told about myself in America.

I MENTIONED TO KATIE OVER THE PHONE THAT I WAS GOING OVER TO Eamon's to clear out Marlin's things. She asked if I wanted help or company. I told her not to worry about it.

"I'm proud of you," she said.

"For what?"

"For starting a new chapter."

I didn't correct her.

Another memory: Katie and I had just started becoming friends and were trading family history. I mentioned my grandmother used to be a rubber tapper. This confused Katie to no end, which delighted me for some reason. I toyed with her, painting a picture of women with beautiful hands going around rubber trees and blessing them with gentle taps of their fingertips like fairy godmothers until rubber flowed out, forming perfect Kate Spade rain boots by the time it hit ground.

"Rubber is *liquid*?" she asked, awed.

"THANKS FOR COMING," EAMON SAID WHEN HE OPENED THE DOOR. HE had asked me to come collect Marlin's things, now that it seemed virtually certain Marlin would not be returning. Looking at Eamon's glum face, I felt a surge of gratitude. Here was a corroborator of my interpretation of events. Eamon, too, had lived with Marlin and found his change unreasonable. More importantly, Eamon also still cared for Marlin despite their fallout. I could tell from how eagerly he asked: "So you're sure he's camping out in his office?"

I nodded. "I think so. I don't know how to confirm it, though."

He waved me into his living room. I sank into his stained leather couch that was too deep for me. No matter how I sat, I ended up either slumping or slouching.

"You're vegetarian, right?" Eamon asked, coming out of the kitchen with a serving tray.

"Yes, that's right."

I ate the crudités he offered, double-dipping baby carrots and celery sticks into the hummus bowl. He sat next to me on the couch, not touching the food.

"I'm still waiting to hear back from the recruiter. I could ask for another tour of Cachi." He looked intently at my face, as if asking permission. I realized with a start that he'd taken to heart what I said about alerting the authorities.

"But you're worried he'll see you and leave?" I guessed.

"Yeah," he said, finally averting his eyes. "I don't want to be the reason he ends up sleeping on the streets or something."

I pulled him into a hug because he had voiced my fear, and because I didn't know what to say in response. His head weighed heavy on my shoulder for a few seconds before his hands came to rest on my back. I cried, my tears darkening Eamon's shirt. When the dampness soaked through, he leaned back and broke our hug, coughing awkwardly. I opened my mouth to apologize. No words emerged. Instead I stuffed more crudités into my mouth to stop it, the crying. We sat side by side on the couch until I felt ready, and then I stood up.

"All his things are in there." Eamon gestured at the guest room.

It was the same room and also not the same room, now devoid of Marlin's resolutely turned back. My body insisted on raising my heartbeat when I walked in, and I experienced Marlin's rejection all over again. I wondered when scientists would get around to discovering the antonymous equivalent of serotonin, its opposite. I didn't buy that depression was caused by low serotonin levels. No, what I felt was way more aggressive than a simple deficiency of certain neurotransmitters. There had to be another neurotransmitter that carried sadness, that handed out hopelessness like drugged candy. After all, even matter had antimatter.

I started with the clothes hanging in the closet. I yanked a dress shirt off its hanger brutishly, hands shaking, which set off a chain reaction that made all the other clothes dance, like someone had started playing a song in a room full of drunks. I swiped them all into a heap on the floor.

The trash bag was almost full by the time I got to the IKEA

desk with two drawers. I leaned the bag against one end of the desk and opened the first drawer, wondering why Marlin had left behind some of his clothes. It was true that as a software engineer he could alternate between the same two T-shirts and not raise an eyebrow at work. And having just a few changes of clothes with him while squatting was probably less troublesome than trying to hide a bag somewhere in the office.

I crouched on the floor and peeked under the bed. I'd looked everywhere else and hadn't seen a sign of Buster. I hoped Marlin hadn't gotten rid of him. It made my heart ache to think of our joint creation destroyed.

"Do you need help?" Eamon asked from the doorway.

I guessed at what it must look like to him, me motionless, kneeling, head almost touching floor.

"I just need a moment," I said. He nodded and left.

I still hadn't decided what to do about Marlin. I wavered between different daydreams. In one of them, I lurked by the Korean deli and confronted Marlin when he emerged for his food run. Sometimes he was silent the whole time I said my piece, exactly like when I'd found him here at Eamon's. Other times he begged me not to expose his squatting as I stood and felt powerful waves of benevolence wash over me.

I thought, too, of dropping off anonymous care packages addressed to him at his office. I'd send nail clippers (he was fastidious that way, or at least he used to be when he lived with me), ramen packets (the fancy, super spicy ones, not the kind that tasted like boiled water someone had farted in), a throw, maybe even a handheld gaming console.

The first drawer of the desk in Eamon's guest room was sparse, holding just a few takeout menus and promotional leaflets. The second drawer was a mess of thick papers variously stapled together. Most of them looked like white papers that Marlin was probably reading for work. Near the bottom of the drawer was something familiar, and it took me a while to process why a feeling of apprehension was welling up within me. I'd held the exact same document in my hands just the other night. What was it doing here?

I pulled it out from the pile: "Application to Register Permanent Residence or Adjust Status." Another of its names: USCIS Form I-485. When I fingered its pages they felt soft and well-thumbed, some corners curling up on themselves like they just wanted to protect their heads in a brawl. What did this mean? Had Marlin been promised green card sponsorship by his employer? Did he see it as a golden opportunity to ditch me while he alone ascended from impermanence to permanence?

I made for the bed and sat down clumsily, Form I-485 deforming in my clenching fist. I flipped through the creased document automatically, the way I'd done so many times before. It was blank; he hadn't claimed it with his name yet. No, it wasn't entirely blank. All the pages were clean except for one. I stared at it. In green ink, Marlin had circled one and only one of the form's many, many questions.

74. Are you accompanying another foreign national who requires your protection or guardianship but who is inadmissible after being certified by a medical officer as being helpless from sickness, physical or mental disability, or infancy, as described in INA section 232(c)?

An avalanche of possible interpretations trembled inside me. I felt my world dissolving once more into signs. I realized I couldn't see anything, and discovered I had my hands over my eyes. I freed them and blinked at the empty room. The form lay by my feet.

I stood up in a daze and walked over to the door to close it. Nearby, lying on the floor tiles, was my tote bag. I squatted and rummaged through it unthinkingly, pulling out fistfuls of wadded restaurant napkins, loose cough drops, drugstore coupons, not one but two squashed granola bars, and, finally, a folded piece of paper.

I spread open the paper and tried to make sense of the dense paragraphs. Slowly, the context returned to me. The words were instructions, steps for how to perform dowsing, given to me by Carol at the end of my fruitless visit to the Dowsers Society of America.

I skimmed the paper, forcing my vision and my breathing both to slow down. Avoid windows, the handout advised, so that external vibrations do not influence the results. I scooted until I had my back against the door, as far away from the guest room's two windows as possible. Steer clear of electrical equipment. Wildly I flitted my eyes around the objects in the room, before remembering my own cell phone. I took it out of the tote bag and slid it across the floor until it skidded into Form I-485, still on the floor.

I crawled to retrieve the form, then settled back against the door. Beyond, the house was quiet. I hoped Eamon was occupying himself with something.

There were more dos and don'ts on the sheet Carol gave me, but I couldn't wait anymore; the interior churning was becoming unbearable. As calmly as I could, I took off my necklace and looped my front door key through it, the way I had done in front of Carol at the Dowsers Society. With a shaky breath I closed my eyes. I stretched out my arm, hovering my pendant over Form I-485, and began.

It was rough going at first, the pendant lurching erratically and without rhythm. Soon it began spinning in smoother circles that felt independent of my manipulations, even though I understood intellectually that it was simply going off momentum. Since I didn't have a pen, I mentally decided that the left side of the immigration form represented the answer "Yes," while the right side would be "No."

Did Marlin circle number 74 on the form because of me? I asked silently.

The pendant whirled and tugged at my fingers. My eyes still closed, I tried to gauge whether it was listing in any particular direction. Yes? No? I screwed my eyelids together tighter, trying to shut out all other sensations except those of the pendant's arcs.

Never had I focused on something that hard before. The moments went by, pulled and stretched. Curiously, the top of my head began to tingle. As soon as my attention darted from the pendant to the tingling, I felt a strange knowing settling into my chest. *This is what happened*, it declared. Marlin wasn't worried about having to declare me "helpless from sickness" to the government. In fact, it was the opposite. He thought I was beginning to see him as the sick one.

I thought about what Eamon had said—Marlin loved his father, far more than I ever knew. Marlin's turn to dowsing was a desperate attempt to continue their bond in some form, but I had been too shocked and judgmental to understand that. I couldn't accept how Marlin could change so much. He knew his attempts to deepen his relationship with his dead father were alarming to me. Maybe Marlin was the clear-eyed one, after all. He'd become a different person, and he saw I couldn't keep up. And so he'd chosen to leave, freeing me from having to answer the question of whether he was well or unwell. Unburdening me.

I opened my eyes. The tingling had vanished. Unsteadily, I maneuvered my limbs until I was on my feet. Yes, that was it, the mystery unraveled.

Day Fifteen (Wednesday)

I wrote Marlin another email. I titled it "I dowsed and now I know," hoping this would intrigue him enough to at least read my words. In my email I described what had happened in Eamon's guest room, the conclusions and understanding that had hit me from out of nowhere.

I don't know if I'll ever hear from you again, I wrote. If I don't, I'll hold on to this version of what happened between us. You left because I was starting to see you as a problem. You thought I would label you "helpless." I can't blame you for that.

As I hit send, I thought briefly about how Katie provoked responses from her manager by making unpalatable suggestions. I wasn't deliberately saying something to Marlin that I didn't believe, but I wasn't a sudden convert to dowsing either. It was true I didn't have exact words to describe what had happened. My best guess was that when I tried dowsing, my mind simply synthesized the

information I'd gathered over the past few weeks and made it co-
here into a narrative. But I still didn't believe in dowsing—at least
not in the way Marlin practiced it, with spirit guides providing answers. So was I just manipulating Marlin into talking to me? Even
so, I like to think that whatever puff of sincerity I'd had while my
eyes were closed counted for something.

Day Sixteen (Thursday)

I was going to claim illness again and work from home, but Lucas messaged me early in the morning, asking if we could move our one-on-one up a day. I took the subway in, calculating my arrival so that it would coincide with lunchtime. As expected, the bullpen was deserted. Trying my best to be inconspicuous, I paused by Josh's desk and rolled my eyes upward so I could observe the ceiling without angling my neck.

There. A camera, not directly over his desk, but opposite and three spots down from it. How long did they keep footage around? A week?

Afterward I pretended to work in the building lobby until it was time to meet Lucas. The sofa reserved for visitors was surprisingly firm. I eyed everyone who came through the glass doors, on alert for anything like a uniform, but there was none. At some point a fire truck drove past, slowly by the sounds of it, its honks brassy and indignant.

I went to the one-on-one fifteen minutes early and sat waiting. To my surprise, my breathing was steady when Lucas walked in and closed the door. It was easier than I'd thought, being an agent of destruction.

"How's it going?" he asked. "You don't look great. Is everything all right?"

At first I was startled, thinking he was referring to my weight gain. Then I thought: Maybe I'm not as calm as I think. Perhaps the stillness I felt within me was not the tranquil repose of a river-polished stone but that of a hunted animal, frozen in shock.

"You can tell me," Lucas said, leaning forward and clasping his hands together. "Did something happen?"

"I'm worried about my visa situation." The words emerged on autopilot. I'd rehearsed the phrase so many times that my body now supplied it reflexively when I was at a loss for words, wanting only to avoid confessing to sabotage.

"You are?" Lucas raised both eyebrows. "Oh, why didn't you say so earlier? What's the lowdown?"

I told him The Date on my visa and described what needed to happen for a green card, as succinctly as I could. I knew he had no idea about any of all that, even though he was supposedly responsible for my career.

"Okay, let's get started, then," he said when I finished. "I'll shoot an email to the HR and legal guys right away."

"What do you mean?"

"You said there's a deadline, right?"

"You're sponsoring my green card? Just like that?"

He laughed. "I know it's been an uphill battle for you here, but you've done good work. You've caught some major bugs. And you don't let things get to you. I could tell from the beta test."

I blinked, trying to read between the lines. Was I being rewarded for tolerating the engineers' absurd behavior? Not letting things get to me—was that what the path to a green card entailed?

After the meeting I walked right up to Josh. He was standing, working with headphones on. I tapped one of his monitors, startling him into looking at me.

"Send me the next installment of your novel," I said. I walked away without waiting for a response. With every step I resolved further to be honest this time, completely. I would tell him what I really thought about Radmonsius and his adventures.

AFTER WORK I CALLED MY MOTHER. SHE WOULD BE DISAPPOINTED BY the green card news, I knew. But I rode the buoyant wave of the day's unexpected turn, finally ready to lay it all out with her. I wanted to tell her how her past life stories had both helped and wounded me.

While the dial tone continued, I imagined her naked again. This time, instead of picturing her body as some ideal that mine could never contort itself into, I saw the bow of her shoulders and the compression of her rib cage, as if she walked through life holding her breath. I saw, too, the wrinkles crackling across her folds, the cellulite mottling darker skin like egg sacs fermenting some secret sorrow. My mother, frail.

She didn't pick up. I left a message. "Call me back," I said. And just like that I was transported to the day I first left Malaysia for America. We were in the airport. My mother was weeping, one hand loosely clasping my arm.

"You're never coming back, are you?" she sobbed. "You'll marry an American and never return, that's what's going to happen."

I remembered the force of my head shaking out vehement denials. No, I swore. Never.

Can promises be kept in halves? Quarters? Slivers?

She flagged down a passing traveler with a rolling suitcase. Would they please take a photo of us, at the moment of our separation?

The stranger looked at my mother's tear-soaked face and refused.

Day Eighteen (Saturday)

I was not surprised at Marlin's response showing up in my in-box, strangely, just as I wasn't surprised he wanted to meet at the Korean deli. The developments on the green card front had overloaded my capacity for shock; I had a sense of floating around in an asteroid-dotted space, my movements not entirely under control, the possibility of impact always looming. Marlin's note was brief, asking me to meet him later that day.

There were hours yet before our meeting. I smoothed the torn halves of Marlin's modulo proposal on the floor. Flipping them over, I wrote on the other side:

QI LING % EDWINA % AMERICA == ?

Shortly after we'd first met, Marlin and I had entrusted each other with our birth names. The exchange felt almost sacred, even though, halfway across the world, our parents had called us by those names for almost two decades—to praise us, to scold us, to bid us home when darkness began to loom.

For a few months, heady with fresh love, Marlin insisted on calling me Qi Ling instead of Edwina. He wanted to be the only person in America to do so. It was a secret, a claim, and a spell all rolled in one. How thrilling it was, to be Edwina under fluorescent office lights, tugging at the revealing neckline concealed under a modest mustard sweater, imagining Marlin's reaction when we would meet after work, in a few hours' time. Then I'd transform into a different, luminous being when he put his hand on my cheek and called me Qi Ling, while the sweater lay limp across the back of my office chair.

He stopped when we started introducing each other to friends and family. Too confusing, he said, giving in to the engineer's need for efficiency at scale. And so that name was put back into a box, reserved for official government business.

I loaded the dating app Katie had installed on my phone the night we had whiskey. I wasn't looking to do anything, or find anyone. Never did I imagine I might soon have French food for the first time with someone I met off the app (thanks for suggesting that, by the way). At that moment, I just wanted to explore my state of preternatural calm.

At Buddhist camp, we'd sat in a loose circle around a camp instructor who told us stories from Buddha's life in forty-minute installments. On the last day, we gathered around her for the climax. I was looking forward to it, yearning for holiness and purity to cap off all the disease, death, and suffering Buddha had witnessed along the way. I wanted to know it had all been for something.

Buddha was well on his way to enlightenment, sitting under the bodhi tree. It had been seven times seven days since he had first crossed his legs among the tree's roots. He had not moved once. Into this tranquility broke in Mara, a demon hell-bent on thwarting Buddha's ascension. When his grotesque visage failed to quail Buddha, Mara summoned his three beautiful daughters. One by one the daughters stripped, parading their lovely naked bodies in front of Buddha, posing in the most tempting positions. But he paid them no mind, whatever pleasures they promised. And that was how Buddha achieved transcendence. He passed his tests.

I thought I, too, could put myself through a trial of enticement. Hands clutching my smartphone, I kept swiping away people of all genders on the dating app without really looking at their faces, using them like worry beads. I don't know how long I swiped for; it felt like an age, smiling faces flashing unceasingly by, the carousel never depleted. It might have gone on forever had my finger not slipped.

I stared down in fascination. I had accidentally swiped yes on a person. It was you, and in your profile you said you were a therapist, a good listener.

I picked up the nearest book and fiddled with its manifold frontiers. Mary Shelley. How I rooted for the monster's impossible dream, ached for it on his behalf, even as I knew what he wanted would hurt him and others. Did I still have the capacity for it, that cruel sympathy?

I remembered my first days in America: lawns of cut grass, chalk scribbles on sidewalks, wind that trembled trees free of their leaves.

All avenues to love, I realized, were acts of imagination. My tenderest bursts of affection for my mother happened when I associated her with death in my mind, as when I imagined her frail, naked flesh. All my unresolved anger toward her, I short-circuited by picturing her dead, beyond communication, so that I could call up waves of regret at not telling her how I really felt when I had the chance. That red-hot ball of future regret powers currents of love in the present, and I think: I do love her after all.

And is that love so pathetic?

America demands yet more supreme leaps of fancy. I juggle forked lives in my head: an intense love for the great nation of the United States should my green card come through, and a heavy loathing for this uncaring, capricious machine of a country should I fail to be legalized. It is an ice cube that never melts on my tongue, and every hour I turn it this way or that, unable to let it sit in one position for too long because of a burning freeze that builds up.

And Marlin. I saw again his face, somber and pinched, as he sat twirling a purple crystal over a diagram of words. His air of concentration gave him a look of grit. I thought maybe we were not so different after all. Who knew what love lay concealed behind his made-up spirits. Just as I ventured into imagination to love my mother, he could be calling forth love for his father using a pendant.

I hoped that one day he would imagine a way back to me, though I had no idea who I would soon become. Since young I'd opened wide to a gush of influences stripped of their contexts. Was I now taking cues from a government form in the same way? Learning how to be a person, a wife, a daughter, from numbered questions? Maybe that was precisely what Marlin was resisting. I imagined him hunched over Form I-485, carefully marking it with green ink.

Looking at your profile picture, I decided I would try to retell

EDGE CASE | 297

the story of Marlin and me. It was the closest thing to time travel. I would venture to alter how I thought about the past, and maybe it would somehow change my present. No matter how my meeting with Marlin would go, I already knew the way I wanted the story to end. I clicked "Message" under your smiling face.

I was paying for my corn silk tea when the Korean deli's door tinkled. I turned and watched Marlin nod to the man who worked there, the mopper who must have told Marlin how I'd asked after him.

I finally felt a squirt of fear when Marlin paced toward me, his expression neutral. My first impulse had been to yank him into a hug, but that impulse was now squashed by terror. I didn't want to start believing he was here to reconcile. If I did, that runaway hope would destroy me later. So I leaned against a shelf of seaweed snacks and chocolate, trying to just look at him without feeling anything.

His hair seemed longer than it should be, given the time that had passed since I last saw him. When he glanced down to put his phone away, I saw streaks of silver fanning out from his crown. He'd always had the stray strand or two of those, but now there were enough that I could easily visualize him with a head full of gray.

"Marlin," I said. I unscrewed the tea bottle so I could have an excuse for tilting my head back. I'd already vowed not to cry.

"You figured it out." He smiled very slightly.

"About you staying in the office? That was Eamon, really. He did a lot." I attempted my own smile. "We were both worried about you."

"I mean dowsing. But—thank you."

I shifted against the shelf. Behind me, plastic packaging crackled. "Was I right?" I asked.

"Mostly." He nodded. "Not bad for first-time dowsing."

"You could have told me you were trying to communicate with your dad. You could have tried to explain—how much he meant to you."

"Would that have changed anything?" His eyes flashed, that familiar glint when he was confident in his reasoning. "Would you have understood why I was dowsing if I'd told you?"

"Maybe. Or—I don't know," I confessed. It was hard to admit it out loud. "I'm sorry."

"Sorry too." His voice softened. "The important thing is, now you get it. Now you see why I spent so much time and energy learning to dowse. I've learned a lot. I'm good at it now. Once we move back to Malaysia, I'll be able to contact my dad."

"Move back?" My hand trembled. I set the tea down on the floor.

"That was one of the things your email didn't mention. I guess that's why you look so surprised."

"My boss just agreed to sponsor my green card. I can't. Remember when we joked about racing each other, see who would get sponsored first?" I put two fingers on his wrist, trying to adopt a joking tone.

Marlin looked lost. "But the spirits said you would come," he said quietly.

My heart broke for him then. How I wanted for him to be right, to get what he was told he would. But it was impossible. I might manage to go along with his vision for a moment—this moment—or maybe even an hour, a day, a week. Yet even if I didn't know myself very well anymore, I was certain I would forever regret not finding out whether that green card would materialize.

I was trying to work out how to explain it all to him when I looked up and read his expression. I saw that he already understood. His brows were dragging down, his mouth a grim hyphen. There was a bit of the old him left after all, the person who quickly grasped the facts at hand and adjusted to the new reality.

My Marlin.

ACKNOWLEDGMENTS

Thank you to—

Sara Birmingham, for listening and understanding, for many brilliant ideas, and for saying that you laughed. I'm so glad to have worked with you on this novel. Alexa Stark, for ushering in numerous early reincarnations of this book, each better than the last. I'm grateful for your patience and frankness.

The design and production teams at Ecco, and Na Kim, for their care.

Somesuch Stories for publishing part of this novel in a different form, and for thought-provoking prompts.

Generous early readers: David Joseph, Lim Kai Ling, Cheryl Loo Qi Ying, Mui Poopoksakul, Johnny Schmidt.

Editors and others who have helped shape my prose: John Amen, Sharon Bakar, Sybil Baker, Michelle Cahill, Andy Cox, Andrew Day, Joanna R. Demkiewicz, Todd Dills, Tammy Ho Lai

Ming, Lauren Rosemary Hook, Lee Hope, Jee Leong Koh, Charles Lambert, Jo Lou, Brian Mihok, Meghan Murphy, Jyothi Natarajan, Suze Olbrich, Debi Orton, R. B. Pillay, Christina Thompson, Jess Zimmerman.

Writers gracious and encouraging: Tash Aw, Brian Bouldrey, Amanda DeMarco, Hanna Alkaf, Caitlin Harper, Z Kennedy-Lopez, Catherine LaSota, Mira T. Lee, Chia-Chia Lin, Lisa Locascio, Juan Martinez, Ivelisse Rodriguez, Preeta Samarasan, Jeremy Tiang, Jeannie Vanasco, Sunny Xiang, Hilary Zaid, Authors '18.

Founts of support: My family, Chlump Chatkupt, Gia Gan, Pamela Ibarra, Saadia Imtiazi, Usman Jafarey, Ruchir Khaitan, Tina Kit, Jimmy Tang, Sarah Wang, everyone at Feminist Press, the RTP crew (no engineers in this book are based on you, don't worry).

Anyone I may have unintentionally left off as I write this during the discombobulating month of October 2020.

David and Murso, for seeing, comforting, recombobulating.

ABOUT THE AUTHOR

YZ CHIN is the author of the story collection *Though I Get Home*, which won the Louise Meriwether First Book Prize and the Asian/Pacific American Award for Literature honor title. Her writing has been published in the *Harvard Review, Gulf Coast, Somesuch Stories, Electric Literature*, Lit Hub, and other outlets. Born and raised in Malaysia, she now lives in New York, where she worked most recently as a software engineer.